CRAYNE'S LAW:
ALL COMPUTERS WAIT AT THE SAME SPEED

No one seriously disputes the advantages of programming in a high-level language. Yet there are still programs, or portions of programs, which are best written in that lowest level of all—the computer's native instruction set. There are two related reasons for this: speed and machine-dependent function.

A friend reported the following benchmarks on the IBM PC for a program which generates prime numbers. Written in interpretive BASIC, the program ran for about 4 hours. The identical BASIC program, compiled, ran in about 2½ hours. But the same function—carefully constructed in assembler to take full advantage of the PC's internal registers—ran in less than 2 minutes, more than 100 times faster.

For the majority of programs which spend most of their time either searching a disk or waiting for the user to key something, this speed advantage means little. But there are many applications where a few assembly language routines can allow a microcomputer to provide the speed and function of a much larger system.

This book, then, is written for the person who—either for business or for pleasure—wants to bypass the barriers of BASIC and delve beneath the depths of DOS.

THE SERIOUS

A POURNELLE USERS GUIDE

ASSEMBLER

CHARLES A. CRAYNE
AND DIAN GIRARD

BAEN computer BOOKS

A Baen Book

Baen Enterprises
8–10 W. 36th Street
New York, N.Y. 10018

First printing, May 1985

ISBN: 0-671-55963-X

Cover art by Robert Tinney. Reproduced with permission of BYTE Publications.

Printed in the United States of America

Distributed by
SIMON & SCHUSTER
MASS MERCHANDISE SALES COMPANY
1230 Avenue of the Americas
New York, N.Y. 10020

CONTENTS

TRADEMARKS

PREFACE

Conventional wisdom is that new programming languages arise not in a continuous stream, but in waves of innovation. Each such generation is supposedly marked by an order of magnitude improvement in functionality and accompanying programmer productivity. The pundits claim that such languages as COBOL, PL/I, and Pascal are of the third generation, and that the query languages and application generators which are now becoming common represent the fourth.

No one seriously disputes the advantages of programming in a high-level language. Yet there are still programs, or portions of programs, which are best written in that lowest level of all—the computer's native instruction set. There are two related reasons for this—speed and machine-dependent function.

One friend of mine reported the following benchmarks on the IBM PC for a program which generates prime numbers. Written in interpretive BASIC, the program ran for about 4 hours. The identical BASIC program, compiled, ran in about 2½ hours—a major improvement. But the same function—carefully con-

1

structed in assembler to take full advantage of the PC's internal registers—ran in less than 2 minutes, more than 100 times faster.

For the majority of programs which spend most of their time either searching a disk or waiting for the user to key something, this speed advantage means little. Indeed, *Crayne's Law* reminds us that "All computers wait at the same speed!" But there are many applications where a few assembly language routines can allow a microcomputer to provide the speed and function normally associated with a much larger system.

This book, then, is written for the person who—either for business or for pleasure—wants to bypass the barriers of BASIC and delve beneath the depths of DOS. Although no specific level of programming experience is required (in the sense that many of the examples are not just code fragments but rather complete working programs), the book does not attempt to teach beginning programming skills. Nor does it contain a detailed explanation of each of the machine instructions since that material is included in the IBM *Macro Assembler* manual.

The book is divided into five major parts. "The DOS Programming Environment" provides an overview of the IBM PC architecture and explains how to write, assemble, and execute a trivial assembly language program. "Programming with DOS Calls" contains a detailed discussion of the DOS service calls, and concludes with a file display program which will operate in the tree-structured directory environment of DOS release 2. "Programming with BIOS Calls" demonstrates how windowing, graphics, nonstandard disk formats, and other advanced features can be added to programs by taking advantage of the functions in IBM'S ROM BIOS. "Programming the Silicon" goes the final mile, explaining how to directly program the device adapters.

Finally, "Interfaces and Ideas" shows how to interface assembly language routines to high-level languages, and also provides a repository for some topics—such as copy-protection schemes—that didn't quite fit anywhere else.

Charles A. Crayne

Part I

The Dos Programming Environment

Chapter 1
THE IBM PC FAMILY

When IBM chose to enter the personal computer market, it brought with it several ideas which were commonplace in medium- and large-scale computers, but which were almost nonexistent in the microcomputer industry. Some of these features, such as parity checked memory and power-on diagnostics, have since become fairly common. The concept that has remained exclusively IBM's however, is that of a diverse family of personal computers, based essentially on the same architecture and technology, with individual members providing specialized functions at some cost in compatability. As of this writing, the IBM PC family consists of 11 members which can be categorized as follows.

The general-purpose personal computers consist of the PC, PC XT, and the Portable PC. These machines all use the Intel 8088 microprocessor and accept most of the same interface adapter boards. The PCjr also uses the 8088, but is packaged quite differently, which leads to programming differences when directly controlling the device adapters.

The PC AT is an upgraded PC XT which uses the

more advanced Intel 80286 microprocessor. This chip has architectural features which allow it to address more memory than the 8088 and which can protect sections of memory against unauthorized changes. These features make this chip desirable for running multiuser operating systems. However the 80286 also has a 8086/8088 compatability mode which means that systems and programs written for the PC and PC XT will operate on the PC AT with little or no changes.

The 3270 PC contains a hardware windowing capability and is designed for direct attachment to an IBM communications controller. In this mode, it will handle four host communication sessions, two scratchpad windows, and one DOS program window. Several models exist, with different graphics capabilities. The older models are build on a PC XT base. The newer ones use the PC AT. Except for the screen handling functions, therefore, programming is similar to the base machines.

The PC XT/370, and a newer version based on the PC AT, are quite different from the rest of the family. They have been upgraded with a special processor board containing a Motorola 68000 microprocessor; a second, specially modified 68000; and a modified Intel 8087 floating point processor. This allows them to execute the IBM 370 instruction set, and thus to directly execute many programs written to run on the IBM mainframes. Needless to say, programming for these machines is beyond the scope of this book.

PC Operating System

When the IBM PC was announced, three operating systems were announced as supporting it. These were PC DOS, written for IBM by Microsoft; the UCSD p-system; and Digital Research's CP/M-86. For a variety of reasons—

primarily IBM's aggressive policy of pricing DOS at a small fraction of the price of the other system—PC DOS has become the industry standard. The other operating systems still exist, and the 3270 PC and the PC XT/370 each have their own unique control programs. But the only serious threat on the horizon are the variants of ATT'S UNIX operating system. These are PC/IX for the PC XT and XENIX for the PC AT.

PC DOS, however, is itself heading towards UNIX functions. When DOS 1.0 appeared, it was obvious that it owed a lot to CP/M. Some programmers maintain that it is easier to convert CP/M programs to DOS than to CP/M-86. PC DOS 1.1 was a maintenance release, but PC DOS 2.0 introduced many new features, including the UNIX concepts of input and output redirection, program piping, and filters. DOS 2.1 was announced as a release specifically to support the PCjr, but was also a maintenance release which fixed several known problems. PC DOS 3.0 was announced to support the PC AT, with no other new functions. At the same time, PC DOS 3.1 was announced for delivery in the spring of 1985, to support the newly announced networking features. Due to publication schedules, the sample programs in this book have been developed and tested under DOS 2.1 on a PC XT, but should work with little or no change on DOS release 3.

Chapter 2
OVERVIEW OF THE 8086/8088
ARCHITECTURE

The "brain" of the IBM Personal Computer is the Intel 8088 microprocessor unit (MPU). Although this unit is quite small physically it has several design features that are commonly found in the much larger "mainframe" computers. It is logically divided into two parts: the Bus Interface Unit (BIU), which contains the segment registers and the instruction pointer, and the Execution Unit (EU), which contains the program registers and the stack and base pointers. Figure 2.1 illustrates the functional organization of the 8088 MPU.

The function of the Bus Interface Unit is to handle all of the memory read and write requests and to keep the instruction stream byte queue (the "pipeline") full. Since the 8088 BIU Interfaces to an 8-bit data bus and the EU works primarily with 16-bit operands, the BIU must make two consecutive bus reads whenever a 16-bit value (such as an address) is required. These functions are performed asynchronously with instruction execution. That is, after each instruction is performed the BIU checks the status of the pipeline. This pipelining technique effectively isolates the Execution Unit from

Figure 2.1—8088 Architecture

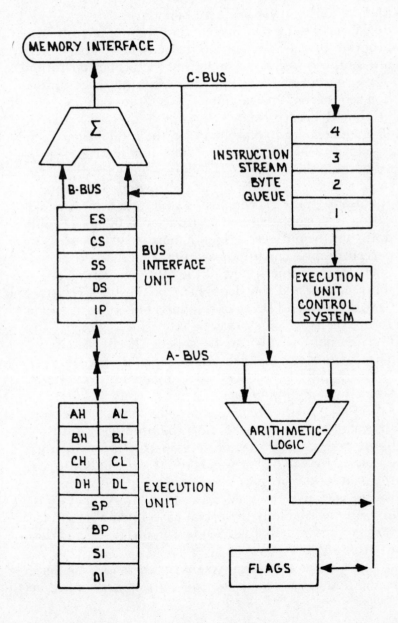

the data bus and avoids placing boundary restrictions on application data. You do not have to worry about placing data on word or byte boundaries.

The pipeline can be accepted or manipulated by the programmer. The only time it needs to be considered are on those rare occasions when the proper operation of a program depends upon knowing the exact timing of a sequence of instructions. [This discussion has been presented here primarily to dispell the myth that if IBM had chosen to base its PC on the Intel 8086 (which is logically identical to the 8088 but interfaces to a 16-bit bus) then the PC would have run twice as fast. In fact, a detailed study of the 8086 and 8088 timing equations yields the conclusion that for a typical application program, the change from an 8-bit to a 16-bit data bus would result in no more than about a 20 percent improvement in execution time.]

The programmers view of the 8088 consists solely of the registers and the flags. Four of the EU's registers (AX, BX, CX, and DX) can be addressed either as single 16-bit registers or as two paired 8-bit registers. The register pair AH/AL can be called AX, BH/BL is the same as BX, and so forth. All of the other registers are 16-bit (two-byte) registers only, and cannot be used for single-byte manipulation.

The 8088 instruction set consists of about 90 basic instructions, each of which can be used with multiple addressing modes. Most of these instructions will work either on byte (8-bit) or word (16-bit) operands. Most of the instructions are either register-to-register or register-to-storage operations. Memory-to-memory operations are only available with special case "string handling" instructions which are dependant upon source and destination index registers.

This book assumes that you have access to a reference manual that describes the function of each machine instruction in detail, and therefore that information has not been duplicated in this book. For quick reference, however, a chart giving a short description of each assembly language instruction (mnemonic) is provided in Appendix A.

Like all language handlers, the IBM macroassembler (which will be considered the standard throughout this book) has its own syntax rules. Figure 2.2 is a program fragment which shows the format. Each instruction appears on a separate line in the source file, and each instruction consists of two parts, although not all parts are required on every line.

<u>Figure 2.2—Instruction Format</u>

```
LABEL:   MOV   AX,CASH              ;CAPTURE MONEY
         CMP   AX,0
         JNZ   LABEL1

    (code omitted for clarity)

;CALCULATE COMMISSION
LABEL1:
```

The first component of an instruction is an optional label. A label which references a machine instruction is followed by a colon. Next is the operator, which is the mnemonic for a machine instruction. Then come the operands, or data, being used by the operator. The number of operands depends upon the specific instruction. In most cases, the operands will consists of a register and a memory reference.

The order of the operands is important. Many systems distinguish between read and write requests by using separate instructions, such as "load" and "store." The IBM macroassembler uses the single mnemonic

"MOV" for both cases, with the direction being from the second operand to the first. Thus, in the example line "MOV AX,CASH" the value at the memory location labeled "CASH" will be loaded into the 16-bit register "AX." If "CASH" does not refer to data item defined as a word, then the assembler will flag this statement as being in error. Notice that the operands are separated by a coma. This is a required character. If it is missing the assembler will also flag the statement. Although labels are generally started in the first column the position of the instruction elements is not critical. Formatting can be done with either spaces or the tab key.

The final element of an instruction is an optional comment. Comments are indicated by a semicolon (;); any part of a line following a semicolon is considered to be a comment. If a semicolon appears in the first position of a line then the entire line is a comment.

Segment Registers

The 8088 instructions work with 16-bit addresses. Sixteen bits are only enough to access a memory address space of 64K bytes. To overcome this limitation, the 8088 BIU indexes all memory requests—for data or instructions—with a 20-bit value computed from one of the four segment registers (CS, SS, DS, or ES). These registers are actually only 16 bits themselves, but they are used as if they had an additional four zero bits appended to them. A segment always begins on a 16-byte boundary and for this reason a group of 16 bytes on a 16-byte boundary is called a "paragraph."

Each of the four segment registers has a specific purpose. The Code Segment (CS) register is automatically used as the index for the instruction pointer. That is, all instruction fetches come from a 64K address space pointed to by the CS register. The Stack Segment (SS) register provides a similar function for all stack operations. In addition, memory requests which are indexed by the Base Pointer register (BP) default to the stack segment. The Data Segment (DS) register provides automatic indexing of all data references—except for those which are relative to the stack, those which are the destination of one of the "string" instructions, and those cases where the programmer has explicitly specified a different segment register. Finally, the Extra Segment (ES) register automatically indexes only the destination operand for the "string" instructions.

Figure 2.3 illustrates one way in which the four segments can be set up in the 1024K [1-megabyte (1M)] total address space. In the example each segment is separate and noncontiguous, but this need not be the case. Segments can overlap or even coincide. In extreme cases, manipulation of the segment registers can be quite tricky, but fortunately, most of the time the assembler and the linker will set up the proper values and the programmer can mostly ignore them.

Arithmetic and Index Registers

There are four general-purpose registers: AX, BX, CX, and DX. As mentioned above, each of these registers can also be treated as two single-byte registers. That is, AX consists of AH, which is the most significant byte of AX, and AL, which is the least significant byte of AX. Likewise, BH and BL make up BX, CH and CL comprise. CX, and DH and DL form DX. Although all of these registers can be used to perform 8- or 16-bit arithmetic, each also has one or more unique functions.

AX is the primary accumulator. Some instructions,

Figure 2.3—Memory Organization

MEMORY REFERENCE NEEDED	SEGMENT REGISTER USED	SEGMENT SELECTION RULE
Instructions	CODE (CS)	Automatic with all instruction prefetch
Stack	STACK (SS)	All stack pushes and pops. Memory references relative to BP base register except data references.
Local data	DATA (DS)	Date references when: relative to stack, destination of string operation, or explicitly overridden.
External Data (global)	EXTRA (ES)	Destination of string operations: Explicitly selected using a segment override.

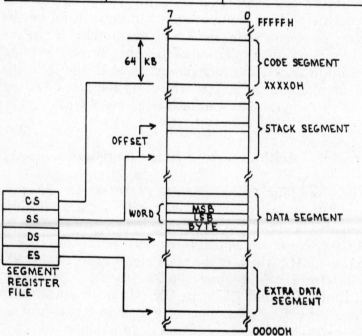

such as Convert Byte to Word (CBW) operate only on the AX register. AH and AL are also the primary parameter registers for calls to PC DOS.

BX is the base register. It is the only one of the general-purpose registers which can be used as an index in address calculations.

CX is used in loop control. For example, the LOOP instruction automatically decrements CX by one and branches if the result is not zero. Other instructions can be used with a repeat prefix which will cause them to iterate the number of times specified by CX, creating a "count loop."

DX is the data register. It is used to pass address parameters to DOS, and specifies the port addresses for direct I/O requests.

Pointer Registers

SP is the stack pointer. It points to the current position in the execution stack. Although it can be set to any value, it is normally changed automatically as a result of such instructions as PUSH, POP, CALL, and RETurn.

BP is the base printer. Like SP, it normally points into the current execution stack. However, it is not changed by stack operations. Therefore it is typically used as a base index for variables which were passed to a subroutine by placing them on the top of the stack.

Index Registers

SI is the source index register. It can be used as an index for any data requests. It is automatically used as the pointer to the source operand by the "string" instructions.

DI is the destination index register. Like SI, it can be used by the programmer as a data index register. It is automatically used as the pointer to the destination operand by the "string" instructions.

Figure 2.4 is a register usage summary.

Figure 2.4—Register Usage Summary

```
GENERAL PURPOSE REGISTERS
    AX   Primary accumulator. Used for all I/O operations
         and for primary parameters for DOS calls.
    BX   Base register. The only general purpose register
         used in address calculations.
    CX   Count register. Used for loop control.
    DX   Data register. Holds address parameters for DOS
         calls, and the port address for I/O.

POINTER REGISTERS
    SP   Stack Pointer
    BP   Base Pointer

INDEX REGISTERS
    SI   Source index.
    DI   Destination indes. (Indexed access to memory
         is required for string instructions.)
```

Addressing Modes

Coding style often depends on the available addressing modes. The 6502, for example, has only single-byte index registers. This forces the programer to put data tables on page boundaries. The 8080 has only limited ability to address memory without using index registers. This leads to a programming style in which the register contents are constantly being saved and reloaded from register save areas.

The 8088 solves both at these problems. The immediate mode works not only for registers, but also for memory locations. This makes it unnecessary to initialize memory constants by first passing the values through a register.

The direct mode is available for most instructions, allowing, for example, the direct addition of a register to a memory location instead of having to load the value into the accumulator, add in the desired register, and then store the accumulator back into memory. The direct mode can be enhanced by several different ways of indexing. Even double indexing is available, which allows for the concept of repeated fields within records within buffers, all controlled with register pointers.

Finally, indexing or double indexing can also take place within the stack segment. This is most useful when the stack is being used for passed parameters and local program variables in order to provide reentrant code.

Addressing modes are summarized in Figure 2.5.

Figure 2.5—Addressing Modes

```
IMMEDIATE
     ADD   AX,1024
     MOV   TEMP,25

DIRECT
     ADD   AX,TEMP
     MOV   TEMP,AX

DIRECT, INDEXED
     ADD   AX,ARRAY[DI]
     MOV   TABLE[SI],AX

IMPLIED
     ADD   AX,[DI]
     MOV   [SI],AX

BASE RELATIVE
     ADD   AX,[BX]
     ADD   AX,ARRAY[BX]
     ADD   AX,ARRAY[BX+SI]
```

```
STACK
      ADD   AX,[BP]
      ADD   AX,ARRAY[BP]
      ADD   AX,ARRAY[BP+SI]
```

Stack Operations

Some machine architectures, like the IBM 360/370 family, have no concept of an execution stack. Others, like the 6502, place the stack at a hardware-defined location. The 8088 allows the stack to be placed anywhere in memory, and lets the programmer work directly within the stack (through register indexing) as well as with the item which is currently on the top of the stack.

Figure 2.6 shows how the stack might look after a subroutine is given control. The calling routine has placed three parameters on the stack before issuing the call instruction. The SS register points to the start (low address) of the stack segment. This address can be anywhere within the 1M address space supported by the 8088. (In actuality, of course, the stack has to be in read/write memory.) The Stack Pointer points to the 16-bit value which is currently on the top of the stack. Note that the illustration has been drawn so that the lowest memory address is toward the bottom of the page. The stack actually grows from high memory addresses toward lower memory addresses. The concept of calling the most recent addition to the stack the "top" is a logical one that comes from the way a human would put a piece of paper on the top of a stack.

The called program could refer to the passed parameters as an offset from the Stack Pointer (SP). But SP is

Figure 2.6—Stack Awaiting Subroutine Operation

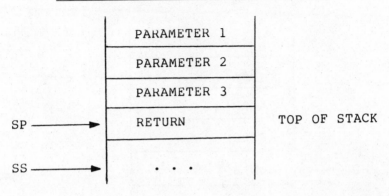

going to move around as the subroutine saves and restores the caller's registers. So a better way is to use the base pointer register, BP. Here is a scenerio which a subroutine might use in order to save registers and access both the passed parameters and its own local variables, all in a way which requires no preallocated storage.

First, the subroutine saves the caller's BP register. Then BP is set equal to SP. SP is then decremented by two bytes for each local variable. The other registers are now saved, as required, by pushing them on the stack. This leaves the configuration shown in Figure 2.7. Note that all of the passed parameters can now be addressed as $BP+n$ and the local variables are addressed as $BP-n$, where n is the offset. When the subroutine is finished, it resets SP to BP and issues a RET n instruction to clean up the stack.

Figure 2.7—Stack During Subroutine Execution

PARAMETER 1	(BP+8)
PARAMETER 2	(BP+6)
PARAMETER 3	(BP+4)
RETURN	(BP+2)
OLD BP	← BP
LOCAL 1	(BP-2)
LOCAL 2	(BP-4)
LOCAL 3	(BP-6)
LOCAL 4	(BP-8)
AX	
BX	
CX	← SP

Chapter 3
PROGRAMMING IN THE .COM
ENVIRONMENT

At first glance the four segment registers—each of which relocates a different type of address reference—seem to make programming on the PC overly complicated. It's true that they add a level of programming complexity which did not exist in previous generations of micro-computers, but they do not have to be used for the majority of programs. By accepting a few simplifying restrictions, not only can the segment registers be mostly ignored, but their existence can solve some of the common problems associated with relocating code.

Without hardware relocation, a microprocessor using a 16-bit addresses operates in an absolute address space of 0 to 64K. Unfortunately the application programmer cannot use this entire address range because it is shared with the operating system, ROM storage, and memory-mapped I/O.

The location of the operating system is particularly critical. If it is placed in low memory, and grows larger for any reason (such as a new release with more features), all of the application programs have to be relinked to a higher address. On the other hand, if the operating system is located in high memory, then it has to be regenerated whenever the amount of read/write memory on the system is changed.

The PC segment registers do away with these problems entirely. By simply accepting the segment register values set by the operating system when it loads the program and ignoring them thereafter, the application program becomes completely independent of the actual hardware address assignments.

Figure 3.1 is an overview of the 1M address space. (For a more detailed breakdown, with specific addresses, see the "System Memory Map" in the *Technical Reference Manual*.) The first 640K can contain read/write memory (RAM). The next 128K is reserved for CRT refresh buffers, although only the 3270 PC currently uses all of it. The top 256K contains the system BIOS and cassette BASIC, which are on the system board, and any ROM code on expansion boards, such as that on the hard disk controller.

The PC's operating system is loaded into low memory. Next to be loaded are any specified device drivers, and any other programs, such as a print spooler, which have to stay resident while the application programs are running. Application programs are loaded at the first available storage above the resident modules.

When DOS loads a program, it checks to see if the load module contains any relocation information. Such a file conventionally has a file name extension of .EXE, and is the most general format of an executable module. However, .EXE files are a bit more complex to program, and will be discussed later. The other acceptable load module format is conventionally called a .COM file.

A program written to become a .COM file has a simplistic view of the universe. It doesn't know anything about segment registers. It believes that it has been loaded into real memory at address 256, just

Figure 3.1—One-Million Byte Address Space

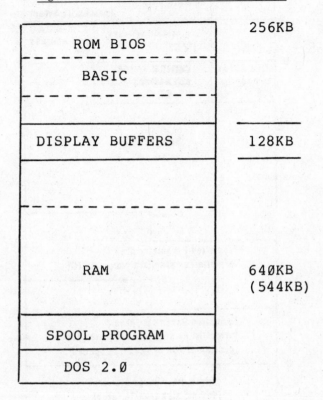

above a predefined work area called the "Program Segment Prefix." This work area is the only reserved area in the program's addressable memory. (This environmental view will be familiar to those who have programmed under CP/M.)

Figure 3.2 contains the description of the PSP, as defined in the DOS reference manual. (The memory addresses are shown in hex.) Again, the similarity to CP/M should be noted. All of the fields in the PSP are set up by DOS when the program is loaded so that no program initialization is required.

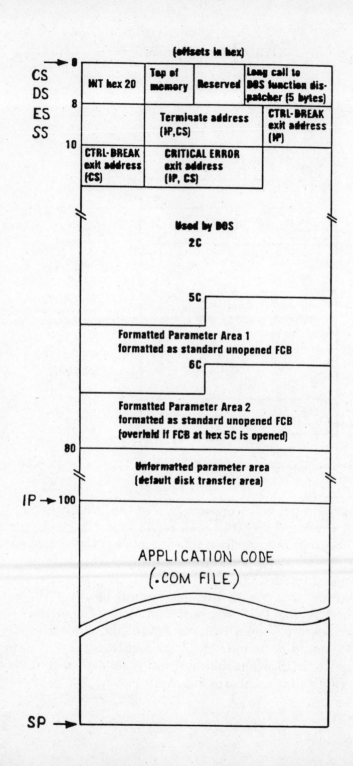

Passing Parameters

The first field of the PSP that the application programmer is likely to use is the unformatted parameter area at hex 80. When a program is invoked by typing its name from the command prompt, DOS places any command line text following the program name into a text buffer at hex 81 and puts the length of that text string (not including the carriage return) in a one-byte count field at location hex 80. Figure 3.3 illustrates this process. It shows a program fragment which tests for the existence of a parameter string and, if one is found, examines each character in the string.

Figure 3.3—Passing Parameters

```
A>   MYPROG   ABCDE

     80   5
     81   ABCDE
```

```
;SCAN INPUT PARAMETER LINE
ENTRY:    MOV    DI,OFFSET CMDSTR
          MOV    CH,0
          MOV    CL,CMDCNT         ;LENGTH OF PARAMETER STRING
          CMP    CX,0              ;ANY PARAMETERS
          JNZ    SCAN0             ;YES - PROCESS THEM
;NO PARAMETERS SUPPLIED - INSERT DEFAULT CODE HERE
          JMP    SCANX
SCAN0:    MOV    AL,[DI]           ;GET 1ST PARAMETER CHARACTER
          AND    AL,0DH            ;CONVERT TO UPPER CASE
;HANDLE PARAMETERS HERE
SCANN:    INC    DI                ;POINT TO NEXT PARAMETER
          LOOP   SCAN0             ;GET NEXT CHARACTER
SCANX:    NOP                      ;ALL PARAMETERS HANDLED
```

Gaining Control from DOS

When DOS loads a .COM program, it builds the PSP and sets all four segment registers to point to it. DOS then loads the program at hex 100, sets the stack pointer to the end of the 64K address space (or the top of real memory, if it happens to be lower) and gives control to the program at its load point. The program, therefore, has very little housekeeping to do. The programmer's primary responsibility is to explain to the macroassembler what DOS has already done.

Although the .COM program does not know about segment registers, the macroassembler does. Because of this the programmer's first job is to define the entire program as a single segment. This is done by surrounding the program with the SEGMENT and ENDS pseudo-ops, as shown in the sample program in Figure 3.6. Next, the assember is informed that all of the segment registers have been set to point to the beginning of the segment via the ASSUME statement. Note that the ASSUME pseudo-op does NOT generate any code. It only sets an expectation level for the assembler to use. This distinction will become critical when we discuss the .EXE environment, where the programmer is responsible for specifically setting the segment registers.

NEAR and FAR Procedures

Another macroassembler construct, which only marginally affects the generated code, is the "procedure." In high-level languages procedure blocks typically control the scope of variable names, keep track of the number and type of passed parameters, and assign storage for local variables. The macroassembler only keeps track of whether a procedure is declared as FAR or NEAR.

A FAR procedure is one that is intended to be called from another code segment. The assembler will generate an intersegment call, which places both the instructions pointer and the code segment register on the stack before transfering control. Any return instructions within the scope of the FAR procedure will be generated as intersegment returns, setting both the instruction pointer and the code segment from the top of the stack.

A call to a NEAR procedure with be generated with an intrasegment (single-segment only) call, which saves only the instruction pointer. Likewise, any return instructions within a NEAR procedure will restore only the instruction pointer. This situation is shown in Figure 3.4.

Figure 3.4—NEAR and FAR Procedures

```
FAR-NAME    PROC FAR
            CALL NEAR-NAME
            RET
FAR-NAME    ENDP

NEAR-NAME   PROC NEAR
            (code omitted for clarity)
            RET
NEAR-NAME   ENDP
```

Since the .COM environment involves only a single segment, we do not actually need to use FAR procedures. Strictly speaking, it is not even necessary to use procedures at all. The assembler will default to considering the entire program as an unnamed NEAR procedure and will only generate intrasegment calls and returns. However, the use of procedures will become important later and therefore they will be used in all of the sample programs, for the sake of compatibility.

The proper use of the NEAR and FAR procedure attributes involves only a couple of simple rules:

1. Each program should have exactly one FAR procedure which is the routine to which DOS will give con-

trol. (This procedure must not contain any embedded subroutines.)

2. All routines called from the main routine must be placed in one or more NEAR procedures. The sample program makes each subroutine a separate procedure, but it is also a common programming practice to group a set of logically related subroutines together into a single procedure.

Returning to DOS

In DOS 1.0 and 1.1 there is basically only one way to effect a normal return to DOS. This is to issue interrupt hex 20 with the code segment register pointing to the program segment prefix. Since, in the .COM environment, CS always points to the PSP and since DOS has placed an INT 20H instruction at the beginning of the PSP, there are several possible techniques to use in executing the interrupt. Four of these are illustrated in Figure 3.5. (DOS 2.0 introduced an additional technique which will be discussed in a later chapter.) The

Figure 3.5—Returning to DOS

```
•     INT   21H

•     JMP   0

•     MOV   AH,0
      INT   21H

•     PUSH  DS
      MOV   AX,0
      PUSH  AX
      RET
```

first three of these, however, work ONLY in the .COM environment. Again, for compatibility with later examples, we will adopt the fourth technique. Note that this method only works when it appears within the scope of a FAR procedure, since it depends upon an intersegment return to cause both the IP and the CS registers to be set from the top of the stack.

The Sample Program

Now let us put these concepts together to form the working program shown in Figure 3.6. This simple program will clear the screen, write a short message to the console, and return to DOS. In doing so it illustrates all of the concepts that we have developed in this chapter.

The first thing the program does is perform its housekeeping: it defines a segment, notifies the assembler that the segment registers will be pointing to it on entry, defines labels for that portion of the PSP that it will be referring to, ORGs to the program load point, and jumps around the data area to the true program entry.

Since all four segment registers point to the same place, code and data can be freely intermixed. However, it is a good idea to always define data areas before referring to them, because of the internal design of the assembler. Thus it has become a common programming practice to place all of the data elements together at the beginning of the program, immediately following a jump to the true entry point. Note that labels on data elements (as well as on pseudo-ops) do not have colons for delimiters. This is important. The assembler does weird things if you make a mistake in this rule.

Figure 3.6—Sample Program

```
PAGE      60,132
TITLE     SAMPLE - SHOWS DOS CALLING CONVENTIONS FOR .COM FILES
PAGE
COMSEG    SEGMENT PARA PUBLIC 'CODE'
          ASSUME  CS:COMSEG,DS:COMSEG,ES:COMSEG,SS:COMSEG
          ORG     80H
CMDCNT    DB      ?                    ;COMMAND LINE COUNT
CMDSTR    DB      80 DUP (?)           ;COMMAND LINE BUFFER
          ORG     100H
START     PROC    FAR
          JMP     ENTRY                ;SKIP DATA AREAS
;-----------------------------------------------------------------
;DATA AREAS
;-----------------------------------------------------------------
LOGO      DB      'Sample Program Executed',13,10,'$'
;-----------------------------------------------------------------
;SCAN INPUT PARAMETER LINE
ENTRY:    MOV     DI,OFFSET CMDSTR
          MOV     CH,0
          MOV     CL,CMDCNT            ;LENGTH OF PARAMETER STRING
          CMP     CX,0                 ;ANY PARAMETERS
          JNZ     SCAN0                ;YES - PROCESS THEM
;NO PARAMETERS SUPPLIED - INSERT DEFAULT CODE HERE
          JMP     SCANX
SCAN0:    MOV     AL,[DI]              ;GET 1ST PARAMETER CHARACTER
          AND     AL,0DH               ;CONVERT TO UPPER CASE
;HANDLE PARAMETERS HERE
SCANN:    INC     DI                   ;POINT TO NEXT PARAMETER
          LOOP    SCAN0                ;GET NEXT CHARACTER
SCANX:    NOP                          ;ALL PARAMETERS HANDLED
;-----------------------------------------------------------------
;START OF MAIN PROGRAM
;-----------------------------------------------------------------
          CALL    CLRSCN               ;CLEAR THE SCREEN
          CALL    IAMHERE              ;DISPLAY MESSAGE
;-----------------------------------------------------------------
;RETURN TO DOS
;-----------------------------------------------------------------
DONE:     PUSH    DS
          MOV     AX,0
          PUSH    AX
          RET
START     ENDP
;-----------------------------------------------------------------
;SUBROUTINES
;-----------------------------------------------------------------
CLRSCN    PROC                         ;CLEAR SCREEN
          PUSH    AX
          MOV     AX,2
          INT     10H
          POP     AX
          RET
CLRSCN    ENDP
IAMHERE   PROC
          PUSH    AX
          PUSH    DX
          MOV     AH,9
          MOV     DX,OFFSET LOGO
          INT     21H
          POP     DX
          POP     AX
```

```
                RET
IAMHERE  ENDP
COMSEG   ENDS
         END        START
```

Code labels, on the other hand *must* end with a terminating colon.

The section of the sample program that scans the input parameter line does not actually accomplish anything the way it is written. A good first exercise for the reader would be to add the necessary code to the program so that it changes the message written to the console if a specific character is recognized in the input string. (Hint: the simplistic uppercase translate routine provided only works on alphabetic characters.)

The two subroutines provided with this sample illustrate two different techniques for manipulating the screen. CLRSCN clears the screen by issuing a direct call to the ROM BIOS. IAMHERE uses a DOS function call to write a character string to the current cursor position. Note that the function keeps writing until it finds a dollar sign. If you forget to supply this terminator the routine will blithely cause all of memory to be dumped to the screen until one is found (if ever).

The problem with IAMHERE, of course, is that it always prints the same message. As part of the exercise suggested above, IAMHERE should be modified so that the address of the message to be displayed is passed to it as a parameter.

Chapter 4
ASSEMBLY AND LINKAGE

In order to create an executable program in assembly language you must type the source code, assemble it, and then link it. These steps are always followed, no matter whether the end result is an .EXE or a .COM file.

The macroassembler converts source code instructions, typed in by the programmer, into machine language that can be read by the computer. This assembler, which executes in two separate passes, expects an .ASM file as input, and produces .MAP, .CRF, .LST, and .OBJ files as output. It is generally advisable to put the macroassembler and the linker on a diskette in drive A:, along with any library files used by the program, and to keep all source code on separate diskettes, which are mounted in drive B:. The object code and .EXE or .COM executable files can then be built on drive A: while the listing file is routed to drive B:. This is especially attractive if you are dealing with a program that has been broken up into sections for assembly, since the source code, backup copy, and listing for each program can be kept conveniently on one diskette while a master diskette holds the generated object code and the final combined program created by the LINK program.

It is very common to run out of disk space while attempting to assemble a program because of the large size of the generated listing (.LST) file. Some programmers prefer to suppress sections of the listing (for routines that have already been debugged) by inserting alternate nonprint (.XLIST) and print (.LIST) commands within the source code. If you are lucky enough to have a hard disk you will have much less difficulty, but if you're dealing with diskettes this is a problem to watch out for.

The assembler needs to know five pieces of information: the names of the source file, object file, cross reference, listing, and map file. It also needs to know which diskettes contain, or will receive, these various files. The best way to give the assembler the information—and to ensure that you don't leave out part of it—is to create a batch file. The batch file only needs to be a single line long and will save you a lot of grief over your development cycle. Figure 4.1 shows a sample batch file that takes a source program from drive A: and routes all of its output to drive B:.

Figure 4.1—Assembly Batch File

```
ECHO OFF
IF NOT EXIST B:%1.ASM GOTO ERROR
MASM B:%1,%1,B:%1,B:%1/X%2
GOTO DONE
:ERROR
ECHO SOURCE FILE NOT ON DRIVE B.
:DONE
```

This batch file uses the limited logic available in batch mode to abort the process if the source code is not present on drive B:. This keeps the assembler from allocating disk space for files that can't actually be built. Without this error proofing, the assembler will create directory entries that can only be purged with CHKDSK.

Linking Your Code

After the program is assembled it must be linked. This process converts the assembler's machine language code into an executable program. If the program is made up of separately assembled routines then the linker is also used to combine them. Like the assembler, LINK must know where the program sections are, and where the final linked program should be written. Figure 4.2 shows a sample batch file that is used to combine three assembled programs (PARSER, ACTION, and SUBRTN) into a program called ADVENTUR. LINK automatically appends an extension to the completed program, and unless you specify otherwise the extension will be .EXE.

Figure 4.2—Linker Batch File

```
LINK PARSER+ACTION+SUBRTN,ADVENTUR,ADVENTUR, /M;
```

This batch file is intended to be used on the logged drive, which holds the assembled program code, and links known programs. For general cases the replacement character (%) would have to be used instead of the actual program names.

If you want to create a .COM program, instead of .EXE code, you must convert the program by using EXE2BIN, a program that is supplied on your DOS diskette. If this is a process you will be going through often (or even more than once) it is well worth while to create a batch file to do the work for you. The program shown in Figure 4.3 does both the LINK and the conversion.

Figure 4.3—EXE to COM Conversion by Batch

```
LINK  B:%1,B:%1,B:%1;
EXE2BIN B:%1 B:%1.COM
DEL  B:%1.EXE
```

EDLIN—The PC Line Editor

The screen editor provided with the IBM DOS is called EDLIN. It is a line editor, which means that you can only work on one line at a time, unlike a full-screen editor which allows you to move the cursor to any position on the display for additions or corrections. Line editors are somewhat limiting and can be frustrating if you're used to a full-screen version. If you have a word processor that can be used in nondocument mode (like WordStar) and you prefer to use it, by all means do so. Just be sure that it creates a file that can be used by the assembler. Document modes frequently use the high-order bit of each byte for formatting information; this will produce assembly errors.

Editing a file with EDLIN is the same whether it is a new file or you're reopening one for changes and additions. Type EDLIN followed by the name of the new file. If you want to edit a file on a drive other than the logged one you must include the drive name: EDLIN B:TEST.TXT.

EDLIN responds with an asterisk, to let you know the file has been opened. You can now type any of the ten EDLIN commands listed in Figure 4.4. One very important thing to remember about EDLIN is that it automatically creates a backup copy of your program each time it is used, unless you abort the edit with a Q for QUIT. Always be sure there is enough space on your working diskette to accommodate this backup.

<u>Figure 4.4—EDLIN Commands</u>

A	Append lines
D	Delete lines
line #	Edit a line
E	End editing the file
I	Insert a line
L	List lines
Q	Quit editing
R	Replace text
S	Search for string
W	Write lines

Opening a New EDLIN File

To begin writing lines to a new file you must first type I, which places the editor in insert mode. The editor will prompt you for input by displaying a 1 on the screen, and once you respond by entering your text and then pressing the enter key (carriage return), it will prompt with the next line number. EDLIN continues to prompt for new lines until you enter CTRL-Break, when it leaves insert mode and displays an asterisk prompt again.

Making Changes

You can type over a line to make changes, or insert and delete characters within it. First you must select the line for editing. This is done by simply typing the number of the line. EDLIN displays the line contents and its number on the screen and positions the cursor under it, at the first character. If you want to completely replace the line, just type over it and end by pressing enter. If the new line is longer than the old one you do NOT have to use insert to add the extra characters. (You don't have to delete extra characters if the new line is shorter either. EDLIN accepts the enter key as the end of the line and discards the extra text.)

If you want to change part of the line instead of retyping it, use the right arrow to move the cursor to the appropriate location and then press the DEL or INS keys to add or delete text. The right arrow key will type out characters one by one as it moves, and the F3 function key can be pressed to type out the entire line. If the right arrow doesn't seem to work, press the Num Lock key once. Remember that DEL does not remove the characters from the screen while you're typing. You have to count the characters you're erasing. (Yes, it's a pain in the neck, but that's the way it works.) When you're through making changes press the enter key to exit from the line.

Deleting Lines

Lines are deleted by typing the line number, followed by the letter D. For example, if you wanted to delete line number 1225, you would type 1225D. You can also delete a series of lines by giving EDLIN the beginning and ending line numbers, separated by a comma: 1225,1253D. EDLIN automatically adjusts line numbers as lines are added or deleted, so always delete lines from the bottom of the file toward the top, if possible. If you are careless while deleting from the top down you may find you've deleted the wrong lines. For example, if you want to delete lines 100, 102, and 103 and begin by deleting line 100, you'll find that line 102 has now become 101 and 103 has become 102, while a totally innocent line has moved into the ranks as 103.

Inserting Lines

Insertions are done with the I command, in the same way that you begin entering lines into a file. The only trick to remember is that insertions are always done *before* the line number you specify. If you type 1000I, then the new line you insert will become 1000 and the existing 1000 will become 1001. EDLIN doesn't allow you to add a specific number of blank lines which you can fill in later. All insertions are done dynamically, one at a time, as you type the text. To get out of insert mode, press CTRL-Break.

Searching for Strings

The command S, followed by a text string, tells EDLIN that you want to see where that string occurs in the file. For example, Slabel3 searches for "label3." It will either display the line and its number or display "NOT FOUND." If it does locate the string and you suspect there may be others, merely press the S key and ENTER again. EDLIN will continue to search through the file for the next occurence. You can also ask EDLIN to search through a specific range of line numbers, by entering the beginning and ending line numbers, separated by a comma: 1225,2000 Slabel3. Adding a question mark between the ending line number and the S command will cause EDLIN to prompt "O.K.?" after each instance it finds. If you want it to stop the search at that position, press enter or Y. Pressing any other key will cause it to continue the search.

Editing Large Files

In the case of very large files, which will not fit in memory, EDLIN automatically reads in from the disk until 75 percent of available memory has been filled. In order to edit the remainder of the file you must first write the current contents of memory back to the diskette (with the W command) and then append the next file section from the diskette. The command A reads in the file until memory is once again 75 percent full. This write and append sequence can be repeated as many times as necessary, until the end of the file is reached. You can also write or append a specific number of lines by typing the number before the command: 100 W or 100 A. If the number of lines exceeds 75 percent of available memory than only the allowable number of lines will be processed.

Debugging Your Program

A fairly good debugger, called—reasonably enough—
DEBUG, comes with your IBM PC DOS system disk.
This program can be used to check registers, single-
step thrugh instructions, and dump memory. It also
includes a disassembler so that the source code can be
checked while the program is running. However, the
names of the original labels are not available and they
are represented by addresses. This makes it imperative
that you have a current hard-copy listing of your program before you begin debugging.

There are 18 DEBUG commands, summarized in Figure 4.5. All of them are single letters. In order to use
these commands the program you want to investigate
must run under DEBUG, which is done by typing DE-
BUG *program-name* (or DEBUG B:*program-name*). Once
the program has finished DEBUG remains in effect
until you type the letter Q, But you must reinvoke
DEBUG to test a second program.

Figure 4.5—DEBUG Commands

COMMAND	DESCRIPTION	FORMAT
A	Assemble statements	A address
C	Compare memory	C range address
D	Dump memory	D address or D range
E	Change memory	E address data
F	Change memory blocks	F range list
G	Go execute (This commands allows you to set optional breakpoints within the program or just execute it.)	G or G = address
H	Hex add/subtract	H value value
I	Read and display input byte	I portaddress
L	Load file or sectors	L address drive sector sector
M	Move a memory block	M range address
N	Define files and parameters	d: path filename.ext
O	Send an output byte	O portaddress byte
Q	Quit DEBUG	Q
R	Display registers and flags (all registers are displayed unless a single one is specified.)	R registername
S	Search for character	S range list
T	Trace, by single step or to a given address	T=address value
U	Unassemble instructions	U address or U range
W	Write a file or diskette sectors	W address drive sector sector

Chapter 5
PROGRAMMING IN THE .EXE
ENVIRONMENT

As you have seen, we can emulate the programming environment commonly found in the previous generation of 8-bit personal computers by leaving all of the segment registers set to the start of the program segment prefix. With just a little more understanding, however, we can take full advantage of the 8088 architecture's capability to address more than 64K, separate code from data, and directly address hardware dependent areas such as the screen refresh buffers.

Registers on Entry

Unlike a .COM file, an .EXE file contains relocation information in addition to the actual code and data. When the DOS loader recognizes this type of file, it sets the segment registers based upon the definitions supplied by the programmer. Figure 5.1 shows the register assignments on entry to the program. Note that, although the DS and ES registers still point to

Figure 5.1—.EXE Memory Map

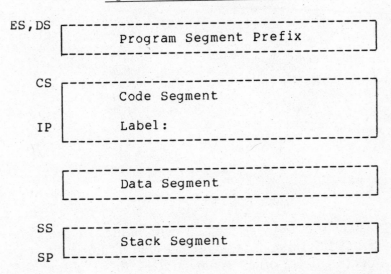

the program segment prefix, the CS and SS registers point to the code and stack segments, respectively. The instruction pointer (IP) now points to the designated entry point instead of an arbitrary hex 100, and the data segment has no initial addressability. The segments are not necessarily loaded in the order shown and, in theory, could be scattered throughout memory.

Segment Definitions

The actual position of the segments in memory depends on the segment definitions in the application program. Each definition consists of an assembly language statement with five fields. The syntax of this statement is summarized in Figure 5.2.

Figure 5.2—Segment Definition

```
                         Align Type      Combine Type   'Class'
                         ----------      ------------
SEGNAME  SEGMENT         PARA              PUBLIC
                         BYTE              COMMON
                         WORD              AT expression
                         PAGE              STACK
         ...                               MEMORY

SEGNAME  ENDS
```

Segment Name

The first field is the segment name. In the current DOS versions, the linkage editor processes segments in the order it encounters them. Since the macroassembler sorts its symbol table, this means that, unless overridden, the segments will be loaded into memory in alphabetical order. However, you shouldn't rely on this fact because it may change in future releases of the linker. The segment name is followed by the reserved word *segment* in the second field.

Align Type

The third field is the alignment type, which is used by the linkage editor to determine the starting position for the segment. The available choices are summarized in Figure 5.3. In actual fact this parameter is not very useful. Since the segment registers can only point to paragraph boundaries, the byte and word parameters are not appropriate. Likewise, since the indexed addressing modes are not sensitive to page boundaries,

Figure 5.3—Align Types

```
PARA (default) - Segment begins on paragraph
     boundary

BYTE - Segment can begin anywhere

WORD - Segment begins on a word boundary

PAGE - Segment begins on a page boundary (the
       address is divisible by 256)
```

the page option does not ease the programming task. This parameter, therefore, should always be set to "PARA."

Combine Types

At first glance, it would seem that if we write our entire program as one assembly language module, the combine type would not matter. This *is* true for the PUBLIC and COMMON combine types, but not in other cases. These commands are summarized in Figure 5.4.

PUBLIC specifies that separately assembled segments with the same name will be concatenated (joined together) at link time. This is the normal specification for code segments, and will allow the combined code to be addressed from a single CS register setting.

COMMON specifies that segments of the same name will share the same space. This is the equivalent function to the COMMON data area specification in FORTRAN. A data segment used to pass parameters from program to program should be specified as COMMON. Data segments which contain local variables used only in one program should instead specify PUBLIC.

AT, followed by an arithmetic expression, specifies

that the described segment is not actually to be loaded into memory. What it does is set up symbolic pointers to an area of memory which has already been loaded by some other process. This technique is required for addressing the program segment prefix, which is created by DOS. It is also useful for working directly with some of the DOS or hardware-maintained data areas, such as the interrupt vector tables or the screen refresh buffers.

STACK indicates that this segment is the stack segment. A separate stack segment is not allowed for .COM files, but it is required for .EXE files. If you don't include a stack segment you will get an error message when you try to link the program.

MEMORY specifies that this segment is to be loaded at a higher memory address than the rest of the segments. This overrides the default load sequence. Obviously, only one segment can be specified with the MEMORY parameter and mean anything. The results of specifying this parameter are affected by the /DSALLO-CATION and /HIGH parameters specified when invoking the linkage editor. In DOS 1.x versions the MEM-

Figure 5.4—Combine Types

```
PUBLIC - Segments will be concatinated to others
         of the same name.

COMMON - Segments will begin at the same address.

AT expression - Segment will be located at the
         paragraph number evaluated from the
         expression (DSECT).

STACK - Segment is part of the stack segment.

MEMORY - Segment will be located at a higher
         address that all other segments being
         linked together.
```

ORY parameter was useful for ordering the segments, so that the programmer could dynamically allocate memory above the end of the defined variables. Starting in DOS 2.0, there are DOS function calls which provide dynamic memory allocation in a more generalized way.

Class Entry

The final parameter in the SEGMENT statement is a name enclosed in single quotation marks, which is used by the linkage editor to group segments. The class parameter is another way to control the order in which segments will be loaded into memory. Specifically, all segments within a load module which have the same class parameter will be loaded contiguously into memory.

As we have already discussed, it is rarely, if ever, necessary to manually position segments in memory. Because of this, we recommend that you use the class parameter only for documentation purposes. That is, all code segments should have the class "CODE," data segments should have the class "DATA," stack segments should have the class "STACK," and so forth.

Establishing Addressability to Segments

In the case of .COM files, the programmer never needs to set the segment registers. The only responsibility you have is to inform the assembler of the action which the loader has already taken. When you work with .EXE files, the same is true for the code segment, but the data segment has no initial addressability. Before attempting to access any variables defined in the data segment, you must point the DS register to it and then tell the assembler what you done. Both of these actions are vital. Figure 5.5 shows a code fragment that does this. Remember that the 8088 architecture does not allow the direct loading of a segment register with an immediate value. Therefore, we first load the value of DSEG (supplied by the linkage editor) into the AX register, and then transfer it into the DS register.

Figure 5.5—Establishing Addressability to Segments

```
;DEFINE DATA SEGMENT
;-----------------------------------------------------------------
DSEG       SEGMENT    PARA PUBLIC 'DATA'
APREFIX    DW         0               ;SEGMENT PREFIX ADDRESS
LOGO       DB         'SKELETON PROGRAM EXECUTED',13,10,'$'
DSEG       ENDS
;-----------------------------------------------------------------
        (code omitted for clarity)

;DEFINE CODE SEGMENT
;-----------------------------------------------------------------
        (code omitted for clarity)

;ESTABLISH LINKAGE FROM DOS
           MOV        AX,DSEG         ;ADDRESS OF DATA SEGMENT
           MOV        DS,AX           ;NOW POINTS TO DATA SEGMENT
           ASSUME     DS:DSEG         ;TELL ASSEMBLER
```

Use of Dummy Segments

In the .COM environment, the program segment prefix was the first 256 bytes of the same segment that contained the code and data. In .EXE programs it is in its own segment. Therefore, variables within this segment that are of interest to the programmer have to be defined using the AT expression form of the segment statement.

A code fragment illustrating this is shown in Figure 5.6. Since DOS initially sets the ES register to point to the program segment prefix you only have to use an

ASSUME statement to let the assembler know that these variables are to be accessed with the ES register. The assembler will automatically generate an ES override prefix on all accesses to these variables.

Figure 5.6—Addressing a Dummy Segment

```
;DEFINE PROGRAM SEGMENT PREFIX
;-----------------------------------------------------------------
PREFIX      SEGMENT    AT Ø
            ORG        8ØH
CMDCNT      DB         ?                 ;COMMAND LINE COUNT
CMDSTR      DB         8Ø DUP (?)        ;COMMAND LINE BUFFER
PREFIX      ENDS

;DEFINE CODE SEGMENT
;-----------------------------------------------------------------
ASSUME      CS:CSEG,SS:STACK,ES:PREFIX

       (code omitted for clarity)

;SCAN INPUT PARAMETER LINE
            MOV        DI,OFFSET CMDSTR
            MOV        CH,Ø
            MOV        CL,CMDCNT          ;LENGTH OF PARAMETER STRING
            CMP        CX,Ø               ;ANY PARAMETERS?
            JNZ        SCANØ              ;YES
;SET UP DEFAULT PARAMETERS HERE
            JMP        SCANX
SCANØ:      MOV        AL,ES:[DI]         ;GET FIRST PARAMETER CHAR.
            AND        AL,ØDH             ;CONVERT TO UPPER CASE
;HANDLE PARAMETERS HERE
SCANN:      INC        DI
            LOOP       SCANØ
SCANX:      NOP
```

Returning to DOS

A serious side effect of having the program segment prefix in a separate segment is that most of the choices presented earlier for returning control to DOS will no longer work. This is because of the requirement that the CS register point to the program segment prefix at termination time. In the .EXE environment, of course, the CS register is pointing at our own code segment.

Figure 5.7 shows a simple way to solve this dilemma. During initialization, the program saves the ES register (which DOS has preset to point to the program segment prefix) into a variable called APREFIX. The timing on this save is critical. It must be done after DS has been changed to point to our data segment, but before ES has been altered. To terminate, the program places this saved address on the stack, followed by a word (two bytes) of zeros. An intersegment return (forced by the fact that it occurs within a FAR procedure) then causes control to be transferred to the INT 20 instruction within the program segment prefix. This technique has the additional advantage that it ensures that the stack has been cleaned up before the program attempts to exit.

Figure 5.7—Returning to DOS

```
           MOV        APREFIX,ES           ;SAVE PREFIX SEGMENT
;RETURN TO DOS
;-----------------------------------------------------------------
DONE:      MOV        AX,APREFIX
           PUSH       AX
           SUB        AX,AX
           PUSH       AX
           RET
```

Figure 5.8 shows the sample program, which has now been updated to run in the .EXE environment. The first thing that had to be done was to define the stack segment. As pointed out previously, this does not mean that the stack will appear first in memory. Actually, because of the naming conventions which we have chosen, it will be placed at the high end of the load module. We have initialized the stack so that it contains an iteration of the word STACK followed by three blanks. Doing this lets you see clearly on a memory dump exactly where the stack is and how much of it has been used.

Figure 5.8—Sample Program

```
PAGE      62,132
TITLE     SKELETON ASSEMBLY PROGRAM
PAGE
;------------------------------------------------------------
;DEFINE STACK SEGMENT
;------------------------------------------------------------
STACK     SEGMENT PARA STACK 'STACK'
          DB      64 DUP('STACK   ')
STACK     ENDS
;------------------------------------------------------------
;DEFINE PROGRAM SEGMENT PREFIX
;------------------------------------------------------------
PREFIX    SEGMENT AT 0
          ORG     80H
CMDCNT    DB      ?                 ;COMMAND LINE COUNT
CMDSTR    DB      80 DUP (?)        ;COMMAND LINE BUFFER
PREFIX    ENDS
;------------------------------------------------------------
;DEFINE DATA SEGMENT
;------------------------------------------------------------
DSEG      SEGMENT PARA PUBLIC 'DATA'
APREFIX   DW      0                 ;SEGMENT PREFIX ADDRESS
LOGO      DB      'SKELETON PROGRAM EXECUTED',13,10,'$'
DSEG      ENDS
;------------------------------------------------------------
;DEFINE CODE SEGMENT
;------------------------------------------------------------
CSEG      SEGMENT PARA PUBLIC 'CODE'
START     PROC    FAR
          ASSUME  CS:CSEG,SS:STACK,ES:PREFIX
;ESTABLISH LINKAGE FROM DOS
          MOV     AX,DSEG           ;ADDRESS OF DATA SEGMENT
          MOV     DS,AX             ;NOW POINTS TO DATA SEGMENT
          ASSUME  DS:DSEG           ;TELL ASSEMBLER
          MOV     APREFIX,ES        ;SAVE PREFIX SEGMENT
;SCAN INPUT PARAMETER LINE
          MOV     DI,OFFSET CMDSTR
          MOV     CH,0
          MOV     CL,CMDCNT         ;LENGTH OF PARAMETER STRING
          CMP     CX,0              ;ANY PARAMETERS?
          JNZ     SCAN0             ;YES
;SET UP DEFAULT PARAMETERS HERE
          JMP     SCANX
SCAN0:    MOV     AL,ES:[DI]        ;GET 1ST PARAMETER CHAR
          AND     AL,0DH            ;CONVERT TO UPPER CASE
;HANDLE PARAMETERS HERE
SCANN:    INC     DI
          LOOP    SCAN0
SCANX:    NOP
;------------------------------------------------------------
;START OF MAIN PROGRAM
;------------------------------------------------------------
          CALL    CLRSCN
```

Figure 5.8 (con't.)

```
            MOV     DX,OFFSET LOGO
            CALL    PRINT
;-------------------------------------------------------------
;RETURN TO DOS
;-------------------------------------------------------------
DONE:       MOV     AX,APREFIX
            PUSH    AX
            SUB     AX,AX
            PUSH    AX
            RET
START       ENDP
;-------------------------------------------------------------
;SUBROUTINES
;-------------------------------------------------------------
CLRSCN      PROC                        ;CLEAR SCREEN
            PUSH    AX
            MOV     AX,2
            INT     10H
            POP     AX
            RET
CLRSCN      ENDP
PRINT       PROC
            PUSH    AX
            MOV     AH,9
            INT     21H
            POP     AX
            RET
PRINT       ENDP
CSEG        ENDS
            END     START
```

The next section defined was the program segment prefix. The segment will not actually be at zero, of course, but this specification reminds us that this is a dummy segment which will overlay our definitions on the actual segment built by DOS.

Next the data segment is defined. It is good programming practice to define all of the segments that contain data labels before you define the code segment. The assembler doesn't handle forward references as well as it might. Most of the time, the result is just inefficient code, but sometimes the assembler gets confused enough that it generates phase errors between passes one and two.

The code segment starts out by establishing addressability to the data segment and then saving the address of the program segment prefix. Actually, in this simple example, we leave the PSP address in the ES register of the duration of the program. In more ambitious programs you would probably drop addressability to the PSP as soon as you had finished processing the passed parameters. The ES register would then be freed for use in string processing.

After a quick pass through the parameters supplied on the command line, the program issues subroutine calls to clear the screen and print the acknowledgment message. The only difference here between this example and the previous one is that the PRINT subroutine has been generalized by having the caller place the message address into the DX register before issuing the CALL statement.

The final action performed in the program is to clean up the stack and return to DOS.

Part II

Programming with DOS Calls

Chapter 6
DOS CONSOLE SERVICES

All DOS function calls are made by placing the function number into the AH register and issuing an INT 21H instruction. Nine of the function calls (shown in Figure 6.1) deal specifically with the console, that is, the keyboard and the display.

Figure 6.1—DOS Console Services

FUNCTION CALL	DESCRIPTION
1	Keyboard input
2	Display output
6	Direct console I/O
7	Direct input without echo
8	Direct input without echo
9	Print string
A	Buffered keyboard input
B	Check keyboard status
C	Clear keyboard buffer and invoke input (AL = 1,6,7,8,A)

55

Print String

The print string function call should already be familiar, since we have used it in the sample programs. Its use is summarized in Figure 6.2. Note that the string must be terminated with a dollar sign ($) and that any carriage control desired must be included in the string. In the example, 13 is the ASCII decimal value for a carriage return, and 10 is the ASCII decimal code for a line feed. This function treats the display as if it were a teletypewriter. No provision has been made to control color, intensity, underlining, and so forth. This is true of all the DOS console function calls.

<u>Figure 6.2—Print String</u>

```
AH = 9
DS:DX points to the character string (which
       must be terminated by a dollar sign).

Calling Sequence:

              MOV        DX,OFFSET LOGO
              CALL       PRINT

    ... (code omitted for clarity)

   PRINT      PROC
              PUSH AX
              MOV  AH,9
              INT  21H
              POP  AX
              RET
   PRINT      ENDP

Actual Print Line:

LOGO DB     'SKELETON PROGRAM EXECUTED',13,1Ø,'$'
```

Buffered Keyboard Input

The printer equivalent input function to print string is buffered keyboard input. This function lets the application program read an entire line, terminated by a carriage return, from the keyboard without having to worry about handling the individual key strokes, echoing characters to the screen, editing, and so on.

In this case the DS:DX register pair points to a buffer. The first byte of this buffer contains the maximum length of data that can be accepted, including the carriage return at the end. If the user attempts to overrun this length, by typing in more than the allowable number of characters, DOS will sound the audible alarm and discard the extra typed characters.

The second byte of the buffer contains the length of the actual input string, *not* including the carriage return. This value is set by DOS. Note that difference carefully. The carriage return occupies a buffer position, but is not included in the returned count field. Therefore the current count will always be at least one less than the maximum count.

The actual message string starts at byte 3. DOS does not clear or pad the remainder of the buffer, so the application must rely on the count field. Other than the fact that the maximum count field does not appear in the program segment prefix, this is the same technique that is used by DOS to pass any parameters to the program that are typed following the program name on the command line. Figure 6.3 summarizes the buffered keyboard input function.

Character Output

There are several reasons why a programmer might want to output characters directly, instead of using the

Figure 6.3—Buffered Keyboard Input

```
AH = ØA
DS:DX Points to the buffer

   1 byte      1 byte

   MAX.         CURR.      INPUT MESSAGE (return)
   COUNT        COUNT
```

DS:DX

Note: The current count does not include the
carriage return.

All editing keys are available.

There is a similarity to the buffer in
the program segment prefix.

print string function, and one of them is the way the
print string function uses a dollar sign as a required
terminator. It is hard to justify that convention on
anything except historical grounds! Figure 6.4 shows
two different ways in which the character output function call can be used in a subroutine to create a print
string function which handles termination differently.
In the first example, the calling sequence is identical to
a print string call (DS:DX points to the string) except
that the string is terminated by a byte of zeros instead
of by a dollar sign. The heart of this routine is the
LODSB instruction which moves the byte pointed to
by the DS:SI register pair into the AL register, and
automatically increments SI. This "moves" the DX register along the string byte by byte, as each character is
read and printed.

The second example expects the length of the string
to be passed in the CX register. No terminator is

Figure 6.4—Character Output

```
AH = 2
DL = the character

The system checks for control/break FOLLOWING output.
```

1. Print string terminated by Ø
   (Expects the message offset in DX.)

```
        PRZER      PROC
                   PUSH  AX
                   PUSH  DX
                   PUSH  SI
                   MOV   SI,DX
        PRZER1:    LODSB
                   CMP   AL,Ø
                   JZ    PRZERX
                   MOV   DL,AL
                   MOV   AH,2
                   INT   21H
                   JMP   PRZER1     ;GET NEXT CHARACTER
        PRZERX:    POP   SI
                   POP   DX
                   POP   AX
                   RET
        PRZER      ENDP
```

2. Print String of Known Length
   (expects the message offset in DX and its length in CX)

```
        PRSTR      PROC
                   PUSH  AX
                   PUSH  CX
                   PUSH  SI
                   MOV   SI,DX
        PRSTR1:    LODSB
                   MOV   DL,AL
                   MOV   AH,2
                   INT   21H
                   LOOP  PRSTR1
                   POP   SI
                   POP   CX
                   POP   AX
                   RET
        PRSTR      ENDP
```

expected. This version makes use of the LOOP instruction, which automatically decrements CX and branches if the result is nonzero.

Other variants can be coded very easily. One common technique, for example, is to include the length of the string as the first byte of the string itself. Another is to set the high order bit on in the last character of the string. Implementing either of these methods requires only minor modifications to the example shown.

Character Input

There are three function calls (1, 7, and 8) that retrieve a character from the keyboard. All three of them check to see if there is currently a character in the DOS type-ahead buffer. If so, it is returned in the AL register (where it can be tested) and deleted from the buffer. If the buffer is empty, then the functions will wait until a key is pressed and a character is available, and then return it as before.

There are two areas of distinction between these functions. Only function 1 echoes the received character to the screen. Function 1 also checks to see if the user has typed the CTRL-break key combination recently. (If so, control is passed to the routine whose address is specified at offset 14 in the program segment prefix.) Function 8 checks for CTRL-break too, but function 7 does not. Figure 6.5 summarizes these combinations. Logically,

Figure 6.5—Character Input Functions

```
AH = 1, 7, or 8

The next character from the buffer is returned in AL.
If the buffer is empty the system waits for a keypress.

    FUNCTION      ECHO TO SCREEN?     CHECK FOR CTRL/BRK?
    ------------------------------------------------------

        1             yes                   yes
        7             no                    no
        8             no                    yes
```

there should be a fourth combination which echoes to the screen but does not check CTRL-break. No such function is supplied, although it could be built up from the direct console I/O function if you really feel that you need it.

Direct Console I/O

Sometimes it is desirable to check for the presence of an input character in the DOS type-ahead buffer, but not to wait for one if there's none there. If DL is set to hex FF, then the function will return the next character from the buffer, if any. Otherwise, it will return zero. If DL is set to any other value, then it is interpreted as a character to be written to the screen.

This function does not wait in either case, nor does it check to see if CTRL-break has been issued. This gives the programmer absolute control over the character I/O operation. The rules for this function are summarized in Figure 6.6.

Figure 6.6—Direct Console I/O

```
 AH = 6
 DL = ØFFH

     This is an input function. It returns
     the keyboard character in AL if one is
     ready. Otherwise it returns a zero.

DL NOT= ØFFH

     Writes the character in DL to the screen.

This function never waits, never checks for CTL/BRK
```

Clear Buffer and Input

This function, illustrated in Figure 6.7, purges the DOS type-ahead buffer, and then links to one of the five input functions already discussed above. Most of the time it is desirable to allow the user to type input before it is needed, but sometimes this is not appropriate. Consider, for example, a disk I/O error subroutine which wishes to ask the user if a retry is desired. Since such an error is not usually predictable, any information in the buffer is highly unlikely to be the response to the question. This function solves that problem by flushing out all of the input buffer characters before it goes on to normal processing.

Figure 6.7—Clear Input Buffer and Perform Function

```
AH = ØCH
AL = 1, 6, 7, or A
```

The keyboard buffer is cleared and the function is invoked from AL. The system is forced to wait for a keystroke.

Keyboard Status

If a program is sophisticated enough to do its own multitasking, by checking several input sources (such as communication lines), then the dispatcher routine may want to know that the console user has pressed a key. However, it may not be the routine that will ultimately process the input. In this case, if the input routine deletes the character from the buffer, then the calling routine must save the returned character and later pass it to the appropriate subroutine. This function, shown in Figure 6.8, solves the problem by leaving the character in the DOS buffer and just returning the status. The keyboard status function could also be used during a long processing routine to check to see if the user has pressed CTRL-break to terminate processing. In that case the calling routine would not even have to check the returned status, since control would not be returned if the CTRL-break routine was invoked.

Figure 6.8—Keyboard Status

```
AH = ØBH

ØFFH is returned in AL if a
character is available. Otherwise,
a zero is returned in AL. A check
is always made for CTRL/BRK.
```

Chapter 7
OTHER CHARACTER CALLS

Printer Output

The IBM PC is designed to support up to three parallel output ports, which are assumed to be printers. DOS recognizes the existence of all three, if present, but the series of character-oriented function calls we are presently studying only supports the first (or standard) printer. This call is identical to function 2, which writes a character to the screen, except that AH is set to 5. In addition, if the printer is not ready, DOS will invoke the critical error handler. This routine will print an error message to the screen and request that the user choose from the three options: Retry, Ignore, or Abort. (This is a change from DOS release 1, where only an error message was issued.)

Since the function is essentially identical to the one for screen output, the print string functions developed in Figure 6.4 will also work for sending strings to the printer just by changing the function number in AH. Another possibility is to modify the function to display the string on the screen and also echo it to the printer if a flag has been set. Figure 7.1 shows an example of this technique.

Figure 7.1—Screen Output Echoed to the Printer

```
Display string terminated by Ø with optional echo
to printer. (Expects  address of string in DS:DX,
PRTFLG=Ø for no echo.)
            PRZER      PROC
            PUSH AX
            PUSH DX
            PUSH SI
            MOV  SI,DX
PRZER1:     LODSB
            CMP  AL,Ø            ;END OF STRING?
            JZ   PRZERX          ;YES - DONE
            MOV  DL,AL           ;CHARACTER TO DISPLAY
            MOV  AH,2            ;DISPLAY CHARACTER FUNCTION NUMBER
            INT  21H             ;INVOKE DOS
            CMP  PRTFLG,Ø        ;ECHO TURNED OFF?
            JZ   PRZER1          ;YES, GO GET NEXT CHARACTER
            MOV  AH,5            ;PRINT CHARACTER FUNCTION NUMBER
            INT  21H             ;INVOKE DOS
            JMP  PRZER1          ;GET NEXT CHARACTER
PRZERX:     POP  SI
            POP  DX
            POP  AX
            RET
PRZER       ENDP
```

Serial Port I/O

DOS provides character-oriented calls for the "standard auxiliary device," which is the first of the PC's two serial ports. Function call 3 waits for a character to be received and returns it in AL. Function call 4 writes the character in DL to the serial port. Since these functions have the same format as the other character input and output function calls, programs written to use the keyboard and display screen can be modified easily to operate a communications line, for example.

The drawback with this technique is that these function calls are unbuffered, do not use interrupts, and do not return any status or error codes. For this reason, serious communications applications need to use more sophisticated techniques.

Date and Time Routines

The PC native hardware (except for the PC AT) does not have a clock, just a timer that ticks about 18.2 times per second. A ROM BIOS routine accumulates these counts in a predetermined memory location. DOS, in turn, uses this information to keep a software clock which keeps track of the elapsed time since January 1, 1980. As shown in Figures 7.2 and 7.3, the time and date values are kept in binary, but in a form that makes both calculation and print editing fairly simple.

<u>Figure 7.2—Date Handling</u>

```
AH = 2A    Get date
   = 2B    Set date

CX = Year, in binary (1980 - 2099)

DH = Month (1=January, 2=February ...
           12=December)

DL = Day of Month (1 - 31)
```

Figure 7.3—Time of Day Handling

```
AH = 2C    Get Time
   = 2D    Set Time

CH = Hours (Ø - 23)

CL = Minutes (Ø - 59)

DH = Seconds (Ø - 59)

DL = 1/1ØØ Seconds (Ø - 99)
```

For the set-date call only, one return code is provided. AL = 0 means the set operation was successful, and AL = FF means that the set request was not valid. For set-time only, one return code is provided. AL = 0 means that the set was successful. AL = FF means the set-time request was not valid. Figure 7.4 shows a sample program that will display the current date and time much like the date and time commands, except that it does not prompt for new values.

Figure 7.4—Time/Date Routine

```
PAGE      62,132
TITLE     DATETIME - SAMPLE DATE & TIME PROGRAM
PAGE
;-----------------------------------------------------------
;DEFINE STACK SEGMENT
;-----------------------------------------------------------
STACK     SEGMENT PARA STACK 'STACK'
          DB      64 DUP('STACK    ')
STACK     ENDS
;-----------------------------------------------------------
;DEFINE PROGRAM SEGMENT PREFIX
;-----------------------------------------------------------
PREFIX    SEGMENT AT Ø
          ORG     8ØH
CMDCNT    DB      ?                     ;COMMAND LINE COUNT
CMDSTR    DB      8Ø DUP (?)            ;COMMAND LINE BUFFER
PREFIX    ENDS
```

```
;-----------------------------------------------------------
;DEFINE DATA SEGMENT
;-----------------------------------------------------------
DSEG      SEGMENT PARA PUBLIC 'DATA'
APREFIX   DW      Ø                   ;SEGMENT PREFIX ADDRESS
LOGO      DB      'It is now '
TIME      DB      '24:ØØ:ØØ.ØØ on '
DATE      DB      '12-31-1984.',13,1Ø,'$'
DSEG      ENDS
;-----------------------------------------------------------
;DEFINE CODE SEGMENT
;-----------------------------------------------------------
CSEG      SEGMENT PARA PUBLIC 'CODE'
START     PROC    FAR
          ASSUME  CS:CSEG,SS:STACK,ES:PREFIX
;ESTABLISH LINKAGE FROM DOS
          MOV     AX,DSEG             ;ADDRESS OF DATA SEGMENT
          MOV     DS,AX               ;NOW POINTS TO DATA SEGMENT
          ASSUME  DS:DSEG             ;TELL ASSEMBLER
          MOV     APREFIX,ES          ;SAVE PREFIX SEGMENT
;-----------------------------------------------------------
;START OF MAIN PROGRAM
;-----------------------------------------------------------
          CALL    CLRSCN              ;CLEAR SCREEN
          MOV     AH,2AH              ;GET DATE
          INT     21H                 ;DOS FUNCTION CALL
          MOV     AX,CX               ;YEAR
          MOV     SI,OFFSET DATE+6    ;OUTPUT LOCATION
          MOV     CX,4                ;OUTPUT FIELD WIDTH
          CALL    BINASC              ;CONVERT TO CHARACTERS
          MOV     AL,DH               ;MONTH
          CBW                         ;CONVERT TO WORD
          MOV     SI,OFFSET DATE      ;OUTPUT LOCATION
          MOV     CX,2                ;FIELD WIDTH
          CALL    BINASC              ;CONVERT TO CHARACTERS
          MOV     AL,DL               ;DAY OF MONTH
          CBW                         ;CONVERT TO WORD
          MOV     SI,OFFSET DATE+3    ;FIELD LOCATION
          CALL    BINASC              ;CONVERT TO CHARACTERS
          MOV     AH,2CH              ;GET TIME FUNCTION
          INT     21H                 ;DOS FUNCTION CALL
          PUSH    CX                  ;REGISTER USED BY BINAS
          MOV     AL,CH               ;HOURS
          CBW                         ;CONVERT TO WORD
          MOV     SI,OFFSET TIME      ;FIELD LOCATION
          MOV     CX,2                ;FIELD WIDTH
          CALL    BINASC              ;CONVERT TO CHARACTERS
          POP     CX                  ;RETRIEVE MINUTES
          MOV     AL,CL               ;MINUTES
          CBW                         ;CONVERT TO WORD
          MOV     SI,OFFSET TIME+3    ;FIELD LOCATION
          MOV     CX,2                ;FIELD WIDTH
          CALL    BINASC              ;CONVERT TO CHARACTERS
          MOV     AL,DH               ;SECONDS
```

```
CBW                                  ;CONVERT TO WORD
MOV       SI,OFFSET TIME+6           ;FIELD LOCATION
CALL      BINASC                     ;CONVERT TO CHARACTERS
MOV       AL,DL                      ;1/100 SECONDS
CBW                                  ;CONVERT TO WORD
MOV       SI,OFFSET TIME+9           ;FIELD LOCATION
CALL      BINASC                     ;CONVERT TO CHARACTERS
          MOV       DX,OFFSET LOGO
          CALL      PRINT
;------------------------------------------------------------
;RETURN TO DOS
;------------------------------------------------------------
DONE:     MOV       AX,APREFIX
          PUSH      AX
          SUB       AX,AX
          PUSH      AX
          RET
START     ENDP
;------------------------------------------------------------
;SUBROUTINES
;------------------------------------------------------------
CLRSCN    PROC                       ;CLEAR SCREEN
          PUSH      AX
          MOV       AX,2
          INT       10H
          POP       AX
          RET
CLRSCN    ENDP
PRINT     PROC
          PUSH      AX
          MOV       AH,9
          INT       21H
          POP       AX
          RET
PRINT     ENDP
;CONVERT BINARY TO ASCII
BINASC    PROC
;CALL WITH            AX = SIGNED BINARY NUMBER
;                     SI = OFFSET OF OUTPUT FIELD
;                     CX = WIDTH OF OUTPUT FIELD
;RETURNS              SI = OFFSET OF 1ST DIGIT
;                     OTHER REGISTERS PRESERVED
          PUSH      DX
          PUSH      CX
          PUSH      BX
          PUSH      DI
          PUSH      AX
          MOV       DI,SI    ;SAVE START OF STRING
BA1:      MOV       BYTE PTR [SI],'0'     ;FILL CHARACTER
          INC       SI       ;POINT TO NEXT FIELD POSITION
          LOOP      BA1      ;LOOP UNTIL DONE
          MOV       BX,10    ;INITIALIZE DIVISOR
BA2:      XOR       DX,DX    ;CLEAR MSB OF DIVIDEND
          DIV       BX       ;DIVIDE BY TEN
```

```
                ADD     DL,'0'   ;CONVERT TO ASCII DIGIT
                DEC     SI       ;STEP BACKWARDS THROUGH BUFFER
                MOV     [SI],DL  ;STORE DIGIT
                CMP     SI,DI    ;OUT OF SPACE?
                JZ      BAX      ;YES - QUIT
                OR      AX,AX    ;ALL DIGITS PRINTED?
                JNZ     BA2      ;NO - KEEP TRUCKING
BAX:            POP     AX
                POP     DI
                POP     BX
                POP     CX
                POP     DX
                RET
BINASC          ENDP
CSEG            ENDS
                END     START
```

Chapter 8
INTRODUCTION TO DISK FILE
OPERATIONS

In the version 1 DOS releases (1.0, 1.1), the file functions are record oriented. By this we mean that you can think of a file as a collection of fixed length records which are moved between program storage and diskette or hard disk by means of READ and WRITE commands. Information about which block is to be transferred is communicated via fields within a control block, called a File Control Block (FCB). The FCB is physically located within the program's data areas.

DOS 2.0 introduced stream-oriented I/O. In this type of data handling you can think of a file as a stream of characters, with a pointer to the current position. Through use of something called a *file handle*, you can move the pointer and GET or PUT some number of characters. All of the file buffering and deblocking functions are contained within DOS.

Although the stream-oriented I/O functions are generally easier to use than the record-oriented I/O functions, it is necessary to understand them both. Record-oriented I/O has to be used in any application that must be able to run under DOS 1.0 or 1.1, and is also used whenever

71

you want to directly manage the file buffers, in order to maximize performance. Let's take a look at record-oriented I/O first.

The File Control Block

The heart of record-oriented I/O is the file control block (FCB), which is shown in Figure 8.1. This control block comes in two flavors, standard and extended. The standard FCB operates on normal file entries. The extended FCB will also work with volume labels, subdirectories, and hidden and system files.

An FCB in which you have set just the drive number, filename, and extension fields is referred to as an *unopened* FCB. When the remaining fields have been

Figure 8.1—File Control Block (FCB)

	−7			
	X'FF'	Zeros		Attribute
0 Drive	Filename (8 bytes) or Reserved device name			
8	Filename extension		Curr. Block	Rec. Size
16 File Size (low)	File Size (high)		Date	Time (DOS 2.0)
24	Reserved for system use			
32 Curr. Record	Random Rec. (low)		Random Rec. (High)	

Byte	Description
0	Drive number
1 - 8	File name
9 - 11	File name extension
12 - 13	Current block number
14 - 15	Logical record size (bytes)
16 - 19	File size (bytes)
20 - 21	Date of last change
22 - 23	Time (DOS 2.0)
24 - 31	Reserved
32	Current record number within current block
33 - 36	Record number relative to start of file

set by either an OPEN or a CREATE function call, the FCB is referred to as an *open* FCB. Descriptions of the various function calls will indicate whether they require an open or an unopened FCB. The program segment prefix contains space for two FCBs. This is important to remember because DOS will parse the command line looking for file specifications. If found, DOS will set up one or both of these areas as unopened FCBs. FCBs, of course, are not limited to the PSP and can be placed wherever you want to put them.

The Disk Transfer Address

One piece of information that is not included in the FCB is the address of the file buffer. This address, called the disk transfer address (DTA), is maintained within DOS, but can be set (and in DOS 2 or later can be retrieved) by the programmer.

The DTA is initially set by DOS to point to offset 80H in the PSP. Of course, this area can only be used as the default file buffer if the record size is 128 bytes or less. Figure 8.2 shows how the application program can set and retrieve the DTA value.

Figure 8.2—Disk Transfer Address (DTA)

- Buffer address for all disk transfers
- Set initially to 80H in the program segment prefix.

```
Setting DTA:

    AH = 1A
    DS:DX = Buffer starting address
    Function call = INT 21H

Retrieving DTA:

    AH = 2F
    Function call = INT 21H
    The data is returned in ES:BX (DOS 2.0 only)
```

Opening a File

The OPEN function call asks DOS to search the indicated file directory for a specific file. If the file is found, data from its directory entry is merged into the FCB, otherwise an error is returned. Figure 8.3 summarizes this process. Following the open, the programmer must check the return code, change the record size field (if it is not 128), and set the current record field for sequential operations or set the random record field for random operation.

<u>Figure 8.3—Opening a File</u>

```
Setting Data:

AH = ØFH
DS:DX = Address of  an unopened FCB

Return Codes:

1. ØFF in AL = File not found
2. Ø in AL and:

      if the drive code was zero (default)
      the code is changed to the actual drive

      the current block size is set to zero

      the record size is set to decimal 128

      the date, time, file size, etc. are set
```

Note that in the FCB the coding for the drive identifier is a little bit different than the convention used elsewhere in DOS. A value of 1 means drive A, 2 indicates drive B, and so on. This allows a zero value to indicate the use of the current default drive. Because the default can be changed during the runnning of a program, OPEN changes the FCB 0 to the value of the current drive.

The OPEN call initializes some, but not all, of the remainder of the FCB fields. Unfortunately, some of the fields it does initialize are likely to be different than the ones you want. Because of this you have several programming responsibilities following the OPEN call.

First, you must check the return code in AL. The only good return code is zero. Currently the only error return is OFFH, which indicates that the file was not found. Good programming practice, however, is to check for zero and take an error branch in all other cases. This will ensure compatibility with future releases, which may include additional error conditions.

The OPEN call sets the record size in the file to 128 (80H). This value was picked for compatibility with prior systems which typically used a physical record size of 128 bytes. The IBM PC, however, uses 512-byte sectors. It is good programming practice to always set the record size field, even if the current default is correct.

Finally, the current record field or the random record field (depending upon the type of access you're going to do) must be set to establish the correct file positioning. There are no default settings for these fields, so they must always be set under program control.

Reading a File Sequentially

The Sequential Read call, if successful, transfers the record specified by the current block and current record fields in the FCB to memory at the address specified by the current DTA. (A block is a group of 128 records.) The current record field is then incremented. An entire file can be read, one record at a time, by just reissuing the DOS call. The DTA, on the other hand, is *not* incremented by this call, so that each file record will be read into the same buffer. Loading a file contiguously into memory could be accomplished by incrementing the DTA address within the program logic, but a better way is provided with the Random Bloc Read call, which will be discussed later.

Figure 8.4—Reading a File (Sequential)

```
AH = 14H
DS:DX = The address of an opened FCB
Function call = INT 21H

Return Codes:

AL = 0    Good read
     01   Attempt to read past end of file
     02   Attempt to read past end of sector
     03   The end of file occurred within the
          record that was passed and the record
          was padded out with zeros
```

Following the Read call, you should always check the return code in AL. A return code of zero indicates not only that the read was successful, but also that the entire record contained data. One reason that this might not happen is that the end of the file has been reached. If the file size is an exact multiple of the record size, then End of File (EOF) will not be detected when the last record is read, but on an attempt to read the (nonexistent) following record. In this case, no data will be transferred and the return code will be set to 01.

If the file size is not a multiple of the record size, as is usual with text files, then the last file sector will only be partially filled. In this case, DOS will transfer the valid information and pad the rest of the record with zeros. The return code, in this case, is set to 03.

The other currently defined return code is 02. This does not show up often, but when it does it means you've got a real problem. This is because it has less to do with your programming than with a hardware dependency in the IBM PC. Normally, you do not have to worry about where your program is loaded into memory. That is because, as we have discussed previously, the segment registers provide automatic relocation for all processor memory accesses. Unfortunately the direct memory access (DMA) hardware which is used to control disk reads and writes does not involve the segment registers. This means that most members of the PC family cannot do a data transfer between disk and memory if the record will cross a 64K physical memory boundary. One solution to this problem is to always use a record size which is smaller that 512 bytes. This will cause DOS to first read the physical sector into a DOS buffer and then move the logical record to the program buffer. The Sequential Read call is summarized in Figure 8.4.

You've probably noticed that no error code is provided to report a true hardware read error. This is because (should such an error occur) DOS will invoke the critical error handler routine via interrupt 24H. This routine will only return control to the application program if the error has been successfully handled or can be ignored. Otherwise the program will be terminated via interrupt 23H. If the program is sophisticated enough to handle hardware problems, it can provide its own routines for either the INT 23H or INT 24H calls.

Reading a File Randomly

The Random Read call is summarized in Figure 8.5. It is very similar to the Sequential Read call except that the record to be read is pointed to by the random record field in the FCB. This four-byte field contains the record number relative to the beginning of the file. That is, the first record is record number zero. When performing this call, **DOS** first sets the current block and current record fields to agree with the random record field. This allows you to switch back and forth between random and sequential processing on the same file if you want to.

Figure 8.5—Reading a File (Random)

```
AH = 21H
DS:DX = The address of an opened FCB

The system takes the value of the random record
field (33-36 in FCB) and sets the current block
and record fields. It then proceeds as if pro-
cessing sequentially.

Return Codes:

AL = 0   Good read
     01  Attempt to read past the end of file
     02  Attempt to read past the end of sector
     03  An end of file marker occurred within
         the record that was passed and the record
         was padded out with zeros.
```

Random Block Read

The Random Block Read call, shown in Figure 8.6, is just a way to load a number of records sequentially into memory with DOS doing some of the bookkeeping. There are only two differences between this call and the Random Read call. Prior to doing a Random Block Read, CX has to be set to the number of blocks to be read. If the return code is zero, then all requested records were read. Otherwise, the return codes mean almost the same as before, but apply to the last record actually read. In addition, CX is set to indicate the

Figure 8.6—Random Block Read

```
AH = 27H
DS:DX = The address of an opened FCB
CX = The record count (must not be 0)

CX number of records are read into the
buffer at the DTA

Return Codes:

AL = 0   All records were okay
     01  The end of file was reached; the
         last record was complete.
     02  The end of segment was reached; as
         many records as would fit in the
         segment were read.
     03  The end of file was reached; the last
         record is a partial record.
```

actual number of records read, and the current block and record fields point to the next unread record.

Regardless of AL, CX returns the actual number of records that were read, and the current block and current record fields point to the next unread record.

Writing a File

For each of the three record-oriented file read calls we've discussed there is a corresponding write call, as shown in Figure 8.7. The only significant difference is that the two return codes which previously reported end of file conditions have been replaced with a single one which indicates that the file write was aborted because there was no room left on the disk.

Figure 8.7—Writing a File

```
AH = Function number
DS:DX = The address of an opened FCB

All writing is done from the current DTA

Write Types:

    AH = 15    Sequential write
         22    Random write
         28    Random block write (if CX is
               0 on entry then no records are
               written)

Return Codes:

AL = 0    Successful write
     01   The diskette is full
     02   There is not enough space in the disk
          transfer segment.
```

Closing a File

It is a good idea to close all files when they are no longer needed. This has to be done by the application program, since for record-oriented operations DOS does not keep track of open files. The function of CLOSE is to update the disk directory. If this is not done, any file which has been changed in size will not have that fact recorded in the directory, leading to loss of information. In addition, if the user physically changes diskettes while there are any open files which have had additional space allocated to them, DOS may later write the file allocation table (FAT) from the previous diskette onto the new diskette, which will destroy access to all files on that diskette. The Close File call is summarized in Figure 8.8.

<u>Figure 8.8—Closing a File</u>

```
AH = 1Ø
DS:DX = The address of an opened FCB
```

- DOS does not keep track of open files
- All files must be closed individually
- A file close updates the directory
- A file close is not necessary for read-only operations.

Return Codes:

```
AL = Ø   The file directory has been updated
         and the file is closed.
     FF  The file was not in the correct
         directory position.
```

End of File (EOF)

If files have been written and closed properly, then DOS knows their physical length. This information is used to signal the program reading the file when the end has been reached. Because of this it is unnecessary, in most cases, to put any kind of special end of file record as the last record in the file, as was common in some prior generation operating systems.

When the file consists of fixed-length records, end of file handling is very straightforward. The CLOSE command set the length into the DOS directory when the file was created or when it was extended. The READ command will return an end of file indication on the first read attempt following the last record in the file.

Variable length records, on the other hand, require slightly different handling. When the file was created, the last WRITE command wrote an entire record, even if the last record was only partially filled. Therefore DOS knows which record is the last record, but not where within that record the valid data stops. Therefore, the application program must adopt some convention which will allow it to recognize the true end of the file. Since text files normally contain only valid ASCII characters, it is an accepted convention to terminate such a file with a special character with a value of 1AH. Variable length binary records usually contain a count field at the beginning of each record, although this convention is not quite as universal as the use of 1AH for ASCII files. EOF techniques summarized in Figure 8.9.

Figure 8.9—End of File (EOF) Effects

```
Fixed Length Records:

    •  The file size is placed in the directory
    •  Read supplies a return code
    •  Close sets the EOF for Write

Variable Length Records:

    •  Read will pad the last record
    •  Write will set the size to full record
    •  ASCII files use hex 1A as the EOF marker
```

The Sample File Display Program

Figure 8.10 combines the record-oriented file access calls which we have been discussing into a sample program that displays an ASCII text file on the console. It is the logical equivalent of the TYPE command supplied with DOS, although the error messages are different.

The first notable difference from the previous program examples is in the definition of the program segment prefix (PSP). Previously we defined the unformatted

Figure 8.10—Sample Program

```
PAGE        62,132
TITLE       Scan - Simple File Display Program
;------------------------------------------------------------------
;DEFINE STACK SEGMENT
;------------------------------------------------------------------
STACK       SEGMENT PARA STACK 'STACK'
            DB      64 DUP('STACK   ')
STACK       ENDS
;------------------------------------------------------------------
;DEFINE PROGRAM SEGMENT PREFIX
;------------------------------------------------------------------
PREFIX      SEGMENT AT 0
            ORG     5CH
FCB         DB      32 DUP (?)
FCBRNO      DB      ?                       ;CURRENT RECORD NUMBER
            ORG     80H
BUFFER      DB      128 DUP (?)             ;FILE BUFFER
PREFIX      ENDS
;------------------------------------------------------------------
;DEFINE DATA SEGMENT
;------------------------------------------------------------------
DSEG        SEGMENT PARA PUBLIC 'DATA'
MSG1        DB      'FILE NOT FOUND',13,10,'$'
DSEG        ENDS
;------------------------------------------------------------------
;DEFINE CODE SEGMENT
;------------------------------------------------------------------
CSEG        SEGMENT PARA PUBLIC 'CODE'
START       PROC    FAR
            ASSUME  CS:CSEG,SS:STACK,DS:PREFIX
;ESTABLISH ADDRESSABILITY TO DATA SEGMENT
            MOV     AX,DSEG                 ;ADDRESS OF DATA SEGMENT
            MOV     ES,AX                   ;NOW POINTS TO DATA SEG.
            ASSUME  ES:DSEG                 ;TELL THE ASSEMBLER
;------------------------------------------------------------------
;START OF MAIN PROGRAM
;------------------------------------------------------------------
            CALL    CLRSCN
            MOV     DX,OFFSET FCB
            MOV     AH,15                   ;OPEN A FILE
            INT     21H
            CMP     AL,0                    ;GOOD RETURN?
            JZ      FILEOK                  ;YES
            MOV     DX,OFFSET MSG1
            PUSH    DS
            PUSH    ES
            POP     DS                      ;PRINT EXPECTS MSG IN DS:DX
            CALL    PRINT
            POP     DS
            JMP     DONE                    ;QUIT
FILEOK:     MOV     CX,1                    ;MARK BUFFER EMPTY
            MOV     FCBRNO,0                ;POSITION TO START OF FILE
READ:       CALL    RDBYTE                  ;READ ONE BYTE FROM FILE
            CMP     AL,1AH                  ;END OF FILE?
            JZ      DONE                    ;YES - QUIT
            MOV     DL,AL
            MOV     AH,2                    ;DISPLAY OUTPUT
            INT     21H
            JMP     READ                    ;GET NEXT FILE BYTE
```

```
; ------------------------------------------------------------
;RETURN TO DOS
; ------------------------------------------------------------
DONE:       PUSH    DS
            XOR     AX,AX
            PUSH    AX
            RET
START:      ENDP
; ------------------------------------------------------------
;SUBROUTINES
; ------------------------------------------------------------
CLRSCN      PROC                         ;CLEAR SCREEN
            PUSH    AX
            MOV     AX,2
            INT     10H
            POP     AX
            RET
CLRSCN      ENDP
PRINT       PROC
            PUSH    AX
            MOV     AH,9
            INT     21H
            POP     AX
            RET
PRINT       ENDP
RDBYTE      PROC
            LOOP    RDBYT2               ;NO PHYSICAL READ IF CX > 1
            PUSH    DX
            MOV     DX,OFFSET FCB
            MOV     AH,14H               ;SEQUENTIAL READ
            INT     21H
            POP     DX
            CMP     AL,0                 ;GOOD RETURN?
            JZ      RDBYT1               ;YES
            CMP     AL,3                 ;EOF IN CURRENT SECTOR?
            JZ      RDBYT1               ;YES, OK
            MOV     AL,1AH               ;MARK AS EOF
            RET
RDBYT1:     MOV     CX,128               ;SHOW FULL BUFFER
            MOV     SI,OFFSET BUFFER
RDBYT2:     LODSB                        ;GET CHAR FROM FILE BUFFER
            RET
RDBYTE      ENDP
CSEG        ENDS
            END     START
```

parameter area so that we could scan any passed
information. In this case, we make use of the fact that
DOS will parse that same information and build an
unopened FCB if it encounters what looks like a file
name. Therefore, we have defined labels for that FCB.
We also have defined a label for the default file buffer.
Since our FCB and file buffer are contained within the
PSP, the only thing that is defined in our data segment

is the error message, which will be issued if the open call can not locate the desired file.

The code segment begins by establishing address-ability to the data segment. Since most accesses will be to the PSP, we have reversed the usual convention and have set the ES register to point to our data segment and left the DS register pointing to the PSP. This will cause us a little problem if we need to issue the error message (since our message print subroutine expects the message to be pointed to by DS:DX), but will help program efficiency if everything runs normally.

After clearing the screen, the program attempts to open the FCB in the PSP. If no file name was entered on the command line, or if DOS can not find that file, then the open will fail. In this case, we issue the error message and exist. Note that in order to do this with our standard PRINT subroutine, we have to temporar-ily point DS to our data segment. We do this with the PUSHes and POPs surrounding the call to PRINT. This works, but is a little bit dangerous in that we have not informed the assembler that we have played games with the data segment register. (This is the sort of thing that lets you make a mistake in addressability that the assembler cannot catch, resulting in a bug that may be difficult to track down. If you decide to do it, be sure and fully document what you've done, and double check your code.)

If the open is okay, we enter the main program loop. The problem here is that we are going to read the file 128 bytes at a time, but we have to write to the console one character at a time. This is because the contents of a text file consist of variable length lines terminated by a carriage return and line feed sequence. The problem is solved by creating a RDBYTE subroutine that will return one character at a time. The main program logic only needs to loop until end of file, signaled by the presence of a 1AH character, is encountered. It then returns to DOS by pushing the address of the PSP (in DS) onto the stack followed by a word of zeros and then executing an intersegment return. This is the same technique we discussed previously.

The RDBYTE subroutine executes a LOOP instruction to test the count in CX. This is also a bit dangerous since it relies on the fact that the main routine is aware of this use of CX and will preserve its value. The subroutine would not be portable to other programs where the main routine did not take this into account. A better technique would be to define a count variable in the data segment and to save and load CX each time the subroutine is entered. This enhancement is left as an exercise to the reader.

If CX is equal to 1, then the buffer is empty and must be read. In this case, the Sequential Read call is issued to fill the buffer. Although the file should end with a 1AH character, there is no guarantee of that it will. So we check the return code from DOS. If an attempt to read beyond the physical end of file has been signaled, then we inform the main routine by generating and returning the EOF character. Otherwise, we set the SI register to point to the beginning of the buffer, and reset CX. The same comments about saving and restoring the CX register within the subroutine also apply to SI.

If the buffer was not empty, or if we have just refilled it, then we obtain the next character from the buffer and place it into AL by executing a LODSB instruction, which also automatically increments SI.

Chapter 9
STREAM-ORIENTED I/O

DOS 2.0 introduced an entirely new way of viewing I/O operations. Although the IBM documentation does not use the term, DOS implemented what is called stream-oriented I/O. The primary difference is that instead of the programmer viewing a file as a collection of fixed length records, the programmer views the file as a continuous stream of characters. Each read or write request transfers the requested number of bytes without regard for physical media boundaries.

When the file is actually a character-oriented device, such as a console, character printer, or communication line, this method seems very natural. Such devices work almost entirely with variable length text strings which are delimited by special characters such as carriage returns, line feeds, horizontal and vertical tab characters, and so on.

With block mode devices like disk drives, on the other hand, record-oriented I/O seems more intuitively correct. Intuition can be misleading, however. Many disk files are text files, for example, with no natural record boundaries. Such files are best treated as continuous streams of characters just like they would be on character devices.

There are also many nontext files which can be handled better as stream files. These are files with variable length records. Such files have not been very common on small computers because the operating systems have not made them very easy to work with, but they are quite common on mainframes. Variable length records typically have the record length as the first two bytes of the record. With stream-oriented I/O, the program can ask to read the first two bytes to get the length and then use that length to get the rest of the record. With record-oriented I/O, the programmer would have to read a predetermined length into a buffer and then deblock the record under program control.

File Handles

In record mode files the basic anchor point was the File Control Block (FCB). Stream mode files do not have a FCB. Instead, the programmer identifies the file via a 16-bit value called a *handle*, or sometimes a *token*. The file handle is supplied to the program as the result of a successful attempt to open or create a file. The program then supplies this value on all subsequent file requests.

Five file handles have been predefined, and are shown in Figure 9.1. These five pseudo devices are always available, and are not opened by the program. The standard input and output devices normally are the two parts of the console, the keyboard and the display. The reason for using the predefined handles, rather than the DOS console services functions, is that the standard input and output devices can be redirected.

Redirection is another concept that was first introduced in DOS 2.0, although it will be familiar to UNIX

Figure 9.1—File Handles ·

Handle	Description
Ø	Standard Input Device
1	Standard Output Device
2	Standard Error Device
3	Standard Auxiliary Device
4	Standard Printer Device

fans. When a program is invoked, either by the command process or through a DOS Exec function request, the invoker can specify the actual files that are to be treated as the standard devices. This is very useful when using .BAT files to string together several programs, since the output of one program can be used as the input to the next program.

The function of the standard error output device is primarily to allow a program to continue sending error messages to the console even when the rest of the console output has been redirected to another file or device. The standard auxiliary device is usually the communications line and the standard printer device is usually the first attached printer, although all of the standard definitions are under the control of the parent process.

ASCIIZ Strings

In record mode requests, the file name was passed to DOS via a fixed length field in the FCB. Provision was made to specify a specific drive, but not a path name. In stream mode, file names are passed as an ASCIIZ string, which is a character string containing (if required) the driver identifier, fully qualified directory path, and file name, followed by a byte of zeros. For example, the assembler statement:

FNAME DB 'C: RBBS DOWNLOAD UTILITY.DOC',0

defines an ASCIIZ string specifying a file in a second level directory on drive C.

Error Return Codes

Record mode requests typically return a one byte code in AL to indicate success or failure. Stream mode requests use a somewhat different scheme. If the request is successful, then the carry flag is cleared and the value in AX is dependent upon the specific function requested. If the requests is unsuccessful, then the carry flag is set and AX contains one of the binary error codes shown in Figure 9.2. Not every possible error code is applicable to every function call, of course. It is

Figure 9.2—Error Return Codes

CODE	DESCRIPTION
1	Invalid function number
2	File not found
3	Path not found
4	Too many open files
5	Access denied
6	Invalid handle
7	Memory control blocks destroyed
8	Insufficient memory
9	Invalid memory block address
10	Invalid environment
11	Invalid format
12	Invalid access code
13	Invalid data
14	unassigned
15	Invalid drive was specified
16	Attempt to remove the current directory
17	Not the same device
18	No more files

the programmers responsibility to test the carry flag upon return from the function call in order to determine what meaning to give to the contents of AX.

Opening a File

Any normal or hidden file whose name matches the specified name can be opened with the parameters shown in Figure 9.3. If successful, the function will return a file handle in AX. This value must be saved by the program and supplied in all subsequent file requests. In record mode, the open function sets the date, time, and attribute fields in the FCB. In stream mode there is no FCB, of course, but there are additional functional calls which will obtain or set the desired information.

Figure 9.3—Opening a File

```
Registers at Invocation:

AH    =  3DH
DS:DX =  Address of ASCIIZ string with file name
AL    =  Access code
         0 = Open for read only
         1 = Open for write only
         2 = Open for reac and write

Returns if Successful:

AX    =  File handle
Read/Write pointer set to beginning of file


Applicable Error Codes:

     2  =  File not found
     4  =  Too many open files
     5  =  Access denied
    12  =  Invalid access code
```

Creating a File

Like record mode requests, the stream Open request will only open an existing file. The Create request (summarized in Figure 9.4) can be used to create a new file. In addition, it can be used with an existing file in order to set it to zero length prior to rewriting it.

Figure 9.4—Creating a File

```
Registers at Invocation:

AH    = 3CH
DS:DX = Address of ASCIIZ string with file name
CX    = File Attribute (hex)

          00 = Normal file
          01 = Read only
          02 = Hidden file
          04 = System file
          08 = Volume label
          10 = Sub-directory
          20 = Archive bit

Returns if Successful:

AX = File handle
File opened for Read/Write

Applicable Error Codes:

    3 = Path not found
    4 = Too many open files
    5 = Access denied
```

The Access Denied error code can have two meanings, depending on the context of the call. If the program is trying to create a new file, then it means that the directory is full. If the program is trying to reset an existing file, than it means that the existing file has been marked read-only.

Reading a File

The three record mode Read requests (sequential, random, and block) have been combined into one in stream mode. This is possible because the function call specifies the number of bytes to read and the buffer address (see Figure 9.5). Note that end of file is not an error condition. Instead, the number of bytes actually read is returned in AX. If this value is zero, then the program has tried to read past the end of the file. If it is greater than zero but less than the requested amount, there are two possible reasons. If the file is a disk file, then the program has just read the remainder of the file. However, if the file is actually a device, then the number of bytes transferred depends upon the characteristics of the device. For example, the keyboard will terminate the transfer when a carriage return is encountered.

Figure 9.5—Reading a File

```
Registers at Invocation:

AH    = 3FH
BX    = File handle
CX    = Number of bytes to read
DS:DX = Buffer address

Returns if Successful:

AX = Number of bytes read

Applicable Error Codes:

     5 = Access denied
     6 = Invalid handle
```

Writing a File

The stream Write function is essentially identical to Read. The programmer has the responsibility to check AX on return to see if all the bytes requested were actually written. Any difference should be considered an error. The most common reason for this difference is that the disk is now full.

Positioning a File

The Read and Write stream functions calls are essentially sequential. That is, the read/write pointer associated with the file is advanced automatically by the number of bytes read or written. To have random access capabilities, we need the Lseek function illustrated in Figure 9.6. As shown, there are three different ways to use this function. Method value 0 allows positioning to an absolute value. This could be used to simulate random access to fixed length records. The CX:DX reg-

Figure 9.6—Positioning a File (Lseek)

```
Registers at Invocation:

AH = 42H
AL = Method Value
        Ø = Absolute offset from beginning of file
        1 = Current location plus offset
        2 = End of file plus offset
DS:DX = Offset in bytes

Returns if Successful:

DS:DX = New absolute position of pointer

Applicable Error Codes:

        1 = Invalid function number
        6 = Invalid handle
```

ister pair would be loaded with the relative record number times the fixed record length.

A method value of 1 specifies relative positioning. This might be used to skip fields within a record or to advance to the next record by skipping the remainder of the current record. The final method could be used with a negative offset to position to the last record in a file, or with a zero offset as one way to determine the length of the file.

Closing a File

Unlike the record mode case, DOS is aware of which stream mode files have been opened by the program. If control is returned through the DOS Exit function call (4CH), then DOS will close all open files and flush all of the internal buffers relating to them. Nevertheless, it is good programming practice to close files when they are no longer needed. The Close function is shown in Figure 9.7.

Figure 9.7—Closing a File

```
Registers at Invocation:

AH = 3EH
BX = File handle

Returns if Successful:

The file will be closed and all internal
buffers flushed.

Applicable Error Codes:

6 = Invalid handle
```

A Sample Stream-Oriented I/O Program

The file scan program from the record mode discussion has been rewritten to use the stream mode function calls exclusively, and is listed in Figure 9.8. Note that the program therefore requires DOS release 2 or later to function. Furthermore, although it is possible to check the DOS release level from the program and issue an appropriate message if not suitable, we have not done so for this sample. Therefore, if run on a DOS 1.x system, the program will blow up!

Figure 9.8—The Sample Program

```
PAGE      62,132
TITLE     Scan2 - File Display Program Using Stream I/O
PAGE
;-----------------------------------------------------------
;DEFINE STACK SEGMENT
;-----------------------------------------------------------
STACK     SEGMENT PARA STACK 'STACK'
          DB       64 DUP('STACK   ')
STACK     ENDS
;-----------------------------------------------------------
;DEFINE PROGRAM SEGMENT PREFIX
;-----------------------------------------------------------
PREFIX    SEGMENT AT Ø
          ORG      8ØH
UPARM     DB       128 DUP (?)      ;UNFORMATTED PARM AREA
PREFIX    ENDS
;-----------------------------------------------------------
;DEFINE DATA SEGMENT
;-----------------------------------------------------------
DSEG      SEGMENT PARA PUBLIC 'DATA'
CHAR      DB       ' '              ;ONE BYTE BUFFER
FNAME     DB       8Ø DUP (' ')     ;FILE NAME INCLUDING PATH
MSG1      DB       16,'FILE NOT FOUND',13,1Ø
MSG2      DB       22,'NO FILE NAME ENTERED',13,1Ø
DSEG      ENDS
;-----------------------------------------------------------
;DEFINE CODE SEGMENT
;-----------------------------------------------------------
CSEG      SEGMENT PARA PUBLIC 'CODE'
START     PROC     FAR
          ASSUME   CS:CSEG,SS:STACK,DS:PREFIX
;ESTABLISH ADDRESSABILITY TO DATA SEGMENT
          MOV      AX,DSEG          ;ADDRESS OF DATA SEGMENT
          MOV      ES,AX            ;NOW POINTS TO DATA SEGMENT
          ASSUME   ES:DSEG          ;TELL ASSEMBLER
```

```
;------------------------------------------------------------
;START OF MAIN PROGRAM
;------------------------------------------------------------
        CALL    CLRSCN
        MOV     SI,OFFSET UPARM  ;FILE NAME PASSED BY DOS
        MOV     DI,OFFSET FNAME  ;FILE NAME FIELD IN OUR DS
        LODSB                    ;GET PARM STRING LENGTH
        CMP     AL,0             ;ANY NAME SUPPLIED?
        JZ      NOFILE           ;NO - SAY SO
        XOR     CX,CX            ;MAKE SURE HIGH BYTE IS ZERO
        MOV     CL,AL            ;INSERT STRING LENGTH
TSTBNK: LODSB                    ;GET CHARACTER
        CMP     AL,' '           ;IS IT BLANK?
        JNZ     NOBLNK           ;NO - GO MOVE NAME
        LOOP    TSTBNK           ;SKIP LEADING BLANKS
NOFILE: PUSH    ES               ;DATA SEGMENT
        POP     DS               ;NOW ALSO IN DS
        MOV     SI,OFFSET MSG2   ;NO FILE MESSAGE
        JMP     BADFIL           ;GO ISSUE MESSAGE
NOBLNK: STOSB                    ;STORE IN FILE NAME
        LODSB                    ;GET NEXT CHARACTER
        LOOP    NOBLNK           ;LOOP UNTIL DONE
        XOR     AX,AX            ;CLEAR REGISTER
        STOSB                    ;TERMINATE STRING
        PUSH    ES               ;POINTER TO DATA SEGMENT
        POP     DS               ;NOW ALSO IN DS
        ASSUME  DS:DSEG          ;TELL ASSEMBLER
;ATTEMPT TO OPEN FILE
        MOV     AH,3DH           ;FILE OPEN REQUEST
        MOV     AL,0             ;READ ONLY
        MOV     DX,OFFSET FNAME  ;FILE NAME
        INT     21H              ;DOS FUNCTION CALL
        JNC     FILEOK           ;NO ERROR BRANCH
        MOV     SI,OFFSET MSG1   ;FILE OPEN ERROR MESSAGE
BADFIL: MOV     BX,2             ;STANDARD ERROR DEVICE
        MOV     AH,40H           ;WRITE DEVICE REQUEST
        LODSB                    ;GET MESSAGE LENGTH
        MOV     CL,AL            ;PUT IN COUNT REGISTER
        MOV     CH,0             ;CLEAR HIGH ORDER BYTE
        MOV     DX,SI            ;POINT TO MESSAGE
        INT     21H              ;INVOKE DOS
        MOV     AL,16            ;SET ERROR RETURN CODE
        JMP     DONEX            ;RETURN TO DOS
FILEOK: MOV     BX,AX            ;SAVE FILE HANDLE
        MOV     DX,OFFSET CHAR   ;POINT TO ONE CHAR BUFFER
READ:   CALL    RDBYTE           ;READ ONE BYTE FROM FILE
        CMP     CHAR,1AH         ;END OF FILE?
        JZ      DONE             ;YES - QUIT
        CALL    PRBYTE           ;PRINT BYTE TO STD OUTPUT
        JMP     READ             ;GET NEXT FILE BYTE
;------------------------------------------------------------
;RETURN TO DOS
;------------------------------------------------------------
DONE:   MOV     AL,0             ;GOOD RETURN CODE
DONEX:  MOV     AH,4CH           ;EXIT REQUEST
        INT     21H              ;INVOKE DOS
START   ENDP
;------------------------------------------------------------
;SUBROUTINES
;------------------------------------------------------------
```

```
CLRSCN    PROC                            ;CLEAR SCREEN
          PUSH      AX
          MOV       AX,2
          INT       10H
          POP       AX
          RET
CLRSCN    ENDP
PRBYTE    PROC
;PRBYTE EXPECTS A POINTER TO A CHARACTER IN DX. IT WRITES THE
;CHARACTER TO THE STANDARD OUTPUT DEVICE. NO ERROR CHECKING
;IS PERFORMED
          PUSH      AX
          PUSH      BX                    ;SAVE REGS
          PUSH      CX                    ;ON ENTRY
          MOV       AH,40H                ;WRITE REQUEST
          MOV       BX,1                  ;STD OUTPUT DEVICE
          MOV       CX,1                  ;COUNT
          INT       21H                   ;INVOKE DOS
          POP       CX
          POP       BX
          POP       AX
          RET
PRBYTE    ENDP
RDBYTE    PROC
;RDBYTE EXPECTS A FILE HANDLE IN BX AND THE LOCATION OF
;A ONE BYTE BUFFER IN DX. ALL REGISTERS ARE PRESERVED
          PUSH      AX                    ;SAVE REGS ON ENTRY
          PUSH      BX
          PUSH      CX
          PUSH      DX
          MOV       AH,3FH                ;READ REQUEST
          MOV       CX,1                  ;ONE BYTE ONLY
          INT       21H                   ;INVOKE DOS
          JC        FEOF                  ;TREAT ANY ERROR AS END OF FILE
          CMP       AX,0                  ;EOF?
          JNZ       RDBYT1                ;NO - RETURN
FEOF:     PUSH      SI
          MOV       SI,DX                 ;CAN NOT USE DX AS INDEX REG
          MOV       BYTE PTR [SI],1AH         ;MARK BUFFER WITH EOF
          POP       SI
RDBYT1:   POP       DX
          POP       CX
          POP       BX
          POP       AX
          RET
RDBYTE    ENDP
CSEG      ENDS
          END       START
```

The program begins, as before, by defining the stack, data, and program segment prefix segments. The primary difference is that the only field currently defined in the program segment prefix is the unformatted parameter area. This is because DOS can not parse a filename and build an unopened FCB if the filename contains any path information. Therefore, our program will have to accept the file name in unformatted form.

The next step is to obtain addressability to the data segment in the ES register. The DS register is left addressing the program segment prefix. This combination was chosen to match the register conventions for the string handling instructions which we will use to move the file name to our data segment.

Next we check to see if any filename information was passed on the command line. This is done by checking the count field at the beginning of the unformatted parameter area in the PSP. If this is nonzero, then we skip any leading blanks. If any count still remains, we move the rest of the string to the FNAME field in our data segment. At this point, we have no further need of the PSP, so we set DS equal to ES via a push/pop sequence. This technique is used because the 8088 architecture contains no instructions which will move one segment register directly to another.

The first DOS function call is now issued to attempt to open the file. If the attempt fails, the carry flag will be set on return and we will fall through the JNC FILEOK instruction. In that case, we write an error message to the standard error output device by using the predefined handle of 2. This will allow the error message to appear on the screen even if the standard output has been redirected to another file or device, such as a printer. Since the stream-oriented functions work with a length parameter, the format of the error messages in the data segment has been changed to provide the length of the message as the first byte. The LODSB instruction that picks up this length also advances the SI register to the first character of the actual message.

If the Open request was successful, then the function call returned the file handle in AX. This value is now moved to BX, which is the proper register to use in subsequent Read requests. This is fine for short programs, but a better practice in the general case would be to save it somewhere in the data segment and reload it each time just before the file handling request is issued.

The program now enters the main loop, alternatively calling RDBYTE and PRBYTE until done. When the program detects that RDBYTE has returned an end-of-file character, the program exits by loading a zero into AL and issuing the Exit function call. This call closes all open files and passes the return code back to DOS so that it can be tested by the parent process.

The RDBYTE subroutine saves all of the registers which it will use and then issues a Read function call for one byte. DOS maintains an internal buffer pool and only performs a physical read if there is no more information in the current buffer. Therefore, most of the time, the Read request will just move one character from the DOS buffer to the program's data field, CHAR.

This program is intended to be used with text files, which will have an end-of-file character as the last byte in the file. However, this can not be guaranteed, so the subroutine will supply such a character if it gets an end-of-file indication from DOS. Additionally, for simplicity, it treats any other error condition as end of file, rather than analyzing the error and producing an appropriate error message.

The PRBYTE subroutine is quite straightforward. It saves its registers on the stack and then sets up a Write function call to write one character to the standard output device, by using the predefined handle of 1. This will allow the output to be redirected to a printer or other file if specified on the command line. Following the DOS call, PRBYTE restores its registers and returns without any error checking.

A good exercise for the reader would be to enhance the program to accept the input file name from the standard input device if it is not provided on the command line.

Chapter 10
DIRECTORY OPERATIONS

Most programs operate on the data contained in a file. The file name itself is either hard coded into the program or passed to it as an invocation parameter. For such programs, the DOS services of OPEN, CLOSE, CREATE, and DELETE are sufficient. However, there is also a class of utility programs which operate on data about files such as the file name, size, attributes, etc. DOS also offers functions to assist the programmer in writing such utilities.

Record-Oriented Directory Functions

The primary record-oriented directory functions are:
    Search for the first entry (AH = 11H0)
    Search for the next entry (AH = 12H).
Each requires as input either a normal or an extended FCB, except that the file name can contain one or more question marks. Each question mark indicates that any character will match that position. Thus, a string of 11 question marks will match any file name, a string of 8

question marks followed by an unambiguous extention will match all file names with that file type, etc. This type of matching is often referred to as "class logic."

If the supplied FCB was a normal FCB, then the search will find only normal file entries. Volume labels, subdirectory names, hidden files, and systems files will be skipped. If the supplied FCB is an extended FCB then the attribute byte in the extended FCB is used to determine which directory entries will be examined. This is an inclusive search except for the volume label bit. That is, if you set the attribute byte to (hidden + system + directory) then all file and directory entries will be searched, but if the volume label bit is set then only the volume label will be returned. Only these bits control the search. The read only and archive attribute bits are ignored for this purpose. The hex definitions of these attribute bits are shown in Figure 10.1

Figure 10.1—Attribute Definitions

01	Read Only	08	Volume Label
02	Hidden File	10	Sub-directory
04	System File	20	Archive

For each match encountered, DOS reads the corresponding directory entry into the current data transfer area (DTA). For a normal search FCB, DOS prefixes this information with the drive identifier. For an extended search FCB, DOS copies the first part of the FCB up through the drive identifier. Therefore, the returned information can be examined either as a directory entry, or opened as a normal or extended FCB. Use of these functions is best shown by an example.

Figure 10.3 (see page 104) is a program which will display the contents of a disk directory in much the same way as does the standard DIR function, but with a few differences. First, this program will display system and hidden files as well as normal entries. Also, instead of displaying the file's creation date and time, it will display the file attributes using the single-letter abbreviations shown in Figure 10.2. And finally, the program reports the sum of the actual file lengths encountered instead of the remaining free space.

Figure 10.2—Attribute Indicators

R	File has been marked for Read Only access
H	Hidden File (Excluded from normal searches)
S	System File (Excluded from normal searches)
A	Archive (Turned on when file is written to)

The program begins by establishing addressability to its data segment in ES while retaining addressability to the PSP in DS. This allows it to move information passed on the command line into its own FCB in its data segment. Once this has been accomplished, the PSP is no longer needed and DS is also pointed to the program's data segment.

After checking the validity of the supplied drive id and setting the current DTA to point to the established feedback area, the program issues the search first request. If this request fails for any reason then it complains and quits. Otherwise, it enters a loop in which it displays the desired directory information on the screen and issues a search next request. The program only exits from the loop when no more entries are returned. The program then displays the number of files and the accumulated total file size, and returns to DOS.

Figure 10.3—Directory List Program

```
PAGE      62,132
TITLE     MDIR - SAmple Directory Display Program
PAGE
;-----------------------------------------------------------
;DEFINE STACK SEGMENT
;-----------------------------------------------------------
STACK     SEGMENT PARA STACK 'STACK'
          DB       64 DUP('STACK   ')
STACK     ENDS
;-----------------------------------------------------------
;DEFINE PROGRAM SEGMENT PREFIX
;-----------------------------------------------------------
PREFIX    SEGMENT AT Ø
          ORG      5CH
QDRIVE    DB       Ø                    ;SUPPLIED DRIVE ID
QNAME     DB       8 DUP (?)            ;SUPPLIED FILE NAME
QEXT      DB       3 DUP (?)            ;SUPPLIED FILE EXTENSION
PREFIX    ENDS
;-----------------------------------------------------------
;DEFINE DATA SEGMENT
;-----------------------------------------------------------
DSEG      SEGMENT PARA PUBLIC 'DATA'
APREFIX   DW       Ø                    ;ADDRESS OF PSP
C1Ø       DW       1Ø                   ;CONSTANT FOR DIVISION
C1ØØØØ    DW       1ØØØØ                ;CONSTANT FOR DIVISION
FILES     DW       Ø                    ;NUMBER OF FILES FOUND
TSIZE     DD       Ø                    ;TOTAL SIZE OF FILES FOUND
XFCB      DB       ØFFH                 ;EXTENDED FCB FLAG
          DB       5 DUP (Ø)            ;FILLER
          DB       22                   ;HIDDEN + SYSTEM + DIRECTORY
SDRIVE    DB       Ø                    ;DEFAULT DRIVE
SNAME     DB       8 DUP ('?')          ;FILE SEARCH NAME
SEXT      DB       3 DUP ('?')          ;FILE SEARCH EXTENSION
          DB       23 DUP (?)           ;FILLER
DIR       DB       7 DUP (?)            ;ECHOED FCB PREFIX
DDRIVE    DB       Ø                    ;ECHOED DRIVE NUMBER
DNAME     DB       8 DUP (?)            ;FILE NAME
DEXT      DB       3 DUP (?)            ;FILE NAME EXTENTION
DFLAGS    DB       Ø                    ;FILE ATTRIBUTE FLAGS
          DB       1Ø DUP (?)           ;FILLER
TIME      DW       Ø                    ;FILE CREATION TIME
DATE      DW       Ø                    ;FILE CREATION DATE
CLUSTER   DW       Ø                    ;STARTING CLUSTER NUMBER
DSIZE     DD       Ø                    ;FILE SIZE
MSG1      DB       'FILE NOT FOUND',13,1Ø,'$'
MSG2      DB       'INVALID DRIVE SPECIFIED',13,1Ø,'$'
MSG3      DB       '   <DIR>'
PNAME     DB       8 DUP (' ')          ;FILE NAME
          DB       ' '
PEXT      DB       3 DUP (' ')          ;FILE EXTENSION
          DB       ' '
```

```
PSIZE     DB        8 DUP (' ')      ;FILE SIZE
          DB        ' '
PFLAGS    DB        5 DUP (' ')      ;ATTRIBUTE FLAGS
          DB        10,13,'$'        ;END OF LINE
PTOTAL    DB        '       File(s)'
PTSIZE    DB        '            bytes total size',13,10,'$'
DSEG      ENDS
;------------------------------------------------------------
;DEFINE CODE SEGMENT
;------------------------------------------------------------
CSEG      SEGMENT PARA PUBLIC 'CODE'
START     PROC      FAR
          ASSUME    CS:CSEG,SS:STACK,DS:PREFIX
          PUSH      AX               ;SAVE VALIDITY FLAGS
;ESTABLISH ADDRESSABILITY TO DATA SEGMENT
          MOV       AX,DSEG          ;ADDRESS OF DATA SEGMENT
          MOV       ES,AX            ;NOW POINTS TO DATA SEGMENT
          ASSUME    ES:DSEG          ;TELL ASSEMBLER
          MOV       APREFIX,DS       ;SAVE ADDRESS OF PSP
;CHECK FOR QUALIFIERS ON SEARCH
          MOV       AL,QDRIVE        ;GET DRIVE ID
          MOV       SDRIVE,AL        ;AND PLACE IN FCB
          CMP       QNAME,' '        ;ANY NAME SUPPLIED?
          JZ        CKEXT            ;NO - CHECK EXTENSION
          MOV       SI,OFFSET QNAME  ;NAME SUPPLIED
          MOV       DI,OFFSET SNAME  ;NAME IN FCB
          MOV       CX,8             ;LENGTH OF NAME
          REP MOVSB                  ;MOVE FILE NAME
CKEXT:    CMP       QEXT,' '         ;ANY EXTENSION?
          JZ        ENDPSP           ;NO - DONE WITH PSP
          MOV       SI,OFFSET QEXT   ;EXTENSION SUPPLIED
          MOV       DI,OFFSET SEXT   ;EXTENSION IN FCB
          MOV       CX,3             ;LENGTH OF EXTENSION
          REP MOVSB                  ;MOVE FILE EXTENSION
ENDPSP:   PUSH      ES
          POP       DS               ;ADDRESS OF DATA SEGMENT
          ASSUME    DS:DSEG          ;TELL ASSEMBLER
;------------------------------------------------------------
;START OF MAIN PROGRAM
;------------------------------------------------------------
          CALL      CLRSCN
;CHECK DRIVE VALIDITY
          POP       AX               ;RETRIEVE DRIVE FLAGS
          CMP       AL,0             ;VALID?
          JZ        SETDTA           ;YES - CONTINUE
          MOV       DX,OFFSET MSG2   ;INVALID DRIVE MSG
          CALL      PRINT            ;PRINT MSG TO SCREEN
          JMP       DONE             ;QUIT
;SET DTA TO DIRECTORY FEEDBACK AREA
SETDTA:   MOV       DX,OFFSET DIR    ;FEEDBACK AREA
          MOV       AH,1AH           ;SET DTA
          INT       21H              ;DOS REQUEST
          MOV       DX,OFFSET XFCB   ;EXTENDED FCB ADDRESS
          MOV       AH,11H           ;SEARCH FIRST
          INT       21H
          CMP       AL,0             ;GOOD RETURN?
```

```
           JZ       FILEOK           ;YES
           MOV      DX,OFFSET MSG1
           CALL     PRINT
           JMP      DONE             ;QUIT
FILEOK:    CALL     PRTDIR           ;PRINT DIRECTORY ENTRY
           MOV      DX,OFFSET XFCB   ;EXTENDED FCB ADDRESS
           MOV      AH,12H           ;SEARCH NEXT
           INT      21H              ;DOS REQUEST
           CMP      AL,Ø             ;GOOD RETURN?
           JZ       FILEOK           ;YES - GO DISPLAY
;PRINT ACCUMULATED TOTALS
           MOV      AX,FILES         ;TOTAL FILES FOUND
           XOR      DX,DX            ;CLEAR HIGH ORDER WORD
           MOV      SI,OFFSET PTOTAL
           MOV      CX,5
           CALL     BINASC           ;CONVERT TO ASCII
           MOV      AX,TSIZE         ;LOW WORD OF TOTAL SIZE
           MOV      DX,TSIZE+2       ;HIGH WORD OF TOTAL SIZE
           MOV      SI,OFFSET PTSIZE
           MOV      CX,8
           CALL     BINASC           ;CONVERT TO ASCII
           MOV      DX,OFFSET PTOTAL
           CALL     PRINT
;------------------------------------------------------------
;RETURN TO DOS
;------------------------------------------------------------
DONE:      MOV      AX,APREFIX       ;ADDRESS OF PSP
           PUSH     AX               ;PLACE ON STACK
           XOR      AX,AX
           PUSH     AX
           RET
START      ENDP
;------------------------------------------------------------
;SUBROUTINES
;------------------------------------------------------------
CLRSCN     PROC                      ;CLEAR SCREEN
           PUSH     AX
           MOV      AX,2
           INT      1ØH
           POP      AX
           RET
CLRSCN     ENDP
PRINT      PROC
           PUSH     AX
           MOV      AH,9
           INT      21H
           POP      AX
           RET
PRINT      ENDP
PRTDIR     PROC
           PUSH     AX
           PUSH     SI
           PUSH     DI
           PUSH     DX
;MOVE FILE NAME TO PRINT LINE
           MOV      SI,OFFSET DNAME
           MOV      DI,OFFSET PNAME
```

```
            MOV     CX,8
            REP MOVSB                ;MOVE FILE NAME
;MOVE FILE EXTENSION TO PRINT LINE
            MOV     SI,OFFSET DEXT
            MOV     DI,OFFSET PEXT
            MOV     CX,3
            REP MOVSB
;MOVE FILE SIZE TO PRINT LINE
            TEST    DFLAGS,16        ;DIRECTORY?
            JZ      MOVSIZ           ;NO - MOVE SIZE INFO
            MOV     SI,OFFSET MSG3   ;<DIR>
            MOV     DI,OFFSET PSIZE
            MOV     CX,8
            REP MOVSB
            JMP     TST1             ;SKIP SIZE CALCULATION
MOVSIZ:     MOV     AX,DSIZE         ;LOW ORDER PART OF SIZE
            MOV     DX,DSIZE+2       ;HIGH ORDER PART OF SIZE
            ADD     TSIZE,AX         ;ACCUMULATE TOTAL SIZE
            ADC     TSIZE+2,DX       ;OF FILES FOUND
            INC     FILES            ;COUNT FILES FOUND
            MOV     SI,OFFSET PSIZE
            MOV     CX,8             ;WIDTH OF OUTPUT FIELD
            CALL    BINASC           ;CONVERT TO ASCII
;TURN ON OR OFF ATTRIBUTE INDICATORS
TST1:       MOV     DI,OFFSET PFLAGS
            MOV     AL,' '
            TEST    DFLAGS,1         ;READ ONLY?
            JZ      TST2             ;NO
            MOV     AL,'R'
TST2:       STOSB                    ;PUT CHAR IN STRING
            MOV     AL,' '
            TEST    DFLAGS,2         ;HIDDEN FILE?
            JZ      TST4             ;NO
            MOV     AL,'H'
TST4:       STOSB
            MOV     AL,' '
            TEST    DFLAGS,4         ;SYSTEM FILE?
            JZ      TST32            ;NO
            MOV     AL,'S'
TST32:      STOSB
            MOV     AL,' '
            TEST    DFLAGS,32        ;ARCHIVE?
            JZ      TSTX             ;NO
            MOV     AL,'A'
TSTX:       STOSB
            MOV     DX,OFFSET PNAME  ;OUTPUT LINE
            CALL    PRINT
            POP     DX
            POP     DI
            POP     SI
            POP     AX
            RET
PRTDIR  ENDP
BINASC  PROC
;CONVERTS A BINARY NUMBER IN DX:AX TO PRINTABLE FORM
;AND PLACES IT IN A FIELD POINTED TO BY SI WITH THE
;FIELD WIDTH IN CX. LEADING ZEROS ARE SUPPRESSED.
```

```
              PUSH    DX
              PUSH    CX
              PUSH    BX
              PUSH    DI
              PUSH    AX
              MOV     DI,SI           ;SAVE START OF STRING
BA1:          MOV     BYTE PTR [SI],' '   ;FILL CHARACTER
              INC     SI              ;POINT TO NEXT FIELD POSITION
              LOOP    BA1             ;LOOP UNTIL DONE
              DIV     C10000          ;DIVIDE BY 10,000
              MOV     BX,AX           ;SAVE QUOTIENT
              MOV     AX,DX           ;MOVE REMAINDER BACK TO AX
BA2:          MOV     CX,4            ;NUMBER OF DIGITS TO PRINT
BA3:          XOR     DX,DX           ;CLEAR HIGH ORDER WORD
              DIV     C10             ;DIVIDE BY TEN
              ADD     DL,'0'          ;CONVERT TO ASCII DIGIT
              DEC     SI              ;STEP BACKWARDS THROUGH BUFFER
              CMP     SI,DI           ;OUT OF SPACE?
              JB      BAX             ;YES - QUIT
              MOV     [SI],DL         ;STORE DIGIT
              OR      AX,AX           ;ALL DIGITS PRINTED?
              JNZ     BA4             ;NO - KEEP TRUCKING
              OR      BX,BX           ;ANY MORE WORK?
              JZ      BAX             ;NO - CAN QUIT
BA4:          LOOP    BA3             ;NEXT DIGIT
BA5:          OR      BX,BX           ;MORE WORK TO DO?
              JZ      BAX             ;NO - CAN QUIT
              MOV     AX,BX           ;GET NEXT 4 DIGITS
              XOR     BX,BX           ;SHOW NO MORE DIGITS
              JMP     BA2             ;KEEP ON TRUCKING
BAX:          POP     AX
              POP     DI
              POP     BX
              POP     CX
              POP     DX
              RET
BINASC        ENDP
CSEG          ENDS
              END     START
```

Stream-Oriented Directory Operations

The corresponding stream-oriented function calls are:
  FIND FIRST (AH=4EH)
  FIND NEXT (AH=4FH)
The primary advantage of using these calls is that they will accept directory path information, while the

record-oriented functions only work on the current directory. This information is passed as a variable-length ASCII string containing the fully qualified diretory information. The filename portion of this string can contain global filename characters. The string is terminated by a byte of zeros.

Since no FCBs are used in stream-oriented functions, the directory information is supplied at the current DTA in a format which contains the information necessary for DOS to keep track of its current position in the directory. This information must be unchanged when the FIND NEXT call is issued. The format of the feedback area is shown in Figure 10.4.

Figure 10.4—Directory Feedback Area

Position	Length	Item
0	21	Reserved for DOS
22	1	File attribute bits
23	2	File creation time
25	2	File creation date
27	4	File size
31	13	File name and extension

The sample program in Figure 10.3 has been modified to use the stream-oriented function calls, and now appears as Figure 10.5. Other than the changed format of the feedback area, the primary difference is in string handling. If the user specifies a fully qualified string, including a filename with global file characters, then it is just a case of moving that string from the PSP to the data segment. On the other hand, if the user uses a shorthand form with just a drive identifier or a directory path, then the program must add "*.*" to the supplied path information. The difficulty arises when the specified string is something like "D⧧ROOT⧧HECTOR". Is "HECTOR" a file name or a directory name? This version of the program assumes that the last portion of the supplied string is a filename unless it ends in ":" or "⧧". Therefore, to list the filenames in a directory named "GAMES", the user must specify something like "B⧧GAMES⧧". Modification of this assumption is left as an exercise for the reader.

Figure 10.5—Modified Directory List Program

```
PAGE      62,132
TITLE     MDIR2 - Directory Program with Stream I/O
PAGE
;-----------------------------------------------------------
;DEFINE STACK SEGMENT
;-----------------------------------------------------------
STACK     SEGMENT PARA STACK 'STACK'
          DB      64 DUP('STACK   ')
STACK     ENDS
;-----------------------------------------------------------
;DEFINE PROGRAM SEGMENT PREFIX
;-----------------------------------------------------------
PREFIX    SEGMENT AT 0
          ORG     80H
UPARM     DB      128 DUP (?)      ;UNFORMATTED PARM AREA
PREFIX    ENDS
;-----------------------------------------------------------
;DEFINE DATA SEGMENT
;-----------------------------------------------------------
DSEG      SEGMENT PARA PUBLIC 'DATA'
APREFIX   DW      0                ;ADDRESS OF PSP
C10       DW      10               ;CONSTANT FOR DIVISION
C10000    DW      10000            ;CONSTANT FOR DIVISION
FILES     DW      0                ;NUMBER OF FILES FOUND
TSIZE     DD      0                ;TOTAL SIZE OF FILES FOUND
SNAME     DB      80 DUP (0)       ;SEARCH NAME FIELD
DIR       DB      21 DUP (?)       ;DOS WORKSPACE
DFLAGS    DB      0                ;FILE ATTRIBUTE FLAGS
TIME      DW      0                ;FILE CREATION TIME
DATE      DW      0                ;FILE CREATION DATE
DSIZE     DD      0                ;FILE SIZE
DNAME     DB      13 DUP (' ')     ;FILE NAME FOUND
MSG1      DB      'FILE NOT FOUND',13,10,'$'
MSG2      DB      '*.*',0
MSG3      DB      '    <DIR>'
```

```
PNAME     DB      8 DUP (' ')     ;FILE NAME
          DB      ' '
PEXT      DB      3 DUP (' ')     ;FILE EXTENSION
          DB      ' '
PSIZE     DB      8 DUP (' ')     ;FILE SIZE
          DB      ' '
PFLAGS    DB      5 DUP (' ')     ;ATTRIBUTE FLAGS
          DB      10,13,'$'       ;END OF LINE
PTOTAL    DB      '       File(s)'
PTSIZE    DB      '              bytes total size',13,10,'$'
DSEG      ENDS
;--------------------------------------------------------------
;DEFINE CODE SEGMENT
;--------------------------------------------------------------
CSEG      SEGMENT PARA PUBLIC 'CODE'
START     PROC    FAR
          ASSUME  CS:CSEG,SS:STACK,DS:PREFIX
          PUSH    AX              ;SAVE VALIDITY FLAGS
;ESTABLISH ADDRESSABILITY TO DATA SEGMENT
          MOV     AX,DSEG         ;ADDRESS OF DATA SEGMENT
          MOV     ES,AX           ;NOW POINTS TO DATA SEGMENT
          ASSUME  ES:DSEG         ;TELL ASSEMBLER
          MOV     APREFIX,DS      ;SAVE ADDRESS OF PSP
          MOV     SI,OFFSET UPARM ;FILE NAME PASSED BY DOS
          MOV     DI,OFFSET SNAME ;FILE NAME FIELD IN OUR DS
          LODSB                   ;GET PARM STRING LENGTH
          CMP     AL,0            ;ANY NAME SUPPLIED?
          JZ      ENDPSP          ;NO - DONE WITH PSP
          XOR     CX,CX           ;CLEAR HIGH ORDER BYTE
          MOV     CL,AL           ;INSERT STRING LENGTH
TSTBNK:   LODSB                   ;GET CHARACTER
          CMP     AL,' '          ;IS IT BLANK?
          JNZ     NOBLNK          ;NO - GO MOVE NAME
          LOOP    TSTBNK          ;SKIP LEADING BLANKS
NOBLNK:   STOSB                   ;STORE IN FILE NAME
          LODSB                   ;GET NEXT CHARACTER
          LOOP    NOBLNK          ;LOOP UNTIL DONE
          XOR     AX,AX           ;CLEAR REGISTER
          STOSB                   ;TERMINATE STRING
ENDPSP:   PUSH    ES
          POP     DS              ;ADDRESS OF DATA SEGMENT
          ASSUME  DS:DSEG         ;TELL ASSEMBLER
;--------------------------------------------------------------
;START OF MAIN PROGRAM
;--------------------------------------------------------------
          CALL    CLRSCN
;APPLY DEFAULTS TO SEARCH STRING
          MOV     DI,OFFSET SNAME
DEF0:     CMP     BYTE PTR [DI],0 ;END OF STRING?
          JZ      DEF1            ;YES
          INC     DI
          JMP     DEF0            ;KEEP LOOKING
DEF1:     CMP     DI,OFFSET SNAME ;NULL STRING?
          JZ      DEF3            ;YES - GO MOVE DEFAULT
          DEC     DI              ;BACK UP ONE CHARACTER
          CMP     BYTE PTR [DI],':'       ;DRIVE ONLY?
          JZ      DEF2            ;YES - USE DEFAULT
```

```
                CMP       BYTE PTR [DI],'\'        ;DIRECTORY ONLY?
                JNZ       SETDTA              ;NO - DON'T TOUCH ANYTHING
        DEF2:   INC       DI                  ;POINT BACK TO END OF STRING
        DEF3:   MOV       SI,OFFSET MSG2      ;'*.*'
                MOV       CX,4
                REP MOVSB                     ;MOVE DEFAULT STRING
        ;SET DTA TO DIRECTORY FEEDBACK AREA
        SETDTA: MOV       DX,OFFSET DIR       ;FEEDBACK AREA
                MOV       AH,1AH              ;SET DTA
                INT       21H                 ;DOS REQUEST
                MOV       DX,OFFSET SNAME     ;FILE SEARCH NAME
                MOV       CX,22               ;HIDDEN + SYSTEM + DIRECTORY
                MOV       AH,4EH              ;FIND FIRST MATCH
                INT       21H
                JNC       FILEOK              ;YES
                MOV       DX,OFFSET MSG1
                CALL      PRINT
                JMP       DONE                ;QUIT
        FILEOK: CALL      PRTDIR              ;PRINT DIRECTORY ENTRY
                MOV       AH,4FH              ;SEARCH NEXT
                INT       21H                 ;DOS REQUEST
                JNC       FILEOK              ;YES - GO DISPLAY
        ;PRINT ACCUMULATED TOTALS
                MOV       AX,FILES            ;TOTAL FILES FOUND
                XOR       DX,DX               ;CLEAR HIGH ORDER WORD
                MOV       SI,OFFSET PTOTAL
                MOV       CX,5
                CALL      BINASC              ;CONVERT TO ASCII
                MOV       AX,TSIZE            ;LOW WORD OF TOTAL SIZE
                MOV       DX,TSIZE+2          ;HIGH WORD OF TOTAL SIZE
                MOV       SI,OFFSET PTSIZE
                MOV       CX,8
                CALL      BINASC              ;CONVERT TO ASCII
                MOV       DX,OFFSET PTOTAL
                CALL      PRINT
        ;-----------------------------------------------------------------
        ;RETURN TO DOS
        ;-----------------------------------------------------------------
        DONE:   MOV       AX,APREFIX          ;ADDRESS OF PSP
                PUSH      AX                  ;PLACE ON STACK
                XOR       AX,AX
                PUSH      AX
                RET
        START   ENDP
        ;-----------------------------------------------------------------
        ;SUBROUTINES
        ;-----------------------------------------------------------------
        CLRSCN  PROC                          ;CLEAR SCREEN
                PUSH      AX
                MOV       AX,2
                INT       10H
                POP       AX
                RET
        CLRSCN  ENDP
        PRINT   PROC
                PUSH      AX
                MOV       AH,9
                INT       21H
                POP       AX
                RET
```

```
PRINT     ENDP
PRTDIR    PROC
          PUSH    AX
          PUSH    SI
          PUSH    DI
          PUSH    DX
;MOVE FILE NAME TO PRINT LINE
          MOV     SI,OFFSET DNAME
          MOV     DI,OFFSET PNAME
          MOV     CX,12
MOV0:     LODSB                        ;GET CHARACTER
          OR      AL,AL                ;TEST FOR END
          JNZ     MOV1                 ;GO STORE CHARACTER
          MOV     AL,' '               ;PAD CHARACTER
          REP STOSB                    ;PAD WITH BLANKS
          JMP     TSTDIR               ;DONE
MOV1:     STOSB                        ;STORE CHARACTER
          LOOP    MOV0                 ;KEEP TRUCKING
;MOVE FILE SIZE TO PRINT LINE
TSTDIR:   TEST    DFLAGS,16            ;DIRECTORY?
          JZ      MOVSIZ               ;NO - MOVE SIZE INFO
          MOV     SI,OFFSET MSG3       ;<DIR>
          MOV     DI,OFFSET PSIZE
          MOV     CX,8
          REP MOVSB
          JMP     TST1                 ;SKIP SIZE CALCULATION
MOVSIZ:   MOV     AX,DSIZE             ;LOW ORDER PART OF SIZE
          MOV     DX,DSIZE+2           ;HIGH ORDER PART OF SIZE
          ADD     TSIZE,AX             ;ACCUMULATE TOTAL SIZE
          ADC     TSIZE+2,DX           ;OF FILES FOUND
          INC     FILES                ;COUNT FILES FOUND
          MOV     SI,OFFSET PSIZE
          MOV     CX,8                 ;WIDTH OF OUTPUT FIELD
          CALL    BINASC               ;CONVERT TO ASCII
;TURN ON OR OFF ATTRIBUTE INDICATORS
TST1:     MOV     DI,OFFSET PFLAGS
          MOV     AL,' '
          TEST    DFLAGS,1             ;READ ONLY?
          JZ      TST2                 ;NO
          MOV     AL,'R'
TST2:     STOSB                        ;PUT CHAR IN STRING
          MOV     AL,' '
          TEST    DFLAGS,2             ;HIDDEN FILE?
          JZ      TST4                 ;NO
          MOV     AL,'H'
TST4:     STOSB
          MOV     AL,' '
          TEST    DFLAGS,4             ;SYSTEM FILE?
          JZ      TST32                ;NO
          MOV     AL,'S'
TST32:    STOSB
          MOV     AL,' '
          TEST    DFLAGS,32            ;ARCHIVE?
          JZ      TSTX                 ;NO
          MOV     AL,'A'
TSTX:     STOSB
          MOV     DX,OFFSET PNAME      ;OUTPUT LINE
          CALL    PRINT
          POP     DX
          POP     DI
```

```
                POP     SI
                POP     AX
                RET
PRTDIR          ENDP
BINASC          PROC
;CONVERTS A BINARY NUMBER IN DX:AX TO PRINTABLE FORM
;AND PLACES IT IN A FIELD POINTED TO BY SI WITH THE
;FIELD WIDTH IN CX. LEADING ZEROS ARE SUPPRESSED.
                PUSH    DX
                PUSH    CX
                PUSH    BX
                PUSH    DI
                PUSH    AX
                MOV     DI,SI            ;SAVE START OF STRING
BA1:            MOV     BYTE PTR [SI],' '        ;FILL CHARACTER
                INC     SI               ;POINT TO NEXT FIELD POSITION
                LOOP    BA1              ;LOOP UNTIL DONE
                DIV     C10000           ;DIVIDE BY 10,000
                MOV     BX,AX            ;SAVE QUOTIENT
                MOV     AX,DX            ;MOVE REMAINDER BACK TO AX
BA2:            MOV     CX,4             ;NUMBER OF DIGITS TO PRINT
BA3:            XOR     DX,DX            ;CLEAR HIGH ORDER WORD
                DIV     C10              ;DIVIDE BY TEN
                ADD     DL,'0'           ;CONVERT TO ASCII DIGIT
                DEC     SI               ;STEP BACKWARDS THROUGH BUFFE[R]
                CMP     SI,DI            ;OUT OF SPACE?
                JB      BAX              ;YES - QUIT
                MOV     [SI],DL          ;STORE DIGIT
                OR      AX,AX            ;ALL DIGITS PRINTED?
                JNZ     BA4              ;NO - KEEP TRUCKING
                OR      BX,BX            ;ANY MORE WORK?
                JZ      BAX              ;NO - CAN QUIT
BA4:            LOOP    BA3              ;NEXT DIGIT
BA5:            OR      BX,BX            ;MORE WORK TO DO?
                JZ      BAX              ;NO - CAN QUIT
                MOV     AX,BX            ;GET NEXT 4 DIGITS
                XOR     BX,BX            ;SHOW NO MORE DIGITS
                JMP     BA2              ;KEEP ON TRUCKING
BAX:            POP     AX
                POP     DI
                POP     BX
                POP     CX
                POP     DX
                RET
BINASC          ENDP
CSEG            ENDS
                END     START
```

A Copy Program with Space Checking

Information obtained from directory searches is not limited to displaying or printing. This same search capability can be used, for example, to build a copy program which is a little bit more bulletproof than the standard copy function. First, we will have the program check to see if there is enough space on the target drive before attempting the copy. If there isn't, we will give the user the options of skipping that particular file, changing the target diskette and retrying the operation, or gracefully terminating the program. Second, if an error occurs while a particular file is being copied, the program will write an error message and continue with the next file.

To accomplish the space checking, we make use of DOS call 36H. This call returns all of the information on sector and cluster sizes necessary to calculate both the total size of a disk or diskette and also the remaining free space. Figure 10.6 summarizes this call.

Figure 10.6—Get Disk Free Space Function

```
At Entry:

    AH=36H

    DL= Drive # (Ø = Default Drive, 1 = A, ...)

Returns:

    AX=FFFFH if invalid

        else

    AX= Number of sectors per cluster

    BX= Number of free clusters

    CX= Number of bytes per sector

    DX= Number of clusters per drive
```

Figure 10.8 shows the copy program, which is an enhancement to the previous directory list program. As each filename meeting the global search characteristics is found, the directory information is displayed as before. Then the program attempts to create a file with the same name and attributes on the target device. If this is successful, then the original file is opened for input. The file is then copied from the source to the target. Both input and output files are then closed. A check for errors is made at each step in the process. If an error is detected, the COPY subroutine returns with the carry flag set, the DOS error code in AL (Figure 9.2) and a value in AH (Figure 10.7) which shows which part of the routine encountered the error.

Figure 10.7—MCOPY Error Codes

```
AH        Meaning

1         Failure during file create request

2         Failure trying to open input file

3         Failure trying to read input file

4         Failure trying to write output file
```

This program illustrates the issues encountered in most practical programs. To make a program truly "user friendly" requires more code in the error-handling routines than it does in the main line sections. Ideally, our copy program should not only detect all of the different possible errors, but should also analyze them and take corrective action. However, for the sake of space, error correction has been abbreviated. The actions which the program actually takes are discussed below.

If there is not enough free space on the target disk, the program will display the remaining space and ask the user what to do. The user can replace the diskette at this time without fear of corrupting the file directory.

If there is sufficient space, but the attempt to create the new directory entry fails, then the directory is probably full. The program issues a message that the file could not be created and waits for instructions as before. Again, the user can skip the file (probably useless in this case), change the target diskette and retry (the usual action), or terminate the program. On any other error, the program will issue a generic error message and move on to the next file. In this case, a partial file has been created on the target disk which will later have to be manually deleted by the user.

Note that all of the errors discussed above are logical errors. That is because DOS itself intercepts physical errors and asks the users to retry, ignore, or abort. To be really bulletproof, the program should use the set interrupt vector function (AH = 25H) to take over interrupt 23H (CTRL-Break exit address) and interrupt 24H (Critical error handler). Other enhancements left to the reader include allowing the user to set various flags to indicate if the archive bit should be turned off in the source directory upon successful copy, if the date and time from the source file should be used in the output directory instead of the current date and time, and if hidden or system files should NOT be copied.

Figure 10.8—Copy Program With Space Checking

```
PAGE      62,132
TITLE     MCOPY - Copy Program with Space Checking
PAGE
;------------------------------------------------------------
;DEFINE STACK SEGMENT
;------------------------------------------------------------
STACK     SEGMENT PARA STACK 'STACK'
          DB      64 DUP('STACK   ')
STACK     ENDS
;------------------------------------------------------------
;DEFINE PROGRAM SEGMENT PREFIX
;------------------------------------------------------------
PREFIX    SEGMENT AT 0
          ORG     6CH
PDRIVE    DB      0                    ;SPECIFIED TARGET DRIVE
```

```
          ORG      80H
UPARM     DB       128 DUP (?)         ;UNFORMATTED PARM AREA
PREFIX    ENDS
;-----------------------------------------------------------
;DEFINE DATA SEGMENT
;-----------------------------------------------------------
DSEG      SEGMENT PARA PUBLIC 'DATA'
APREFIX   DW       0                   ;ADDRESS OF PSP
C10       DW       10                  ;CONSTANT FOR DIVISION
C10000    DW       10000               ;CONSTANT FOR DIVISION
TDRIVE    DB       0                   ;TARGET DRIVE
FILES     DW       0                   ;NUMBER OF FILES FOUND
TSIZE     DD       0                   ;TOTAL SIZE OF FILES FOUND
RDHAND    DW       0                   ;INPUT FILE HANDLE
WRHAND    DW       0                   ;OUTPUT FILE HANDLE
SPTR      DW       SNAME               ;END OF STRING POINTER
TPTR      DW       TNAME               ;END OF STRING POINTER
SNAME     DB       80 DUP (0)          ;SEARCH NAME FIELD
TNAME     DB       80 DUP (0)          ;TARGET DIRECTORY
DIR       DB       21 DUP (?)          ;DOS WORKSPACE
DFLAGS    DB       0                   ;FILE ATTRIBUTE FLAGS
TIME      DW       0                   ;FILE CREATION TIME
DATE      DW       0                   ;FILE CREATION DATE
DSIZE     DD       0                   ;FILE SIZE
DNAME     DB       13 DUP (' ')        ;FILE NAME FOUND
MSG1      DB       'File Not Found',13,10,'$'
MSG2      DB       '*.*',0
MSG3      DB       'Only'
MSG3A     DB       '          Bytes Left on Target Drive',13,10,'$'
MSG4      DB       'Retry, Skip, or Abort (R,S,A) $'
MSG5      DB       'Invalid File Specification',13,10,'$'
MSG6      DB       13,10,'$'
MSG7      DB       'Cannot Create Output File',13,10,'$'
MSG8      DB       'Error During File Copy',13,10,'$'
PNAME     DB       8 DUP (' ')         ;FILE NAME
          DB       ' '
PEXT      DB       3 DUP (' ')         ;FILE EXTENSION
          DB       ' '
PSIZE     DB       8 DUP (' ')         ;FILE SIZE
          DB       ' '
PFLAGS    DB       5 DUP (' ')         ;ATTRIBUTE FLAGS
          DB       10,13,'$'           ;END OF LINE
PTOTAL    DB       '      File(s)'
PTSIZE    DB       '           bytes total size',13,10,'$'
BUFFER    DB       512 DUP (?)         ;SECTOR BUFFER
DSEG      ENDS
;-----------------------------------------------------------
;DEFINE CODE SEGMENT
;-----------------------------------------------------------
CSEG      SEGMENT PARA PUBLIC 'CODE'
START     PROC     FAR
          ASSUME   CS:CSEG,SS:STACK,DS:PREFIX
          PUSH     AX                  ;SAVE VALIDITY FLAGS
;ESTABLISH ADDRESSABILITY TO DATA SEGMENT
          MOV      AX,DSEG             ;ADDRESS OF DATA SEGMENT
          MOV      ES,AX               ;NOW POINTS TO DATA SEGMENT
          ASSUME   ES:DSEG             ;TELL ASSEMBLER
          MOV      APREFIX,DS          ;SAVE ADDRESS OF PSP
          MOV      AL,PDRIVE           ;GET TARGET DRIVE
          MOV      TDRIVE,AL           ;AND SAVE IN DS
```

```
          MOV     SI,OFFSET UPARM  ;FILE NAME PASSED BY DOS
          MOV     DI,OFFSET SNAME  ;FILE NAME FIELD IN OUR DS
          LODSB                    ;GET PARM STRING LENGTH
          CMP     AL,0             ;ANY NAME SUPPLIED?
          JZ      ENDPSP           ;NO - DONE WITH PSP
          XOR     CX,CX            ;CLEAR HIGH ORDER BYTE
          MOV     CL,AL            ;INSERT STRING LENGTH
          CALL    SKPBNK           ;SKIP LEADING BLANKS
          JCXZ    ENDPSP           ;IF NOTHING LEFT
          CALL    NOBLNK           ;MOVE UNTIL BLANK
          MOV     SPTR,DI          ;SAVE END OF STRING POINTER
          DEC     CX               ;ADJUST FOR SEPARATING BLANK
          JCXZ    ENDPSP           ;IF NOTHING LEFT
          MOV     DI,OFFSET TNAME  ;POINT TO TARGET STRING
          CALL    SKPBNK           ;SKIP ADDITIONAL BLANKS
          JCXZ    ENDPSP           ;IF NOTHING LEFT
          CALL    NOBLNK           ;MOVE REST OF 2ND STRING
          MOV     TPTR,DI          ;SAVE END OF STRING POINTER
ENDPSP:   PUSH    ES
          POP     DS               ;ADDRESS OF DATA SEGMENT
          ASSUME  DS:DSEG          ;TELL ASSEMBLER
;-------------------------------------------------------------
;START OF MAIN PROGRAM
;-------------------------------------------------------------
          CALL    CLRSCN
;CHECK DRIVE VALIDITY
          POP     AX               ;RECOVER VALIDITY FLAGS
          OR      AH,AL            ;COMBINE FLAGS
          JZ      DEF              ;OK
          MOV     DX,OFFSET MSG5   ;INVALID DRIVE SPECS
          CALL    PRINT
          JMP     DONE
;APPLY DEFAULTS TO SEARCH STRING
DEF:      MOV     DI,OFFSET SNAME
DEF0:     CMP     BYTE PTR [DI],0  ;END OF STRING?
          JZ      DEF1             ;YES
          INC     DI
          JMP     DEF0             ;KEEP LOOKING
DEF1:     CMP     DI,OFFSET SNAME  ;NULL STRING?
          JZ      DEF3             ;YES - GO MOVE DEFAULT
          DEC     DI               ;BACK UP ONE CHARACTER
          CMP     BYTE PTR [DI],':'     ;DRIVE ONLY?
          JZ      DEF2             ;YES - USE DEFAULT
          CMP     BYTE PTR [DI],'\'     ;DIRECTORY ONLY?
          JNZ     SETDTA           ;NO - DON'T TOUCH ANYTHING
DEF2:     INC     DI               ;POINT BACK TO END OF STRING
DEF3:     MOV     SI,OFFSET MSG2   ;'*.*'
          MOV     CX,4
          REP MOVSB                ;MOVE DEFAULT STRING
;SET DTA TO DIRECTORY FEEDBACK AREA
SETDTA:   MOV     DX,OFFSET DIR    ;FEEDBACK AREA
          MOV     AH,1AH           ;SET DTA
          INT     21H              ;DOS REQUEST
          MOV     DX,OFFSET SNAME  ;FILE SEARCH NAME
          MOV     CX,6             ;HIDDEN + SYSTEM
          MOV     AH,4EH           ;FIND FIRST MATCH
          INT     21H
          JNC     FILEOK           ;YES
          MOV     DX,OFFSET MSG1
          CALL    PRINT
```

```
          JMP      DONE              ;QUIT
-FILEOK: CALL      PRTDIR            ;PRINT DIRECTORY ENTRY
          CALL     CKSPCE            ;CHECK AVAILABLE SPACE
          JNC      GOCOPY            ;COPY FILE
ASK:      CALL     ASKOP             ;ASK WHAT TO DO
          CMP      AL,'S'            ;SKIP?
          JZ       SKIP              ;SKIP THIS FILE
          CMP      AL,'R'            ;RETRY?
          JZ       FILEOK            ;RECHECK SPACE
          CMP      AL,'A'            ;ABORT?
          JZ       NOMORE            ;QUIT
          JMP      ASK               ;ASK QUESTION AGAIN
GOCOPY:   CALL     COPY              ;COPY FILE
          JNC      SKIP              ;GOOD COPY - GO DO NEXT FILE
          CMP      AH,1              ;ERROR DURING CREATE?
          JNZ      BADFIL            ;NO - FILE IS BAD
          MOV      DX,OFFSET MSG7    ;CREATE ERROR MSG
          CALL     PRINT
          JMP      ASK               ;ASK FOR GUIDANCE
BADFIL:   MOV      DX,OFFSET MSG8    ;GENERALIZED ERROR MSG
          CALL     PRINT
SKIP:     MOV      AH,4FH            ;SEARCH NEXT
          INT      21H               ;DOS REQUEST
          JNC      FILEOK            ;YES - GO DISPLAY
;PRINT ACCUMULATED TOTALS
NOMORE:   MOV      AX,FILES          ;TOTAL FILES FOUND
          XOR      DX,DX             ;CLEAR HIGH ORDER WORD
          MOV      SI,OFFSET PTOTAL
          MOV      CX,5
          CALL     BINASC            ;CONVERT TO ASCII
          MOV      AX,TSIZE          ;LOW WORD OF TOTAL SIZE
          MOV      DX,TSIZE+2        ;HIGH WORD OF TOTAL SIZE
          MOV      SI,OFFSET PTSIZE
          MOV      CX,8
          CALL     BINASC            ;CONVERT TO ASCII
          MOV      DX,OFFSET PTOTAL
          CALL     PRINT
;----------------------------------------------------------------
;RETURN TO DOS
;----------------------------------------------------------------
DONE:     MOV      AX,APREFIX        ;ADDRESS OF PSP
          PUSH     AX                ;PLACE ON STACK
          XOR      AX,AX
          PUSH     AX
          RET
START     ENDP
;----------------------------------------------------------------
;SUBROUTINES
;----------------------------------------------------------------
CLRSCN    PROC                       ;CLEAR SCREEN
          PUSH     AX
          MOV      AX,2
          POP      AX
          RET
CLRSCN    ENDP
PRINT     PROC
          PUSH     AX
          MOV      AH,9
          INT      21H
          POP      AX
```

```
          RET
PRINT     ENDP
PRTDIR    PROC
          PUSH    AX
          PUSH    SI
          PUSH    DI
          PUSH    DX
;MOVE FILE NAME TO PRINT LINE
          MOV     SI,OFFSET DNAME
          MOV     DI,OFFSET PNAME
          MOV     CX,12
MOV0:     LODSB                       ;GET CHARACTER
          OR      AL,AL               ;TEST FOR END
          JNZ     MOV1                ;GO STORE CHARACTER
          MOV     AL,' '              ;PAD CHARACTER
          REP STOSB                   ;PAD WITH BLANKS
          JMP     MOVSIZ              ;DONE
MOV1:     STOSB                       ;STORE CHARACTER
          LOOP    MOV0                ;KEEP TRUCKING
;MOVE FILE SIZE TO PRINT LINE
MOVSIZ:   MOV     AX,DSIZE            ;LOW ORDER PART OF SIZE
          MOV     DX,DSIZE+2          ;HIGH ORDER PART OF SIZE
          MOV     SI,OFFSET PSIZE
          MOV     CX,8                ;WIDTH OF OUTPUT FIELD
          CALL    BINASC              ;CONVERT TO ASCII
;TURN ON OR OFF ATTRIBUTE INDICATORS
          MOV     DI,OFFSET PFLAGS
          MOV     AL,' '
          TEST    DFLAGS,1            ;READ ONLY?
          JZ      TST2                ;NO
          MOV     AL,'R'
TST2:     STOSB                       ;PUT CHAR IN STRING
          MOV     AL,' '
          TEST    DFLAGS,2            ;HIDDEN FILE?
          JZ      TST4                ;NO
          MOV     AL,'H'
TST4:     STOSB
          MOV     AL,' '
          TEST    DFLAGS,4            ;SYSTEM FILE?
          JZ      TST32               ;NO
          MOV     AL,'S'
TST32:    STOSB
          MOV     AL,' '
          TEST    DFLAGS,32           ;ARCHIVE?
          JZ      TSTX                ;NO
          MOV     AL,'A'
TSTX:     STOSB
          MOV     DX,OFFSET PNAME     ;OUTPUT LINE
          CALL    PRINT
          POP     DX
          POP     DI
          POP     SI
          POP     AX
          RET
PRTDIR    ENDP
BINASC    PROC
;CONVERTS A BINARY NUMBER IN DX:AX TO PRINTABLE FORM
;AND PLACES IT IN A FIELD POINTED TO BY SI WITH THE
;FIELD WIDTH IN CX. LEADING ZEROS ARE SUPPRESSED.
          PUSH    DX
```

```
          PUSH   CX
          PUSH   BX
          PUSH   DI
          PUSH   AX
          MOV    DI,SI          ;SAVE START OF STRING
BA1:      MOV    BYTE PTR [SI],' '       ;FILL CHARACTER
          INC    SI             ;POINT TO NEXT FIELD POSITION
          LOOP   BA1            ;LOOP UNTIL DONE
          DIV    C10000         ;DIVIDE BY 10,000
          MOV    BX,AX          ;SAVE QUOTIENT
          MOV    AX,DX          ;MOVE REMAINDER BACK TO AX
BA2:      MOV    CX,4           ;NUMBER OF DIGITS TO PRINT
BA3:      XOR    DX,DX          ;CLEAR HIGH ORDER WORD
          DIV    C10            ;DIVIDE BY TEN
          ADD    DL,'0'         ;CONVERT TO ASCII DIGIT
          DEC    SI             ;STEP BACKWARDS THROUGH BUFFER
          CMP    SI,DI          ;OUT OF SPACE?
          JB     BAX            ;YES - QUIT
          MOV    [SI],DL        ;STORE DIGIT
          OR     AX,AX          ;ALL DIGITS PRINTED?
          JNZ    BA4            ;NO - KEEP TRUCKING
          OR     BX,BX          ;ANY MORE WORK?
          JZ     BAX            ;NO - CAN QUIT
BA4:      LOOP   BA3            ;NEXT DIGIT
BA5:      OR     BX,BX          ;MORE WORK TO DO?
          JZ     BAX            ;NO - CAN QUIT
          MOV    AX,BX          ;GET NEXT 4 DIGITS
          XOR    BX,BX          ;SHOW NO MORE DIGITS
          JMP    BA2            ;KEEP ON TRUCKING
BAX:      POP    AX
          POP    DI
          POP    BX
          POP    CX
          POP    DX
          RET
BINASC    ENDP
MISC      PROC
SKPBNK:   LODSB                 ;GET CHARACTER
          CMP    AL,' '         ;IS IT BLANK?
          JNZ    SKPBNX         ;NO - GO MOVE NAME
          LOOP   SKPBNK         ;SKIP LEADING BLANKS
SKPBNX:   RET
NOBLNK:   STOSB                 ;STORE IN FILE NAME
          LOOP   NOBLN1         ;IF ANY MORE CHARACTERS
          RET
NOBLN1:   LODSB                 ;GET NEXT CHARACTER
          CMP    AL,' '         ;FOUND A BLANK?
          JNZ    NOBLNK         ;NO - GO STORE
          RET
CKSPCE:   PUSH   AX
          PUSH   BX
          PUSH   CX
          PUSH   DX
          MOV    DL,TDRIVE      ;TARGET DRIVE
          MOV    AH,36H         ;GET DISK FREE SPACE
          INT    21H            ;DOS REQUEST
          MUL    CX             ;CALC BYTES PER CLUSTER
          MUL    BX             ;CALC BYTES AVAILABLE
          CMP    DX,DSIZE+2     ;ENOUGH SPACE?
          JA     CKSPC2         ;YES
```

```
             JB        CKSPC1            ;NO
             CMP       AX,DSIZE          ;CHECK LOW ORDER WORD
             JAE       CKSPC2            ;OK
  CKSPC1:    MOV       SI,OFFSET MSG3A   ;SPACE FIELD IN MSG3
             MOV       CX,8              ;FIELD WIDTH
             CALL      BINASC            ;CONVERT TO ASCII
             MOV       DX,OFFSET MSG3    ;REMAINING SPACE MSG
             CALL      PRINT             ;DISPLAY MESSAGE
             STC                         ;SHOW OUT OF SPACE
             JMP       CKSPCX            ;RETURN
  CKSPC2:    CLC                         ;SHOW SPACE OK
  CKSPCX:    POP       DX
             POP       CX
             POP       BX
             POP       AX
             RET
  ASKOP:     MOV       DX,OFFSET MSG4    ;RETRY, SKIP, ETC.
             CALL      PRINT
             MOV       AX,0C01H          ;READ RESPONSE
             INT       21H               ;DOS REQUEST
             AND       AL,0DFH           ;UC XLATE
             PUSH      AX
             MOV       DX,OFFSET MSG6    ;CRLF
             CALL      PRINT
             POP       AX
             RET
  ;COPY INPUT FILE TO OUTPUT
  COPY:      MOV       SI,OFFSET DNAME   ;FILE NAME FOUND
             MOV       DI,SPTR           ;END OF SOURCE DIRECTORY
  COPYM1:    LODSB
             STOSB                       ;MOVE TO OUTPUT STRING
             CMP       AL,0              ;END?
             JNZ       COPYM1            ;KEEP TRUCKING
             MOV       SI,OFFSET DNAME   ;USE SAME NAME FOR OUTPUT
             MOV       DI,TPTR           ;END OF DIRECTORY STRING
  COPYM2:    LODSB
             STOSB                       ;MOVE TO OUTPUT STRING
             CMP       AL,0              ;END?
             JNZ       COPYM2            ;NO - KEEP IT MOVING
             MOV       DX,OFFSET TNAME   ;FILE NAME TO COPY
             XOR       CX,CX             ;CLEAR HIGH BYTE
             MOV       CL,DFLAGS         ;FILE ATTRIBUTE
             MOV       AH,3CH            ;CREATE FILE
             INT       21H               ;DOS REQUEST
             JNC       COPY1             ;GOOD RETURN
             MOV       AH,1              ;FAILURE DURING CREATE
             RET
  COPY1:     MOV       WRHAND,AX         ;SAVE HANDLE
  ;OPEN INPUT FILE
             MOV       DX,OFFSET SNAME   ;SOURCE NAME
             MOV       AL,0              ;INPUT ONLY
             MOV       AH,3DH            ;OPEN REQUEST
             INT       21H               ;DOS REQUEST
             JNC       COPY2             ;GOOD RETURN
             MOV       AH,2              ;FAILURE DURING OPEN
             RET
  COPY2:     MOV       RDHAND,AX         ;SAVE HANDLE
  ;COPY FILE
  COPY3:     CALL      RDBUFF            ;READ ONE SECTOR
             JC        COPY4             ;READ ERROR
```

```
          CMP     AX,0            ;END OF FILE?
          JZ      COPY4           ;YES - GO CLOSE FILES
          CALL    WRBUFF          ;WRITE ONE SECTOR
          JNC     COPY3           ;KEEP IT MOVING
          MOV     AH,4            ;FAILURE DURING WRITE
COPY4:    PUSH    AX              ;SAVE RETURN CODE
          MOV     BX,RDHAND       ;INPUT FILE
          MOV     AH,3EH          ;CLOSE
          INT     21H             ;DOS REQUEST
          MOV     BX,WRHAND       ;OUTPUT FILE
          MOV     AH,3EH          ;CLOSE
          INT     21H             ;DOS REQUEST
;INCREMENT TOTALS
          MOV     AX,DSIZE
          MOV     DX,DSIZE+2
          ADD     TSIZE,AX        ;ACCUMULATE TOTAL SIZE
          ADC     TSIZE+2,DX      ;OF FILES FOUND
          INC     FILES           ;COUNT FILES FOUND
          POP     AX              ;GET RETURN CODE
          CMP     AX,0            ;NORMAL END OF FILE?
          JZ      COPY5           ;YES
          STC                     ;SHOW ERROR RETURN
COPY5:    RET
RDBUFF:   PUSH    BX
          PUSH    CX
          PUSH    DX
          MOV     BX,RDHAND       ;INPUT FILE HANDLE
          MOV     CX,512          ;ONE SECTOR
          MOV     DX,OFFSET BUFFER
          MOV     AH,3FH          ;READ FILE
          INT     21H             ;DOS REQUEST
          POP     DX
          POP     CX
          POP     BX
          RET
WRBUFF:   PUSH    BX
          PUSH    CX
          PUSH    DX
          MOV     BX,WRHAND       ;OUTPUT FILE HANDLE
          MOV     CX,AX           ;WRITE BUFFER
          MOV     DX,OFFSET BUFFER
          MOV     AH,40H          ;WRITE FILE REQUEST
          INT     21H             ;DOS REQUEST
          JC      WRBUFX          ;ERROR ON WRITE
          CMP     AX,CX           ;WRITE OK?
          JZ      WRBUFX          ;YES
          STC                     ;NO - MARK ERROR
WRBUFX:   POP     DX
          POP     CX
          POP     BX
          RET
MISC      ENDP
CSEG      ENDS
          END     START
```

Part III

Programming With BIOS Calls

Chapter 11
VIDEO OUTPUT

The primary reasons for coding in assembly language—
enhanced function and improved execution speed—are
also the incentives for coding **BIOS** interrupts instead
of **DOS** calls. The price you pay is loss of compatibility.
Most computers which are based on the Intel 8086/8088
family of microprocessors will run **MS DOS**, the generic version of **PC DOS**. The number of machines
which have implemented the same calling sequences
as IBM at the BIOS level, however, is much smaller. As
a general rule, therefore, software which is written for
distribution (even if limited only to friends) should be
written using **DOS** function calls whenever practical.

There are several areas, however, where the DOS
function calls are woefully inadequate. The most obvious
of these is in dealing with the display screen. Modern
display technology treats the screen as a two-dimensional
surface, with data fields directly accessible by row and
column coordinates. In addition, each field, or even
each individual character, has attributes such as color,
intensity, automatic underlining, and so forth. Finally,
the screen surface can be logically subdivided into mul-

tiple windows which can be individually scrolled up or down, or made to appear and disappear as required.

DOS, on the other hand, thinks of the screen as a "glass" teleprinter, which prints bright characters on a dark background, left to right, top to bottom, just as a typewriter prints on a piece of paper. DOS 2.0 did supply a device driver named ANSI.SYS, which allows keyboard redefinition, cursor positioning, and some screen attribute manipulation under program control. Not only is this function limited in scope and somewhat awkward to use, but since it is an optional feature requiring user action to implement, it does not solve the compatibility issue since there is no guarantee that it will be present in any given machine environment. To truly unlock the power of the IBM display adapters requires that the programmer drop down to at least the BIOS call level.

Display Adapter Characteristics

No level of programming can cause the hardware to do more than it is physically capable of. Since IBM has more than one type of display adapter for the PC (four as of this writing), we need to briefly review the basic differences.

Ignoring for a moment the more recent announcements, IBM offers a choice of two display adapters. The Monochrome adapter operates in character mode only, with one screen of 25 rows of 80 characters. Each character has a corresponding attribute character which does not take up a screen position. The standard character is green on a dark background. Different attribute bits specify the nondisplay, highlight, underline, reverse video, and blink characteristics. It is important to understand that although the word monochrome means essentially the same thing as black and white, the IBM Monochrome adapter is quite different—from a programming standpoint—than a Color/Graphics adapter with a black and white monitor attached.

The Color/Graphics adapter also has a character mode, or more precisely, multiple character submodes. It has eight independent pages of 25 rows of 40 characters, or four independent pages of 25 rows of 80 characters. Each page keeps track of its own cursor position. The active page (the one currently displayed) can be selected under program control to give the appearance of an instantaneous rewrite of the screen.

The Color/Graphics adapter gives up the hardware underline capability in order to support 16 foreground and 8 background colors (counting black and white as colors). On a RGB monitor, the color attributes are always honored. The adapter can, however, turn off the color burst signal fed to a composite monitor. This capability, combined with the two different screen sizes, gives four different character modes. In addition, the adapter can operate in one of three different graphic modes.

Determining the Current Environment

Since code written for distribution needs to be able to run on different adapter/display combinations, it is important to be able to determine (and sometimes alter) the current video state. Figure 11.1 shows the register settings involved. Note that the Monochrome adapter has its own unique code. This allows us to distinguish between the Monochrome adapter and Color/Graphics adapter in 80 × 25 black and white mode. The current video mode can be altered by issuing the same interrupt with AH set to 0 and AL set to the desired value (using the same codes returned by the get mode call).

Figure 11.1—Get Video Mode

```
Registers at Invocation of INT 10H: AH = 15 (0fH)
Returns:
AL = 0 -    40x25      Character      Black & white
     1 -    40x25      Character      Color
     2 -    80x25      Character      Black & white
     3 -    80x25      Character      Color
     4 -    320x200    Dots           Color
     5 -    320x200    Dots           Black & white
     6 -    640x200    Dots           Black & white
     7 -    80x25      Character      Monochrome Adaptor
AH = The number of character columns on the screen.
BH = The current active display page.
```

Cursor Positioning

The current cursor position can be determined by issuing the video BIOS interrupt (10H) with register AH set to 3, and BH set to the relative page number (always 0 for the Monochrome adapter). This call returns the current row in DH and the current column in DL. (Position 0,0 is the upper left corner of the screen.) Additionally, the starting and ending lines for the cursor shape are returned an CH and CL. A new cursor position can be set by issuing the interrupt with AH = 2 and DH/DL set to the desired row and column. As before, BH contains the page number. The sample program for this chapter includes subroutines to perform these functions.

Scrolling Windows

Neither of the IBM display adapters has any hardware scrolling capabilities. The video BIOS routines, however, provide some very powerful scrolling functions. The BIOS calls will scroll either up or down any arbitrary rectangular section of the screen by the number of lines specified. As the scroll takes place, the new blank line(s) which appear at the top or bottom of the screen are preset to the desired attribute. This allows a window to be maintained in a particular color, for example, without the rest of the program being aware of it. The register parameters for the scrolling functions are shown in Figure 11.2.

Figure 11.2—Video Scrolling

```
Registers at invocation of INT 10H:

  AH = 6 Scroll active, page UP

      7 Scroll active, page DOWN

  BH = The attribute to be used on blank line

  CH,CL = Row, column of upper left corner of window

  DH,DL = Row, column of lower right corner of window
```

Attribute Characters

Each character position on the screen has associated with it an attribute character, which does not take a screen position. There are essentially two different techniques for manipulating these attribute characters. One method is to write the screen character and its corresponding attribute character at the same time. This would be appropriate where a character or field has different attributes than its neighbors. For example, a data entry program that wished to highlight fields found to be in error would use this technique. The other method is to preset the attribute characters in various

Figure 11.3—Attribute Characters

```
 7      6      5      4      3      2      1      Ø
-----------------------------------------------------
 B      R      G      B      I      R      G      B
 L      E      R      L      N      E      R      L
 I      D      E      U      T      D      E      U
 N             E      E      E             E      E
 K             N             N             N
                             S
                             I
                             T
                             Y
=====================================================
      BACKGROUND              FOREGROUND
FOREGROUND COLOR COMBINATIONS:

 Ø - Black          8 - Dark Gray
 1 - Blue           9 - Light Blue
 2 - Green         1Ø - Light Green
 3 - Cyan          11 - Light Cyan
 4 - Red           12 - Light Red
 5 - Magenta       13 - Light Magenta
 6 - Brown         14 - Yellow
 7 - Light Gray    15 - White

Monochrome Attributes:

   Ø - Non-display
   1 - Underline
   7 - Normal
 112 - Reverse video
  +8 - Highlight
+128 - Blink
```

portions of the screen and then write only the screen characters when the screen is updated. A program which maintained one or more windows would likely use this method.

The attribute characters themselves are bit-mapped as shown in Figure 11.3. Note that the blink bit and the intensity bit apply to the foreground only. (By foreground, we mean the dots that make up the displayed character itself. Background means the rest of the character cell.)

The use of any of the nondefault attributes raises some compatibility issues between the Monochrome and the Color/Graphics adapters. For example, characters which are written to display as blue on the Color/Graphics adapter will display as underlined on the Monochrome adapter. A more subtle problem exists on the Color/Graphics adapter when attached to a noncolor monitor. Shades of colors that are quite readable all too often merge into indistinguishable shades of gray in this case.

Writing to the Screen

The two video function calls that write to the screen are very similar. Both write a character or a string of identical characters to the active screen at the current cursor position. The cursor is not advanced by this action and must be controlled with the set cursor call. All 256 possible character combinations are valid display characters. Therefore, any combination that the program wants to treat as control characters must be trapped by the program prior to issuing the video call. The most common characters that are usually trapped are carriage return, line feed, and horizontal tab. Register conventions for these calls are illustrated in Figure 11.4.

Figure 11.4—Video Write Functions

```
Registers at invocation of INT 10H:

    AH = 9 - Write character and attribute

        10 - Write character only

    AL = The character to write

    BH = Display page

    BL = Attribute character (AH = 9 ONLY)

    CX = Count of characters to write
```

Other Character Mode Functions

In addition to the functions already discussed, there are several other video function calls which can be used in character mode. Many editor programs use an underlining cursor for overtyping and a block cursor for inserting. The shape of the cursor can be set with the Set Cursor Type call. The active page can be changed with the Select Active Page call. Both the Monochrome and Color/Graphic adapters have hardware provisions for supporting a light pen, although the light pen will not work if the adapter is attached to a monitor with a slow decay phosphor, such as that used on the IBM Monochrome display. Finally, sometimes the program needs to determine the current contents of a screen position. The register conventions for these functions are shown in Figure 11.5.

The Sample Program

Figure 11.6 shows our old friend, the SCAN program, modified to use the video BIOS calls instead of DOS

Figure 11.5—Miscellaneous Video Calls

Set Cursor Type

```
AH = 1
CH = Start line for cursor (0-31)
CL = End line for cursor (0-31)
```

Setting the start line greater than the cell size will turn off the cursor.

Read Light Pen Postion

```
AH = 4
```

Returns:

```
AH = 0 - Light pen not triggered.
AH = 1 - Valid data in following registers:

    DH,DL = Row, column of light pen position
    CH = Raster line (0-199)
    BX = Pixel column (0-319,639)
```

Set Active Display Page

```
AH = 5
AL = New page value (0-7 for 40x25, 0-3 for
                     80x25)
```

Read Attribute/Character

```
AH = 8
BH = Display page
```

Returns:

```
    AL = Character read
    AH = Attribute of character read
```

calls. The program is essentially unchanged up to the point that it determines that the file name is valid. It then checks the current video state using the GETVID subroutine. This subroutine saves both the current mode and the screen size. If the program is running on either the Monochrome adapter or on the Color/Graphics adapter with the mode set to black and white then the program will use normal video in the text window and reverse video in the title bar. Otherwise the attribute settings are altered to use color.

Next, the program divides the video screen up into two windows. The top line on the screen becomes the title bar. The rest of the screen becomes the text window. The name of the file being displayed, along with path descriptors (if any), is displayed in the title bar. This window will remain unchanged for the duration of program execution.

The program then enters a loop, reading from the disk and writing to the screen via the DISPCH subroutine until the entire file has been displayed. The program then exits, as before, by issuing a DOS EXIT call with a return code of zero to indicate successful completion.

Figure 11.6—The Sample Program

```
PAGE      62,132
TITLE     Scan3 - File Display Program Using Video Bios Calls
PAGE
;-------------------------------------------------------------
;DEFINE STACK SEGMENT
;-------------------------------------------------------------
STACK     SEGMENT PARA STACK 'STACK'
          DB      64 DUP('STACK   ')
STACK     ENDS
;-------------------------------------------------------------
;DEFINE PROGRAM SEGMENT PREFIX
;-------------------------------------------------------------
PREFIX    SEGMENT AT 0
          ORG     80H
UPARM     DB      128 DUP (?)      ;UNFORMATTED PARM AREA
PREFIX    ENDS
;-------------------------------------------------------------
;DEFINE DATA SEGMENT
;-------------------------------------------------------------
DSEG      SEGMENT PARA PUBLIC 'DATA'
VIDCOL    DB      79                    ;MAXIMUM VIDEO COLUMN
```

```
VIDMOD   DB       7                    ;CURRENT VIDEO MODE
FGND     DB       7                    ;TEXT ATTRIBUTE VALUE
BGND     DB       70H                  ;TITLE BAR ATTRIBUTE
CHAR     DB       ' '                  ;ONE BYTE BUFFER
FNAME    DB       80 DUP (' ')         ;FILE NAME INCLUDING PATH
MSG1     DB       16,'FILE NOT FOUND',13,10
MSG2     DB       22,'NO FILE NAME ENTERED',13,10
DSEG     ENDS
;------------------------------------------------------------
;DEFINE CODE SEGMENT
;------------------------------------------------------------
CSEG     SEGMENT PARA PUBLIC 'CODE'
START    PROC     FAR
         ASSUME   CS:CSEG,SS:STACK,DS:PREFIX
;ESTABLISH ADDRESSABILITY TO DATA SEGMENT
         MOV      AX,DSEG              ;ADDRESS OF DATA SEGMENT
         MOV      ES,AX                ;NOW POINTS TO DATA SEGMENT
         ASSUME   ES:DSEG              ;TELL ASSEMBLER
;------------------------------------------------------------
;START OF MAIN PROGRAM
;------------------------------------------------------------
         MOV      SI,OFFSET UPARM      ;FILE NAME PASSED BY DOS
         MOV      DI,OFFSET FNAME      ;FILE NAME FIELD IN OUR DS
         LODSB                         ;GET PARM STRING LENGTH
         CMP      AL,0                 ;ANY NAME SUPPLIED?
         JZ       NOFILE               ;NO - SAY SO
         XOR      CX,CX                ;MAKE SURE HIGH BYTE IS ZERO
         MOV      CL,AL                ;INSERT STRING LENGTH
TSTBNK:  LODSB                         ;GET CHARACTER
         CMP      AL,' '               ;IS IT BLANK?
         JNZ      NOBLNK               ;NO - GO MOVE NAME
         LOOP     TSTBNK               ;SKIP LEADING BLANKS
NOFILE:  PUSH     ES                   ;DATA SEGMENT
         POP      DS                   ;NOW ALSO IN DS
         MOV      SI,OFFSET MSG2       ;NO FILE MESSAGE
         JMP      BADFIL               ;GO ISSUE MESSAGE
NOBLNK:  STOSB                         ;STORE IN FILE NAME
         LODSB                         ;GET NEXT CHARACTER
         LOOP     NOBLNK               ;LOOP UNTIL DONE
         XOR      AX,AX                ;CLEAR REGISTER
         STOSB                         ;TERMINATE STRING
         PUSH     ES                   ;POINTER TO DATA SEGMENT
         POP      DS                   ;NOW ALSO IN DS
         ASSUME   DS:DSEG              ;TELL ASSEMBLER
;ATTEMPT TO OPEN FILE
         MOV      AH,3DH               ;FILE OPEN REQUEST
         MOV      AL,0                 ;READ ONLY
         MOV      DX,OFFSET FNAME      ;FILE NAME
         INT      21H                  ;DOS FUNCTION CALL
         JNC      FILEOK               ;NO ERROR BRANCH
         MOV      SI,OFFSET MSG1       ;FILE OPEN ERROR MESSAGE
BADFIL:  MOV      BX,2                 ;STANDARD ERROR DEVICE
         MOV      AH,40H               ;WRITE DEVICE REQUEST
         LODSB                         ;GET MESSAGE LENGTH
         MOV      CL,AL                ;PUT IN COUNT REGISTER
         MOV      CH,0                 ;CLEAR HIGH ORDER BYTE
         MOV      DX,SI                ;POINT TO MESSAGE
         INT      21H                  ;INVOKE DOS
         MOV      AL,16                ;SET ERROR RETURN CODE
         JMP      DONEX                ;RETURN TO DOS
FILEOK:  MOV      BX,AX                ;SAVE FILE HANDLE
```

```
            MOV     DX,OFFSET CHAR   ;POINT TO ONE CHAR BUFFER
            CALL    GETVID           ;GET CURRENT VIDEO STATE
            CMP     VIDMOD,3         ;GRAPHICS OR MONOCHROME?
            JA      CLEAR            ;YES - USE DEFAULTS
            TEST    VIDMOD,1         ;COLOR ON?
            JZ      CLEAR            ;NO
            MOV     BGND,72H         ;GREEN ON GRAY
            MOV     FGND,1CH         ;LIGHT RED ON BLUE
CLEAR:      CALL    CLRSCR           ;CLEAR VIDEO WINDOW
            CALL    TITLE            ;PUT FILE NAME AT TOP OF SCREEN
READ:       CALL    RDBYTE           ;READ ONE BYTE FROM FILE
            MOV     AL,CHAR          ;GET CHARACTER
            CMP     AL,1AH           ;END OF FILE?
            JZ      DONE             ;YES - QUIT
            CALL    DISPCH           ;PRINT BYTE TO VIDEO SCREEN
            JMP     READ             ;GET NEXT FILE BYTE
;------------------------------------------------------------
;RETURN TO DOS
;------------------------------------------------------------
DONE:       MOV     AL,0             ;GOOD RETURN CODE
DONEX:      MOV     AH,4CH           ;EXIT REQUEST
            INT     21H              ;INVOKE DOS
START       ENDP
;------------------------------------------------------------
;SUBROUTINES
;------------------------------------------------------------
VIDSUBS PROC                         ;VIDEO SUBROUTINES
GETVID:     PUSH    AX
            MOV     AH,15            ;GET VIDEO STATE
            INT     10H              ;VIDEO REQUEST
            MOV     VIDMOD,AL        ;CURRENT VIDEO MODE
            MOV     VIDCOL,AH        ;NUMBER OF COLUMNS
            DEC     VIDCOL           ;MAXIMUM COLUMN NUMBER
            POP     AX
            RET
CLRSCR:     PUSH    AX
            PUSH    BX
            PUSH    CX
            PUSH    DX
            MOV     AX,0600H         ;CLEAR WINDOW
            MOV     CX,0             ;START=ROW 1 COL 1
            JMP     CLRSC1           ;SKIP SCROLL SETUP
SCROLL:     PUSH    AX
            PUSH    BX
            PUSH    CX
            PUSH    DX
            MOV     AX,0601H         ;SCROLL UP ONE LINE
            MOV     CX,0100H         ;START=ROW 1 COL 1
CLRSC1:     MOV     BH,FGND          ;TEXT ATTRIBUTE
            MOV     DH,24            ;END=ROW 25
            MOV     DL,VIDCOL        ;END=MAX COL NO.
            INT     10H              ;VIDEO BIOS REQUEST
            MOV     DX,1800H         ;ROW 25 COL 1
            CALL    SETCSR           ;SET CURSOR
            MOV     AH,11            ;CHECK INPUT STATUS
            INT     21H              ;DOS SERVICE REQUEST
            POP     DX
            POP     CX
            POP     BX
            POP     AX
            RET
```

```
SETCSR: PUSH    AX
        PUSH    BX
        MOV     BX,0            ;PAGE 0
        MOV     AH,2            ;SET CURSOR
        INT     10H             ;VIDEO BIOS REQUEST
        POP     BX
        POP     AX
        RET
GETCSR: PUSH    BX
        PUSH    CX
        MOV     AH,3            ;READ CURSOR POSITION
        MOV     BH,0            ;VIDEO PAGE 0
        INT     10H             ;VIDEO BIOS REQUEST
        POP     CX
        POP     BX
        RET
DISPCH: PUSH    AX
        PUSH    BX
        PUSH    CX
        PUSH    DX
        CMP     AL,10           ;LINE FEED CHAR?
        JZ      DISPC4          ;YES - IGNORE
        CMP     AL,13           ;CARRIAGE RETURN
        JZ      DISPC2          ;GO SCROLL
        CMP     AL,9            ;TAB CHAR?
        JNZ     DISPC1          ;GO DISPLAY CHAR
        MOV     AH,3            ;GET CURRENT CURSOR POS
        INT     10H             ;VIDEO BIOS REQUEST
        ADD     DL,8            ;EXPAND TAB
        AND     DL,0F8H         ;TRUNCATE TO BOUNDRY
        CMP     DL,VIDCOL       ;PAST END OF SCREEN?
        JA      DISPC2          ;YES - GO SCROLL
        MOV     AH,2            ;SET CURSOR
        INT     10H             ;VIDEO BIOS REQUEST
        JMP     DISPC4          ;DONE
DISPC1: MOV     AH,10           ;WRITE CHAR
        MOV     BH,0            ;PAGE 0
        MOV     CX,1            ;ONE CHARACTER
        INT     10H             ;VIDEO BIOS REQUEST
        CALL    GETCSR          ;READ CURSOR POSITION
        CMP     DL,VIDCOL       ;END OF PHYSICAL LINE?
        JNZ     DISPC3          ;NO PROBLEM
DISPC2: CALL    SCROLL          ;SCROLL UP SCREEN
        JMP     DISPC4          ;EXIT
DISPC3: INC     DL              ;INCREMENT CURSOR POSITION
        CALL    SETCSR          ;SET CURSOR POSITION
DISPC4: POP     DX
        POP     CX
        POP     BX
        POP     AX
        RET
TITLE:  PUSH    AX
        PUSH    BX
        PUSH    CX
        PUSH    DX
        MOV     DX,0            ;TOP OF SCREEN
        CALL    SETCSR          ;SET CURSOR
        MOV     AH,9            ;WRITE CHAR AND ATTRIBUTE
        MOV     BH,0            ;VIDEO PAGE
        MOV     CL,VIDCOL       ;MAX COLUMN
        INC     CL              ;SCREEN WIDTH
```

```
        MOV     CH,Ø
        MOV     AL,' '              ;BLANK
        MOV     BL,BGND             ;TITLE BAR ATTRIBUTE
        INT     1ØH                 ;VIDEO BIOS CALL
        MOV     SI,OFFSET FNAME     ;FILE NAME
        CALL    PRINT               ;PRINT FILE NAME
        CALL    SCROLL              ;START LISTING AT BOTTOM
        POP     DX
        POP     CX
        POP     BX
        POP     AX
        RET
PRINT:  LODSB                       ;GET CHAR
        CMP     AL,Ø                ;END OF STRING?
        JNZ     PRINT1              ;NO - CONTINUE
        RET
PRINT1: CALL    DISPCH              ;DISPLAY CHARACTER
        JMP     PRINT               ;GET NEXT CHARACTER
VIDSUBS ENDP
RDBYTE  PROC
;RDBYTE EXPECTS A FILE HANDLE IN BX AND THE LOCATION OF
;A ONE BYTE BUFFER IN DX. ALL REGISTERS ARE PRESERVED
        PUSH    AX                  ;SAVE REGS ON ENTRY
        PUSH    BX
        PUSH    CX
        PUSH    DX
        MOV     AH,3FH              ;READ REQUEST
        MOV     CX,1                ;ONE BYTE ONLY
        INT     21H                 ;INVOKE DOS
        JC      FEOF                ;TREAT ANY ERROR AS END OF FILE
        CMP     AL,Ø                ;EOF?
        JNZ     RDBYT1              ;NO - RETURN
FEOF:   PUSH    SI
        MOV     SI,DX               ;CAN NOT USE DX AS INDEX REG
        MOV     BYTE PTR [SI],1AH       ;MARK BUFFER WITH EOF
        POP     SI
        JMP     RDBYT1              ;RETURN
RDBYT1: POP     DX
        POP     CX
        POP     BX
        POP     AX
        RET
RDBYTE  ENDP
CSEG    ENDS
        END     START
```

The DISPCH subroutine, after saving registers on the stack, checks for special characters. Since this example is designed to display files in which each line is terminated by both a carriage return and a line feed, the routine treats carriage return as a new line character and invokes the SCROLL subroutine to scroll the window. Line feed characters are treated as redundant and discarded. Horizontal tab characters are handled by doing a direct cursor movement to the next tab position, defined in this case as a multiple of 8 columns. A program that allowed the user to set tab positions arbitrarily would use a table lookup function at this point.

All other characters are written to the screen. Since the video BIOS call does not move the cursor position, the routine obtains the current cursor position and tests for the end of the current line. If the last position of the line has just been filled, SCROLL is called. Otherwise, the column position is incremented and the BIOS routine is called to update the cursor position.

When SCROLL is called, it points to the text window by specifying the upper left corner, which is fixed, and the lower right corner, which is dependent upon the screen width. It then requests that the window be scrolled up one line, specifying the attribute character that should be used to initialize the new blank line at the bottom of the window.

The use of the BIOS calls creates one minor problem. DOS normally only checks to see if the operator has keyed the CRTL-break abort sequence during a DOS console request. The SCROLL subroutine solves this problem by issuing a DOS CHECK INPUT request after each window scroll operation. There is no need to check the result of this call, since—if CRTL-break has been signaled— control will never be returned from the DOS call.

If you have the proper equipment configuration available, test this program on the Monochrome display and in the various combinations of screen width and color on and off on the Color/Graphics adapter, and verify that the program properly adapts itself to the various environments.

Chapter 12
GRAPHICS

As we have seen, DOS thinks of the display screen as a character printer. Graphics through DOS calls is, therefore, limited to what can be built with the various graphic characters provided—mostly in the upper half of the extended ASCII character set. If your machine is equipped only with the IBM Monochrome Display Adapter, that is all the graphics function you have. The Color/Graphics adapter, on the other hand, has an all points addressable mode which allows treating the screen as an array of dots. The maximum resolution of the original adapter is 640 dots horizontally by 200 dots vertically in one color, or 320 × 200 in four colors. Newer boards from IBM and other vendors have greatly increased both the number of colors and the total number of dots.

There are two ways to take advantage of the all points addressable capability. The first makes use of the fact that the IBM BIOS provides a routine which writes normal text to the screen in 320 × 200 and 640 × 200 graphics modes. This routine makes use of a character table in ROM. The table, however, only de-

140

fines the ASCII characters from 0-7FH. For the upper half of the extended ASCII codes, the routine assumes that someone has set the 1FH interrupt vector to the segment and offset values of their own table. The routine then uses this table with no validity checking.

To build such a table, we only need to know that the system routine divides the screen up into character cells of 8 × 8 dots each. For building special graphics characters, all 64 dots may be freely used. If we are building a custom character font, however, we need to leave some room between letters. The normal uppercase letter is built in a 5-dot-wide by 7-dot-high character cell which occupies the upper left portion of the 8 × 8 total cell. Lower case letters use the bottom row of dots to form descenders. Of course, these are all just guidelines. You are free to use any dots at any time for any purpose. How it looks on the screen is the only real requirement.

Since a cell is 8 × 8 and since a byte has 8 bits, it takes 8 bytes to specify each of the 128 cells in a table. Each byte represents one row of dots, starting from the top. Figure 12.1 shows the encoding for the standard backslash character. The '1's in the matrix represent the dots which will be turned on. The '0's are dots that will be turned off.

Figure 12.1—Backslash Character Cell Map

```
DB    0C0H,60H,30H,18H,0CH,6,2,0      ;BACKSLASH


              11000000   C0
              01100000   60
              00110000   30
              00011000   18
              00001100   0C
              00000110   06
              00000010   02
              00000000   00
```

Of course we are not limited to one table. Once the character has been written to the screen, the table is no longer needed. Thus we can mix any number of fonts—alphabetic or graphic—on a single screen just by changing the pointer to the appropriate table before writing the character.

Figure 12.2 shows a sample program which displays the Hebrew alphabet. The program begins by checking the current video mode (Figure 11.1). If the system is currently running on the Monochrome Adapter, then the program will complain and quit. In all other cases, the program will save the current mode and reinitialize the screen in 320×200 graphics mode. This is done even if already in that mode, since this also acts as a clear screen function. Next, it gets and saves the current system 1FH interrupt vector and replaces it with the address of its own table. The saving and later restoring of the previous pointer is a nice touch, but it's usually unnecessary since no standard system table exists and most other user programs are not going to expect to come back later and find their pointer still there.

After displaying a message to let the user know how to terminate, the program enters a loop reading the keyboard. Each character typed is first checked to see if it is the ESC character. If so, the program restores the previous video environment and exits to DOS. Otherwise, it relocates most printable character up into the range where they will be displayed from the custom character set. Control characters, and a few punctuation marks, are left unchanged. Of course, no real program would translate in so simplistic a fashion, but it does illustrate the technique.

The other method of handling graphics is to adapt our programs to write one dot at a time. This is done by first issuing the BIOS function call to put the

Figure 12.2—Hebrew Character Set Example

```
PAGE      60,132
TITLE     CHARSET - Demonstration of Alternate Character Sets
PAGE
;-----------------------------------------------------------
;DEFINE STACK SEGMENT
;-----------------------------------------------------------
STACK     SEGMENT PARA STACK 'STACK'
          DB      64 DUP('STACK   ')
STACK     ENDS
;-----------------------------------------------------------
;DEFINE DATA SEGMENT
;-----------------------------------------------------------
DSEG      SEGMENT WORD PUBLIC 'DATA'
APREFIX   DW      0               ;ADDRESS OF PSP
OLDMODE   DB      0               ;PREVIOUS VIDEO MODE
OLDCHAR   DD      0               ;PREVIOUS GRAPHICS POINTER
MSG1      DB      'Program Requires Graphics Adapter',13,10,'$'
MSG2      DB      'Press ESC to Exit',13,10,'$'
;-----------------------------------------------------------
; HEBREW GRAPHIC CHARACTER EXTENSIONS (INTERRUPT 1FH)
;-----------------------------------------------------------
; For use without vowels:
HEBREW    DB      000H,022H,012H,01AH,02CH,024H,022H,000H ; aleph
          DB      000H,03CH,004H,014H,004H,004H,03EH,000H ; bet
          DB      000H,03CH,004H,004H,004H,004H,03EH,000H ; vet
          DB      000H,00CH,004H,004H,004H,01CH,014H,000H ; gimel
          DB      000H,03EH,004H,004H,004H,004H,000H,000H ; dalet
          DB      000H,03EH,002H,022H,022H,022H,022H,000H ; hay
          DB      000H,018H,008H,008H,008H,008H,008H,000H ; vav
          DB      020H,01CH,00AH,008H,008H,008H,000H,000H ; zayin
          DB      000H,07EH,022H,022H,022H,022H,022H,000H ; chet
          DB      000H,02EH,02AH,022H,022H,022H,01CH,000H ; tet
          DB      000H,01CH,004H,004H,000H,000H,000H,000H ; yod
          DB      000H,03CH,002H,012H,002H,002H,03CH,000H ; kaf
          DB      000H,03CH,002H,002H,002H,002H,03CH,000H ; chaf
          DB      000H,03EH,004H,004H,004H,004H,004H,004H ; final chaf
          DB      020H,020H,03EH,002H,004H,008H,010H,000H ; lamed
          DB      000H,02EH,012H,022H,022H,022H,02EH,000H ; mem
          DB      000H,03EH,012H,012H,012H,012H,01EH,000H ; final mem
          DB      000H,00CH,004H,004H,004H,004H,01CH,000H ; nun
          DB      000H,018H,008H,008H,008H,008H,008H,008H ; final nun
          DB      000H,03EH,012H,012H,012H,012H,01CH,000H ; sameh
          DB      000H,022H,022H,012H,00AH,006H,03CH,000H ; ayin
          DB      000H,03EH,022H,02AH,032H,002H,03EH,000H ; pay
          DB      000H,03EH,022H,022H,032H,002H,03EH,000H ; fay
          DB      000H,03EH,022H,032H,002H,002H,002H,002H ; final fay
          DB      000H,022H,014H,008H,004H,002H,03EH,000H ; tzadee
          DB      000H,024H,024H,028H,030H,020H,020H,020H ; final tzadee
          DB      000H,03EH,002H,022H,024H,028H,020H,020H ; kof
          DB      000H,03CH,004H,004H,004H,004H,004H,000H ; resh
          DB      000H,02AH,02AH,02AH,02AH,032H,03EH,000H ; shin/sin
          DB      000H,03EH,022H,02AH,022H,022H,062H,000H ; tav
          DB      000H,03EH,022H,022H,022H,022H,062H,000H ; tav
;
;
; For use with vowels:
          DB      000H,000H,022H,012H,01AH,02CH,024H,022H ; aleph
          DB      000H,000H,03CH,004H,014H,004H,004H,03EH ; bet
          DB      000H,000H,03CH,004H,004H,004H,004H,03EH ; vet
          DB      000H,000H,00CH,004H,004H,004H,01CH,014H ; gimel
          DB      000H,000H,03EH,004H,004H,004H,004H,004H ; dalet
          DB      000H,000H,03EH,002H,022H,022H,022H,022H ; hay
          DB      000H,000H,018H,008H,008H,008H,008H,008H ; vav
          DB      000H,020H,01CH,00AH,008H,008H,008H,008H ; zayin
          DB      000H,000H,07EH,022H,022H,022H,022H,022H ; chet
          DB      000H,000H,02EH,02AH,022H,022H,022H,01CH ; tet
```

```
        DB      000H,000H,01CH,004H,004H,000H,000H,000H ; yod
        DB      000H,000H,03CH,002H,012H,002H,002H,03CH ; kaf
        DB      000H,000H,03CH,002H,002H,002H,002H,03CH ; chaf
        DB      000H,000H,07EH,004H,004H,004H,004H,004H ; final chaf
        DB      004H,004H,004H,004H,000H,000H,000H,000H ;   its tail
        DB      020H,020H,03EH,002H,002H,004H,008H,010H ; lamed
        DB      000H,000H,02EH,012H,022H,022H,022H,02EH ; mem
        DB      000H,000H,03EH,012H,012H,012H,012H,01EH ; final mem
        DB      000H,000H,00CH,004H,004H,004H,004H,01CH ; nun
        DB      000H,000H,018H,008H,008H,008H,008H,008H ; final nun
        DB      008H,008H,008H,008H,000H,000H,000H,000H ;   its tail
        DB      000H,000H,03EH,012H,012H,012H,012H,01CH ; sameh
        DB      000H,000H,022H,022H,012H,00AH,006H,03CH ; ayin
        DB      000H,000H,03EH,022H,02AH,032H,032H,03EH ; pay
        DB      000H,000H,03EH,022H,022H,032H,002H,03EH ; fay
        DB      000H,000H,03EH,022H,022H,032H,002H,002H ; final fay
        DB      002H,002H,002H,002H,000H,000H,000H,000H ;   its tail
        DB      000H,000H,022H,014H,008H,004H,002H,03EH ; tzadee
        DB      000H,000H,022H,022H,024H,028H,030H,020H ; final tzadee
        DB      020H,020H,020H,020H,000H,000H,000H,000H ;   its tail
        DB      000H,000H,07EH,002H,042H,042H,044H,048H ; kof
        DB      040H,040H,040H,040H,000H,000H,000H,000H ;   its tail
        DB      000H,000H,03CH,004H,004H,004H,004H,004H ; resh
        DB      002H,000H,02AH,02AH,02AH,02AH,032H,03EH ; shin
        DB      020H,000H,02AH,02AH,02AH,02AH,032H,03EH ; sin
        DB      000H,000H,03EH,022H,02AH,022H,022H,062H ; tav
        DB      000H,000H,03EH,022H,022H,022H,022H,062H ; tav

        DB      000H,008H,000H,008H,000H,000H,000H,000H ; shvah
        DB      000H,01CH,008H,008H,000H,000H,000H,000H ; kamatz
        DB      000H,03AH,010H,012H,000H,000H,000H,000H ; kamatz + shvah
        DB      000H,01CH,000H,000H,000H,000H,000H,000H ; patach
        DB      000H,01CH,000H,002H,000H,000H,000H,000H ; patach + shvah
        DB      000H,014H,000H,008H,000H,000H,000H,000H ; segol
        DB      000H,02AH,000H,012H,000H,000H,000H,000H ; segol + shvah
        DB      000H,008H,000H,000H,000H,000H,000H,000H ; chirik
        DB      000H,014H,000H,000H,000H,000H,000H,000H ; tzereh
        DB      000H,020H,008H,002H,000H,000H,000H,000H ; kubutz
        DB      008H,000H,018H,008H,008H,008H,008H,008H ; cholam
        DB      080H,000H,000H,000H,000H,000H,000H,000H ; just the dot
        DB      000H,000H,018H,008H,008H,028H,008H,008H ; shuruk
        DB      000H,000H,000H,000H,008H,000H,000H,000H ; center dot
        DB      46*8 DUP(000H)
DSEG    ENDS
;-------------------------------------------------------------
;DEFINE CODE SEGMENT
;-------------------------------------------------------------
CSEG    SEGMENT BYTE PUBLIC 'CODE'
START   PROC    FAR
        ASSUME  CS:CSEG,DS:DSEG,ES:DSEG,SS:STACK
        MOV     AX,DSEG         ;ADDRESS OF DATA SEGMENT
        MOV     DS,AX           ;NOW POINTS TO DATA SEGMENT
        MOV     APREFIX,ES      ;SAVE PREFIX ADDRESS FOR EXIT
        MOV     ES,AX           ;NOW POINTS TO DATA SEGMENT ALSO
;GET AND SAVE THE CURRENT VIDEO MODE
        MOV     AH,15           ;GET CURRENT VIDEO MODE
        INT     10H             ;VIDEO BIOS CALL
        MOV     OLDMODE,AL      ;SAVE MODE
        CMP     AL,7            ;CHECK FOR MONO ADAPTER
        JNZ     GRAPH           ;GRAPHICS ADAPTER IN CONTROL
        MOV     DX,OFFSET MSG1  ;NOT GRAPHICS MESSAGE
        CALL    PRINT           ;DISPLAY MESSAGE
        JMP     DONE            ;TERMINATE PROGRAM
GRAPH:  MOV     AL,4            ;MEDIUM RES COLOR
        MOV     AH,0            ;SET MODE
        INT     10H             ;VIDEO BIOS CALL
;-------------------------------------------------------------
;INVOKE ALTERNATE CHARACTER SET
;-------------------------------------------------------------
```

```
;GET OLD CHARACTER POINTER
        PUSH    ES                      ;CALL DESTROYS ES
        MOV     AL,1FH                  ;TABLE VECTOR
        MOV     AH,35H                  ;GET VECTOR
        INT     21H                     ;DOS REQUEST
        MOV     OLDCHAR,BX              ;SAVE OLD TABLE
        MOV     OLDCHAR+2,ES            ;ENTRY ADDRESS
        POP     ES
        MOV     DX,OFFSET HEBREW        ;START OF TABLE
        MOV     AH,25H                  ;SET INTERRUPT VECTOR
        INT     21H                     ;DOS REQUEST
;WRITE EXIT MSG TO SCREEN
        MOV     DX,OFFSET MSG2          ;EXIT MSG
        CALL    PRINT                   ;DISPLAY ON SCREEN
;WAIT FOR KEYPRESS
WAIT:   MOV     AH,7                    ;GET CHAR WITHOUT ECHO
        INT     21H                     ;DOS REQUEST
        CMP     AL,27                   ;ESC?
        JZ      RESTORE                 ;YES - QUIT
        CMP     AL,48                   ;INTERCEPTED RANGE?
        JB      DISPLAY                 ;NO
        ADD     AL,80                   ;FORCE USE OF TABLE
DISPLAY: MOV    DL,AL                   ;CHARACTER TO WRITE
        MOV     AH,2                    ;OUTPUT CHAR
        INT     21H                     ;DOS FUNCTION CALL
        JMP     WAIT                    ;READ NEXT KEY
;------------------------------------------------------------
;RESTORE OLD VIDEO MODE
;------------------------------------------------------------
RESTORE: MOV    AL,OLDMODE              ;PREVIOUS VIDEO MODE
        MOV     AH,0                    ;SET MODE FUNCTION
        INT     10H                     ;VIDEO BIOS CALL
        MOV     DX,OLDCHAR              ;PREVIOUS TABLE OFFSET
        PUSH    DS                      ;NEED DS FOR CALL
        MOV     DS,OLDCHAR+2            ;PREVIOUS TABLE SEGMENT
        MOV     AH,25H                  ;SET INTERRUPT VECTOR
        INT     21H                     ;DOS REQUEST
        POP     DS
;------------------------------------------------------------
;RETURN TO DOS
;------------------------------------------------------------
DONE:   MOV     AX,APREFIX              ;ADDRESS OF PSP
        PUSH    AX                      ;PLACE ON STACK
        XOR     AX,AX                   ;OFFSET = ZERO
        PUSH    AX                      ;PLACE ON STACK
        RET                             ;RETURN TO DOS
START   ENDP

;------------------------------------------------------------
;SUBROUTINES
;------------------------------------------------------------
PRINT   PROC                            ;DISPLAY TO SCREEN
        PUSH    AX
        MOV     AH,9                    ;PRINT STRING FUNCTION
        INT     21H                     ;DOS REQUEST
        POP     AX
        RET
PRINT   ENDP
CSEG    ENDS
        END
```

adapter into the desired graphics mode, and then issuing another BIOS call for each dot to be written. The trick, of course, is choosing the correct algorithm to select the dots to be turned on to form the desired shape.

The sample program in Figure 12.3 illustrates techniques to draw lines, circles, and ellipses. Most other shapes can be fashioned from these primitives. The program begins, as did the previous example, by getting and saving the current video mode. Again as before, if the current mode is the Monochrome Adapter, then the program complains and gives up. Otherwise, it sets the mode to 320 × 200 color.

Next, just to liven up the screen a bit, we set the color palette to a choice of green, red, or yellow on a blue background. This involves issuing the video BIOS call (interrupt 10H) with AH = 11 (set palette), BH = 0 (palette number), and BL = 1 (background color). The palette and background color numbers are the same as those described in the BASIC "COLOR" statement. Then we draw a white circle and set of red lines.

The heart of the program is the POINT subroutine. This code first performes a validity check on the x and y coordinates of the requested point as passed in the DI (Row) and SI (column) registers. If all is well, it then sets up the appropriate registers and issues the BIOS interrupt call. Note that the value for color is taken from a variable in the data segment rather than being passed as a parameter. This was done so that the program could set the color once and then issue a sequence of point calls which would all use the same color. Not obvious from the example is the fact that if the high-order bit of COLOR is set then the dot is exclusive "or"-ed with the current screen contents. This technique is valuable in animation, because it allows a moving object to temporarily overlay the background scene rather than erasing it.

The subroutine called CIRCLE actually generates an ellipse. A circle is, of course, simply a special case in which the aspect ratio is 1:1. In fact, to draw something which looks like a circle on the color monitor, we actually have to draw an ellipse. This is because the dot spacing is not the same in the horizontal and vertical directions. The sample program uses an aspect ratio of 5:6 to attempt to correct for this visual distortion. A different ratio may look better on your own monitor, depending upon how it is adjusted.

Since CIRCLE requires more temporary variables than can be held all at once in the various registers, it has been written to use the stack for both its passed parameters and its local storage. This technique means that the subroutine can be separately compiled and linked with another program without the calling program having to allow for any working storage for the subroutine. It also makes the subroutine re-entrant, although that is only of concern in multi-tasking environments.

In polar coordinates, a circle is defined by the pair of relationships $X = R*$Cosine Theta and $Y = R*$Sine Theta. This relationship does not lend itself well to a good algorithm when working with integer dot positions, however. Instead, we prefer to step along one coordinate one dot at a time and calculate the other coordinate. For that part of the circle that lies in the range of 0 to 45 degrees, we use the following algorithm: $Y = Y + 1$ $X = X - Tan(1/ASPECT)$. For the range 45 to 90 degrees, we step X and calculate Y. The other three quadrants need no calculation. As each point in the first quadrant is calculated, we take advantage of symmetry to locate the corresponding point in the other three quadrants. Additionally, any time that the calculated coordinate is more than one dot position away from the previous point, the routine fills in the intermediate points. This not only makes a more solid-looking cirle, but is critical if a fill routine is to be invoked later.

The line routine could also have been written to use the stack for passing parameters, but is shown here as it might be called from another assembly language routine with the parameters already in the registers. It starts out by normalizing the order of the line ends. That is, it will always draw the line from left to right regardless of which end was specified first. This allows all possible lines to be considered as one of four cases; whether the line slopes up or down, and whether the slope is greater than or less than 45 degrees.

Consider Case 1. $(Y2 - Y1)$ is positive and greater than $(X2 \times X1)$. In this case, we step along the Y axis one dot at a time. We then approximate the slope of the line by adding $(X2 - X1)$ into an accumulator and comparing it to $(Y2 - Y1)$. If less, then we write a dot at the current X position and try again. If greater or equal, then we increment X, write a dot, subtract $(Y2 - Y1)$ from the accumulator and loop. The effect of this is to build a solid line out of little stairsteps. The other cases are essentially identical except for which coordinate we step along and whether we increment or decrement the other coordinate.

If none of the above makes sense to you, don't worry about it. The routines work, as the sample program demonstrates. Just copy them and use them as they are.

Figure 12.3—Sample Graphics Program using BIOS Calls

```
PAGE     60,132
TITLE    GRAPHICS - Sample Graphics Program using Bios Calls
PAGE
;------------------------------------------------------------
;DEFINE STACK SEGMENT
;------------------------------------------------------------
STACK    SEGMENT PARA STACK 'STACK'
         DB      64 DUP('STACK    ')
STACK    ENDS
;------------------------------------------------------------
;DEFINE DATA SEGMENT
;------------------------------------------------------------
```

```
DSEG      SEGMENT WORD PUBLIC 'DATA'
COLOR     DB      0
DIR       DW      0
APREFIX   DW      0               ;ADDRESS OF PSP
OLDMODE   DB      0               ;PREVIOUS VIDEO MODE
MSG1      DB      'Program Requires Graphics Adapter',13,10,'$'
MSG2      DB      'Press Any Key to Exit','$'
DSEG      ENDS
;-----------------------------------------------------------
;DEFINE CODE SEGMENT
;-----------------------------------------------------------
CSEG      SEGMENT BYTE PUBLIC 'CODE'
START     PROC    FAR
          ASSUME  CS:CSEG,DS:DSEG,ES:DSEG,SS:STACK
          MOV     AX,DSEG         ;ADDRESS OF DATA SEGMENT
          MOV     DS,AX           ;NOW POINTS TO DATA SEGMENT
          MOV     APREFIX,ES      ;SAVE PREFIX ADDRESS FOR EXIT
          MOV     ES,AX           ;NOW POINTS TO DATA SEGMENT ALSO
;GET AND SAVE THE CURRENT VIDEO MODE
          MOV     AH,15           ;GET CURRENT VIDEO MODE
          INT     10H             ;VIDEO BIOS CALL
          MOV     OLDMODE,AL      ;SAVE MODE
          CMP     AL,7            ;CHECK FOR MONO ADAPTER
          JNZ     GRAPH           ;GRAPHICS ADAPTER IN CONTROL
          MOV     DX,OFFSET MSG1  ;NOT GRAPHICS MESSAGE
          CALL    PRINT           ;DISPLAY MESSAGE
          JMP     DONE            ;TERMINATE PROGRAM
GRAPH:    MOV     AL,4            ;MEDIUM RES COLOR
          MOV     AH,0            ;SET MODE
          INT     10H             ;VIDEO BIOS CALL
          MOV     AH,11           ;SET COLOR PALETTE
          MOV     BH,0            ;GREEN/RED/YELLOW
          MOV     BL,1            ;ON BLUE BACKGROUND
          INT     10H             ;VIDEO BIOS CALL
;-----------------------------------------------------------
;CREATE A FEW SHAPES
;-----------------------------------------------------------
;DRAW A CIRCLE IN THE CENTER OF THE SCREEN
          MOV     COLOR,3
;CALL CIRCLE(X,Y,RADIUS,NUMER,DENOM)
          MOV     AX,160          ;X ORIGIN
          PUSH    AX
          MOV     AX,100          ;Y ORIGIN
          PUSH    AX
          MOV     AX,40           ;RADIUS
          PUSH    AX
          MOV     AX,5            ;ASPECT NUMERATOR
          PUSH    AX
          MOV     AX,6            ;ASPECT DENOMINATOR
          PUSH    AX
          CALL    CIRCLE
;DRAW A SET OF DIAGONAL LINES
          MOV     COLOR,2
          MOV     SI,20           ;X1
          MOV     DI,180          ;Y1
          MOV     AX,300          ;X2
          MOV     BX,20           ;Y2
LOOP:     PUSH    SI
          PUSH    DI
          PUSH    AX
          PUSH    BX
          CALL    LINE
```

```
              POP       BX
              POP       AX
              POP       DI
              POP       SI
              ADD       SI,20              ;MOVE X1 TO RIGHT
              SUB       AX,20              ;MOVE X2 TO LEFT
              JNZ       LOOP               ;DRAW NEXT LINE
;WRITE EXIT MSG TO SCREEN
              MOV       DX,OFFSET MSG2     ;EXIT MSG
              CALL      PRINT              ;DISPLAY ON SCREEN
;WAIT FOR KEYPRESS
              MOV       AH,0CH             ;CLEAR BUFFER AND INPUT
              MOV       AL,7               ;WITHOUT ECHO
              INT       21H                ;DOS REQUEST
;-----------------------------------------------------------
;RESTORE OLD VIDEO MODE
;-----------------------------------------------------------
              MOV       AL,OLDMODE         ;PREVIOUS VIDEO MODE
              MOV       AH,0               ;SET MODE FUNCTION
              INT       10H                ;VIDEO BIOS CALL
;-----------------------------------------------------------
;RETURN TO DOS
;-----------------------------------------------------------
DONE:         MOV       AX,APREFIX         ;ADDRESS OF PSP
              PUSH      AX                 ;PLACE ON STACK
              XOR       AX,AX              ;OFFSET = ZERO
              PUSH      AX                 ;PLACE ON STACK
              RET                          ;RETURN TO DOS
START         ENDP


;-----------------------------------------------------------
;SUBROUTINES
;-----------------------------------------------------------
POINT         PROC      NEAR               ;[SI=X,DI=Y]
              PUSH      AX
              PUSH      BX
              PUSH      CX
              PUSH      DX
              PUSH      SI
              PUSH      DI
;CLIP POINTS OUTSIDE SCREEN
              CMP       SI,0               ;LEFT EDGE
              JL        POINTX
              CMP       SI,319             ;RIGHT EDGE
              JA        POINTX
              CMP       DI,0               ;TOP
              JL        POINTX
              CMP       DI,199             ;BOTTOM
              JA        POINTX
              MOV       DX,DI              ;ROW
              MOV       CX,SI              ;COLUMN
              MOV       AL,COLOR           ;COLOR VALUE
              MOV       AH,12              ;WRITE DOT
              INT       10H                ;VIDEO BIOS CALL
POINTX:       POP       DI
              POP       SI
              POP       DX
              POP       CX
              POP       BX
              POP       AX
              RET
POINT         ENDP
```

```
;Draws a circle at center at center (X,Y) with aspect ratio
;numer/denom; radius in column units

CIRCLE   PROC     NEAR
         PUSH     BP                      ;SAVE CALLER'S FRAME POINTER
         MOV      BP,SP                   ;ESTABLISH LOCAL FRAME
         SUB      SP,14                   ;RESERVE LOCAL STORAGE
;ESTABLISH LABELS FOR PARAMETERS ON STACK
XX       EQU      WORD PTR [BP+12]        ;X ORIGIN
YY       EQU      WORD PTR [BP+10]        ;Y ORIGIN
RADIUS   EQU      WORD PTR [BP+8]         ;RADIUS OF CIRCLE
NUMER    EQU      WORD PTR [BP+6]         ;NUMERATOR OF ASPECT
DENOM    EQU      WORD PTR [BP+4]         ;DENOMINATOR OF ASPECT
XP       EQU      WORD PTR [BP-2]         ;PREVIOUS X CO-ORDINATE
YP       EQU      WORD PTR [BP-4]         ;PREVIOUS Y CO-ORDINATE
ASPECT   EQU      WORD PTR [BP-6]         ;ASPECT RATIO * 1000
IASPECT  EQU      WORD PTR [BP-8]         ;INVERSE ASPECT * 1000
C1000    EQU      WORD PTR [BP-10]        ;CONSTANT 1000
CURX     EQU      WORD PTR [BP-12]        ;WORK AREA
CURY     EQU      WORD PTR [BP-14]        ;WORK AREA
         MOV      AX,NUMER                ;GET ASPECT NUMER
         MOV      C1000,1000              ;SCALE FACTOR
         IMUL     C1000                   ;SCALE BY 1000
         IDIV     DENOM                   ;AX=ASPECT*1000
         MOV      ASPECT,AX               ;SAVE ASPECT
         MOV      AX,DENOM                ;GET DENOM IN AX
         IMUL     C1000                   ;SCALE DENOMINATOR
         IDIV     NUMER                   ;AX=INV ASPECT*1000
         MOV      IASPECT,AX              ;SAVE
;Y=Y+1 X=X-TAN(INV ASPECT)
         MOV      AX,RADIUS               ;GET RADIUS
         MOV      XP,AX                   ;1st PREVIOUS X
         IMUL     C1000                   ;SCALE
         MOV      CURY,0                  ;ZERO INIT Y VALUE
CR5:     PUSH     AX
         PUSH     DX
         ADD      AX,500                  ;ROUND
         ADC      DX,0
         IDIV     C1000                   ;RESCALE X
         MOV      BX,AX                   ;1st quad
         PUSH     BX                      ;NEW CALCULATED X
CR5A:    ADD      AX,XX                   ;ADD X ORIGIN
         MOV      DI,YY                   ;Y ORIGIN
         SUB      DI,CURY
         MOV      SI,AX                   ;GET X TO PLOT
         CALL     POINT                   ;CALL POINT ROUTINE
         SUB      SI,BX                   ;GET 2nd QUAD
         SUB      SI,BX                   ;X+ORIGIN
         CALL     POINT
         ADD      DI,CURY                 ;GET 3rd QUAD
         ADD      DI,CURY                 ;Y+ORIG
         CALL     POINT
         ADD      SI,BX                   ;GET 4th QUAD
         ADD      SI,BX                   ;X+ORIGIN
         CALL     POINT
         INC      BX
         CMP      BX,XP                   ;X GAP?
         JAE      CR6                     ;NO
         MOV      AX,BX                   ;SET INTERMEDIATE POINT
         JMP      CR5A                    ;GO PLOT IT

;CX NOW AT ORIGINAL POINT
```

```
CR6:    POP     BX              ;CALCULATED X
        MOV     XP,BX           ;PREVIOUS X
        INC     CURY            ;NEW Y
        MOV     AX,CURY         ;Y
        IMUL    IASPECT
        IDIV    BX              ;TAN*INV ASPECT
        XOR     DX,DX           ;REMAINDER
        MOV     CURX,AX         ;CURX=TAN*INV ASPECT
        IDIV    IASPECT         ;AX=TAN
        CMP     AX,1            ;TAN=1?
        POP     DX
        POP     AX
        JAE     CR7             ;GO TO NEXT SECTOR
        NEG     CURX            ;TO DEC X
        ADD     AX,CURX         ;NEW X VALUE
        ADC     DX,-1           ;NEGATIVE CARRY
        JMP SHORT CR5           ;PLOT NEW POINT

;PLOT 45 TO 90 DEGREES

CR7:    MOV     AX,CURY         ;NEXT Y
        MOV     YP,AX           ;INIT PREVIOUS Y
        IMUL    C1000           ;DX:AX=Y*1000
        MOV     CURY,BX         ;LAST X VALUE
        DEC     CURY            ;NEXT X
CR8:    PUSH    AX
        PUSH    DX
        ADD     AX,500          ;ROUND
        ADC     DX,0
        IDIV    C1000
        MOV     BX,AX           ;1st QUAD Y
        PUSH    BX
CR8A:   ADD     AX,YY           ;ADD Y ORIGIN
        MOV     SI,XX           ;X ORIGIN
        ADD     SI,CURY
        MOV     DI,AX           ;Y
        CALL    POINT
        SUB     SI,CURY         ;2nd QUAD
        SUB     SI,CURY         ;X
        CALL    POINT
        SUB     DI,BX           ;3rd QUAD
        SUB     DI,BX           ;Y
        CALL    POINT
        ADD     SI,CURY         ;4th QUAD
        ADD     SI,CURY         ;X
        CALL    POINT
        DEC     BX
        CMP     BX,YP           ;GAP?
        JBE     CR9             ;NO
        MOV     AX,BX
        JMP     CR8A            ;PLOT INTERMEDIATE POINT
CR9:    POP     BX
        MOV     YP,BX           ;SAVE PREVIOUS Y
        SUB     DI,YY           ;Y-Y ORIGIN
        NEG     DI              ;Y ORIGIN ADJUST
        XCHG    SI,DI           ;SI=Y
        CMP     CURY,0          ;90 DEG?
        JS      CR11            ;YES, EXIT
        DEC     CURY            ;NEW X
        MOV     AX,CURY
        IMUL    ASPECT          ;ASPECT*1000
        IDIV    SI
```

```
            MOV     CURX,AX         ;DELTA Y
            POP     DX
            POP     AX
            XOR     BX,BX
            CMP     CURX,Ø          ;SIGN CHECK
            JNS     CR1Ø            ;POSITIVE
            MOV     BX,-1           ;NEGATIVE CARRY
CR1Ø:       ADD     AX,CURX         ;NEW X VALUE
            ADC     DX,BX           ;HI WORD CARRY
            JMP     CR8             ;PLOT NEXT POINT
CR11:       MOV     SP,BP           ;FREE LOCAL STORAGE
            POP     BP              ;RESTORE CALLER'S FRAME
            RET     1Ø              ;FREE PASSED PARAMETERS
            RET
CIRCLE      ENDP
;------------------------------------------------
; LINE - Draws lines in normal or XOR mode
;------------------------------------------------
LINE        PROC    NEAR            ;[SI=X1,DI=Y1,AX=X2,BX=Y2]
            MOV     DX,Ø
            CMP     SI,AX
            JBE     NOXCHG
            XCHG    SI,AX
            XCHG    DI,BX
NOXCHG:     SUB     AX,SI
            MOV     BP,AX           ;BP HOLDS X DIFFERENCE CONSTANT
            SUB     BX,DI
            MOV     CX,1
            JNS     NOTNEG
            NEG     CX
            NEG     BX
NOTNEG:     MOV     [DIR],CX
            MOV     AX,BX           ;SAVE Y DIFFERENCE CONSTANT IN AX
            CALL    POINT           ;WRITE DOT
            CMP     BP,BX
            JLE     CASE1           ;DELTA X LTE DELTA Y
            JMP     CASE2           ;DELTA X GT DELTA Y
CASE1:      CMP     [DIR],1
            JNE     CASE3           ;NEGATIVE Y
            MOV     CX,AX
LP1:        DEC     CX
            JS      DONEL1
            INC     DI
            ADD     DX,BP
            CMP     AX,DX
            JA      SKP1
            SUB     DX,AX
            INC     SI
SKP1:       CALL    POINT           ;WRITE DOT
            JMP     SHORT LP1
DONEL1:     RET
CASE3:      MOV     CX,AX
LP3:        DEC     CX
            JS      DONEL3
            DEC     DI
            ADD     DX,BP
            CMP     AX,DX
            JA      SKP3
            SUB     DX,AX
            INC     SI
SKP3:       CALL    POINT           ;WRITE DOT
            JMP     SHORT LP3
```

```
DONEL3:  RET
CASE2:   CMP    [DIR],1
         JNE    CASE4              ;NEGATIVE Y
         MOV    CX,BP
LP2:     DEC    CX
         JS     DONEL2
         INC    SI
         ADD    DX,AX
         CMP    BP,DX
         JA     SKP2
         SUB    DX,BP
         INC    DI
SKP2:    CALL   POINT              ;WRITE DOT
         JMP    SHORT LP2
DONEL2:  RET
CASE4:   MOV    CX,BP
LP4:     DEC    CX
         JS     DONEL4
         INC    SI
         ADD    DX,AX
         CMP    BP,DX
         JA     SKP4
         SUB    DX,BP
         DEC    DI
SKP4:    CALL   POINT              ;WRITE DOT
         JMP    SHORT LP4
DONEL4:  RET
LINE     ENDP
PRINT    PROC                      ;DISPLAY TO SCREEN
         PUSH   AX
         MOV    AH,9               ;PRINT STRING FUNCTION
         INT    21H                ;DOS REQUEST
         POP    AX
         RET
PRINT    ENDP
CSEG     ENDS
         END
```

Chapter 13
KEYBOARD HANDLING

As we have seen in Chapter 6, the DOS keyboard input routines are functionally fairly rich. For this reason, there is not the same need to escape to BIOS calls as there is—for example—in screen handling. There are three situations, however, in which the use of the BIOS keyboard functions is desirable.

The first, of course, is because DOS is not re-entrant. Any routine such as an interrupt handler which might gain control during a DOS function call cannot itself issue DOS function calls. Secondly, there are times when a program would like to know what the current keyboard state is, prior to any keys being pressed. And finally, there are a few special cases in which the program would like to know which physical key has been pressed, as compared to the ASCII character associated with it.

All of these functions are possible with interrupt 16H, the BIOS keyboard function call. If this interrupt is issued with 0 in AH, the call will return the scan code of the next key pressed (or currently at the head of the type-ahead buffer) in AH, and the ASCII equivalent in

155

AL. The scan code is simply the number of the physical key activated, as shown in Figure 13.1. No two keys have the same scan code, even if they translate to the same ASCII value. Use of scan codes can, for example, distinguish between the left shift key (42) and the right shift key (54). There are also keys which have no defined ASCII values, such as the 10 function keys. DOS handles these as extended ASCII characters, returning zero on the first call, and the scan code on the next call. With the BIOS call, only one call is required. AL in such cases will be set to zero, but the true scan code will be present in AH.

If the interrupt is issued with AH = 1, then the result will be similar to the first case except that the routine will not wait for a key to be pressed if the buffer is empty. Instead, the zero flag will be set if the buffer is empty, and reset if a keypress is available. In the latter case, the scan code and ASCII values will be returned as before, but the character will not be removed from the buffer. This is similar to DOS function call 6, the direct console I/O request.

If AH = 3, then the interrupt will return the current state of the keyboard state indicators, as shown in Figure 13.2, in the AL register. The use of these flags, in conjunction with the keyboard scan codes, allows a program to define many more keyboard states than are recognized by the standard translate tables. Carried to the extreme, each physical key could be assigned up to 256 different meanings, based upon all possible combinations of the shift and shift lock keys.

Other than developing a Chinese word processor, the obvious use of working directly with scan codes is to customize the keyboard and put the various keys logically where we wish IBM had chosen to place them physically. The difficulty, of course, is that only those programs which we ourselves write can benefit from

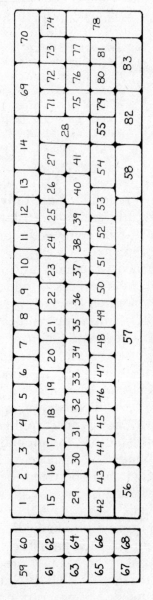

Figure 13.1—Keyboard Scan Codes

157

Figure 13.2 - Keyboard State Indicators

```
Hex Code              Meaning

80                    Insert State is Active
40                    Caps Lock State is Active
20                    Num Lock State is Active
10                    Scroll Lock State is Active
08                    Alt Key is Depressed
04                    Ctrl Key is Depressed
02                    Left Shift Key is Depressed
01                    Right Shift Key is Depressed
```

our own keyboard redesign, since only those programs will use our carefully crafted translate tables. To impose our standards upon commercial programs requires that we go a step further.

The PC's keyboard is actually an intelligent peripheral with its own microprocessor which interrupts the main system whenever a key is depressed or released. This invokes a BIOS interrupt handler which reads the scan code from the keyboard, and translates it in accordance with the current state of the various shift keys. We can steal that interrupt, if we choose, and perform our own interpretation. An example of this technique is shown in Figure 13.3. In this case, we have redefined the keyboard to a "non-typist" configuration. That is, when translation is active, the alphabetic keys are reordered into alphabetic sequence. All other keys are left untouched. Switching between the normal and the reconfigured keyboard is done by pressing and releasing the "Scroll Lock" key.

Since the program will be loaded as an extension of DOS, the segment register handling has been simplified by designing it to be a .COM program. Therefore, it must be run through the EXE2BIN utility after being assembled and linked. The program begins by jumping around the resident code to the initialization section. This section clears the screen, sets interrupt 9 to our own routine, issues a message that the routine has been loaded, and terminates specifying that the new interrupt routine and its associated translate table are to remain resident as an extension to DOS.

When a key is pressed or released, the keyboard microprocessor will interrupt the main microprocessor. Our routine will get control at label NEWKEY and issue an interrupt 16H to get the current keyboard state. If the Scroll Lock has not been toggled, then the routine will jump to the beginning of the ROM BIOS routine. If Scroll Lock *is* active, then the routine reads the keyboard to get the most recent scan code. The scan codes follow the layout in Figure 13.1 except that the high order bit is turned off when a key is depressed and on when the key is released. Also, if for some reason the computer has not been able to read the keyboard scan codes for a while and the keyboard buffer fills up, then the keyboard will signal this by passing a scan code of 255 to indicate that data has been lost.

The interrupt routine must check to see if the overrun scan code has been encountered. If so, it skips the translation step.

Otherwise, it establishes addressability to the translate table and translates the scan code to the new value. Since it doesn't make a lot of sense to have a single physical key issue a different scan code on break as it did on make, the break bit is saved in AH and recombined with AL after the translation has taken place. Finally, the routine jumps into the BIOS routine at a point following the keyboard read.

The technique illustrated here, of jumping into the middle of a ROM routine, is not recommended since it implies both a knowledge of internal ROM addresses and of the ROM routine's internal logic, both of which are subject to change by IBM without notice. It has been used here only to keep the sample program free of code that is not relevant to the specific topic being discussed. The entry points given have been validated for the ROM currently being supplied with the PC XT and with the expansion unit for the original PC. An alternate entry point is given in the program comments for the ROM in the older PCs.

Figure 13.3 - Sample Keyboard Translate Program

```
PAGE      60,132
TITLE     XKEY - SAMPLE KEYBOARD TRANSLATION PROGRAM
PAGE
;-------------------------------------------------------------
;ESTABLISH DUMMY SEGMENT FOR BIOS ENTRY POINTS
;-------------------------------------------------------------
BSEG      SEGMENT AT 0F000H
          ASSUME  CS:BSEG
          ORG     0E987H
BIOS:     NOP
          ORG     0E996H          ;E998 FOR ORIGINAL ROM
BIOS1:    NOP
BSEG      ENDS
;-------------------------------------------------------------
;ESTABLISH COMMON SEGMENT FOR INITIALIZATION CODE
;-------------------------------------------------------------
COMSEG    SEGMENT PARA PUBLIC 'CODE'
          ASSUME  CS:COMSEG,DS:COMSEG,ES:COMSEG,SS:COMSEG
          ORG     100H
START     PROC    FAR
          JMP     INIT            ;INITIALIZATION CODE
;-------------------------------------------------------------
;TRANSLATE TABLES
;-------------------------------------------------------------
TABLE     DB      0,1,2,3,4,5,6,7,8,9,10,11,12,13,14
          DB      15,30,48,46,32,18,33,34,35,23,36,26,27,28
          DB      29,37,38,50,49,24,25,16,19,31,39,40,41
          DB      42,43,20,22,47,17,45,21,44,51,52,53,54,55
          DB      56,57,58,59,60,61,62,63,64,65,66,67,68
          DB      69,70,71,72,73,74,75,76,77,78,79,80,81,82,83
;-------------------------------------------------------------
;NEW KEYBOARD INTERRUPT ROUTINE
;-------------------------------------------------------------
NEWKEY:   STI                     ;ALLOW INTERRUPTS
          PUSH    AX
          MOV     AH,2            ;GET SHIFT STATUS
          INT     16H             ;KEYBOARD BIOS CALL
          TEST    AL,16           ;SCROLL LOCK IN EFFECT?
          JNZ     XLAT            ;YES - WE MUST HANDLE
          POP     AX              ;CLEAN UP STACK
```

```
          JMP   FAR PTR BIOS          ;ENTER BIOS ROUTINE
XLAT:     IN    AL,60H                ;READ KEYBOARD
;SET UP STACK TO MATCH BIOS EXPECTATIONS
          PUSH  BX
          PUSH  CX
          PUSH  DX
          PUSH  SI
          PUSH  DI
          PUSH  DS
          PUSH  ES
          CMP   AL,255                ;OVERRUN SCAN CODE?
          JZ    NOXLAT                ;YES - DON'T TRANSLATE
          PUSH  CS                    ;GET ADDRESSABILITY
          POP   DS                    ;TO OUR DATA SEGMENT
          MOV   BX,OFFSET TABLE       ;POINT TO TRANSLATE TABLE
          MOV   AH,AL                 ;SAVE BREAK BIT IN AH
          AND   AX,807FH              ;AND CLEAR IT IN AL
          XLAT  TABLE                 ;GET NEW SCAN CODE
          OR    AL,AH                 ;RESTORE BREAK BIT
;MATCH BIOS ADDRESSING CONVENTIONS
NOXLAT:   MOV   BX,40H                ;BIOS DATA AREA
          MOV   DS,BX                 ;AS CURRENT DATA SEGMENT
          ASSUME DS:NOTHING           ;DROP DS ADDRESSABILITY
          CLD                         ;BIOS EXPECTS THIS
          JMP   FAR PTR BIOS1         ;JUMP INTO BIOS ROUTINE
;-----------------------------------------------------------
;NON-RESIDENT DATA
;-----------------------------------------------------------
MSG1      DB    'Keyboard Translation Routine Now Resident'
          DB    13,10,'Use the Scroll Lock key to select the '
          DB    'Alternate Keyboard',13,10,'$'
;-----------------------------------------------------------
;INITIALIZATION CODE
;-----------------------------------------------------------
INIT:     CALL  CLRSCN                ;CLEAR THE SCREEN
          MOV   AH,25H                ;SET INTERRUPT VECTOR
          MOV   AL,9                  ;INTERRUPT NUMBER
          MOV   DX,OFFSET NEWKEY      ;NEW INTERRUPT ADDRESS
          INT   21H                   ;DOS SERVICE REQUEST
          MOV   DX,OFFSET MSG1        ;INITIALIZATION MESSAGE
          CALL  PRINT                 ;DISPLAY MESSAGE
;-----------------------------------------------------------
;TERMINATE BUT STAY RESIDENT
;-----------------------------------------------------------
DONE:     MOV   DX,OFFSET MSG1        ;PAST RESIDENT CODE
          INT   27H                   ;TERMINATE AND STAY RESIDENT
START     ENDP
;-----------------------------------------------------------
;SUBROUTINES
;-----------------------------------------------------------
CLRSCN    PROC                        ;CLEAR SCREEN
          PUSH  AX
          MOV   AX,2
          INT   10H
          POP   AX
          RET
CLRSCN    ENDP
PRINT PROC
```

```
          PUSH    AX
          PUSH    DX
          MOV     AH,9
          INT     21H
          POP     DX
          POP     AX
          RET
PRINT     ENDP
COMSEG    ENDS
          END     START
```

Chapter 14
DISK OPERATIONS

The DOS disk functions deal with logical files, located through directories which are also maintained by DOS. The file structure—how the individual sectors are grouped into files—is concealed from the programmer. In general, this is a good thing, but at times there is a need to see the disk as it really is. To do so, we make use of interrupt 13H, the BIOS disk driver, whose register conventions are illustrated in Figure 14.1.

Other than the drive number, which must be 0–3 for diskette and 80H or 81H for hard drives, these values are not range checked. This allows for the use of this interrupt with non-standard diskette formats, such as might be found on diskettes created on certain non-IBM systems or as part of some copy-protect schemes. If the operation is successful, the carry flag and the AH register are set to zero. If an error was detected, the carry flag is set to 1 and the AH register contains one of the error codes shown in Figure 14.2. In most cases, AL is set to the number of sectors actually read or written. It is critical to understand that no motor start delay is taken for a read operation. Therefore it is quite normal

Figure 141—INT 13 Register Conventions

```
AH = 0     Reset Diskette System
     1     Read Status of Last Operation into AL
     2     Read Consecutive Sectors
     3     Write Consecutive Sectors
     4     Verify Consecutive Sectors
     5     Format Track

AL =       Number of sectors (maximum of one track)

ES:BX =    Address of Buffer for Read or Write

CH =       Track Number

CL =       Sector Number

DH =       Head Number

DL =       Drive Number
```

for the first read after a period of inactivity to return with a "not ready" error. The program should always allow at least three retrys before assuming that the error is permanent.

Figure 14.2—INT 13 Status Codes

```
80     Time Out
40     Seek Operation Failed
20     Controller Chip Failed
10     Bad CRC on Read Operation
09     Attempt to Cross 64K Physical Boundry
08     DMA Overrun Condition
04     Sector ID not Found
03     Write Attempt to Protected Disk
02     No Address Marks Found on Track
01     Invalid Command Code
```

Reading or writing a sector using INT 13 is pretty straightforward, but deciding which sector to read and finding something useful to do with the data retreived in this format can be a bit more complicated. To provide a practical example, the sample program for this chapter has been designed to read any sector from a diskette formatted in the standard way; display the sector contents on the screen in both ASCII and hex; allow the user to edit the data on the screen; and to rewrite the modified sector. For the sake of simplicity, some of the features that would make the program easier to use under certain circumstances have been left out. For example, the program is set up for diskettes formatted as double-sided, nine sectors per track. It will work fine on other formats, but requires a little bit more user activity. Such enhancements are left—as usual—as an exercise for the reader.

Use of the program is mostly explained by the menu screen, but there are a few tricks that require explanation. One can step through the target diskette sector by sector or track by track using the indicated commands. However, it is also possible to go directly to any track and sector desired. This is done by pressing the tab key. The cursor will then be moved successively to the various fields on the status line and new values can be typed directly into those fields. Note that the field labeled "status" is displayed only. It is not possible to tab to that field. After all of the desired fields have been changed, either continue tabbing until the cursor is back in the command field, or press the "home" key at any time to skip the remaining fields.

To edit the current sector, either in ASCII or hex, press the appropriate function key. The cursor will be placed in the upper left corner of the appropriate screen window. To change any field, just type over it. The cursor arrow keys will move the cursor to any character within the window, but will not allow movement outside of the window. Attempting to move the cursor below the last line of the window will terminate the edit and move the cursor back to the command field. Attempting to cross any other window boundary will simply have no effect. The edit can also be terminated by pressing the "home" key. At the completion of the edit, the program will update the other window to match what has been changed in the current window, and will return the cursor to the command field. The actual sector has not been changed at this point—only the buffer. Diskette update will only take place when the 'W' command is entered.

The program, after establishing addressability and initalizing variables, enters a logical loop at label LOOP reading single letter commands from the keyboard and executing them. Any input which is not a valid command simply causes a re-display of the main command menu. Most of the commands increment or decrement either the sector or track number and read the indicated sector. The actual disk operations are all performed through a common subroutine, DISKIO, located at the end of the program. This routine simply picks up the necessary parameters from the data segment variables, places them in the appropriate registers, and issues the BIOS call. No error checking is done at this point.

DISKIO is called from RSECT, which sets up the retry count and checks the return code. It also checks to make sure that the track number specified is valid, in order to protect the diskette's seek mechanism from attempting to overreach itself if a bad value is entered. On any error, RSECT decrements the retry count and retrys the operation until the count goes to zero. WSECT is the corresponding entry point to write a sector. It sets up the retry count and the write function code and then jumps into RSECT's comman logic.

The rest of the program is primarily concerned with screen and keyboard handling, ASCII and hex conver-

programming techniques can be learned by examining
this code, but the majority of the system inferface calls
used have already been described in previous chapters.

Figure 14.3—Disk Edit Utility Program

```
PAGE 60,132
title DISKEDIT - Sample Disk Utility Program
;Macro Definitions
DOSCALL MACRO    FUNCT
        IFNB     <FUNCT>
        MOV      AH,FUNCT          ;DOS FUNCTION REQUESTED
        ENDIF
        INT      21H      ;REQUEST DOS SERVICE - FUNCTION IN (AH)
        ENDM
;DEFINE STACK SEGMENT
STACK   SEGMENT PARA STACK 'STACK'
        DB       64       DUP('STACK    ')
STACK   ENDS
;DEFINE DATA SEGMENT
DSEG    SEGMENT PARA    PUBLIC  'DATA'
;DISK_BASE AND ITS ASSOCIATED VARIABLES MUST BE FIRST
;IN THE DATA SEGMENT BECAUSE OF THE INDEXING TECHNIQUE
;USED TO BUILD THE STATUS LINE AT THE BOTTOM OF THE SCREEN
DISK_BASE       LABEL   BYTE
FUNC    DB       ?                 ;FUNCTION CODE
;0 - RESET
;1 - STATUS
;2 - READ SECTORS
;3 - WRITE SECTORS
;4 - VERIFY SECTORS
;5 - FORMAT TRACK
;6 - READ TRACK
;7 - READ ID
;8 - READ DELETED DATA
;9 - WRITE DELETED DATA
DRIVE   DB       ?                 ;DRIVE NUMBER (0->3)
HEAD    DB       ?                 ;HEAD NUMBER (0 OR 1)
TRACK   DB       ?                 ;TRACK NUMBER
SECTOR  DB       ?                 ;SECTOR NUMBER
NOSECTS DB       ?                 ;NUMBER OF SECTORS
BUFSEG  DW       ?                 ;SEGMENT OF BUFFER AREA
BUFOFF  DW       ?                 ;OFFSET OF BUFFER AREA
STATUS  DB       0                 ;MAIN STATUS FROM NEC
CMDTBL  DB       27
        DW       DONE
        DB       0
        DW       CNTRL
        DB       9        ;TAB CHAR
        DW       CMDIN
        DB       'R'
        DW       READ
        DB       'W'
        DW       WRITE
        DB       'N'
        DW       RDNXT
        DB       'L'
```

```
            DW      RDPRV
            DB      'I'
            DW      RNTRK
            DB      'D'
            DW      RLTRK
TBLEND      DB      0
            DW      CMENU
CNTTBL      DW      DISPCB,EDITHEX,EDITASC
CCRPOS      DB      0           ;CURSOR POSITION WITHIN FIELD
CLNPOS      DW      7           ;CURRENT POSITION IN TABLE FOR INPUT
;FORMAT TABLE
CLNTBL0     DB      6           ;# OF ENTRIES IN TABLE
            DW      1800H,CMDMSG1
            DB      0
            DW      1807H,DRIVE
            DW      180BH,CMDMSG8
            DB      0
            DW      1811H,HEAD
            DW      1815H,CMDMSG2
            DB      0
            DW      181CH,TRACK
            DW      181FH,CMDMSG4
            DB      0
            DW      1827H,SECTOR
            DW      182BH,CMDMSG5
            DB      2
            DW      1833H,STATUS
            DW      1842H,CMDMSG7
            DB      3
            DW      184EH
APREFIX     DW      0                   ;SAVE ADDRESS OF PSP
CMDMSG1     DB      'Drive:$'
CMDMSG2     DB      'Track:$'
CMDMSG4     DB      'Sector:$'
CMDMSG5     DB      'Status:$'
CMDMSG7     DB      'Command:$'
CMDMSG8     DB      'Head:$'
MENUMSG     DB      'DISK EDIT UTILITY',13,10,10
            DB      'COMMAND LIST',13,10,10
            DB      '   F1  - DISPLAY CURRENT BUFFER',13,10
            DB      '   F2  - EDIT HEX DATA ON SCREEN',13,10
            DB      '   F3  - EDIT ASCII DATA ON SCREEN',13,10
            DB      '   D   - DECREMENT PHYSICAL TRACK NUMBER',13,10
            DB      '   I   - INCREMENT PHYSICAL TRACK NUMBER',13,10
            DB      '   L   - DECREMENT PHYSICAL SECTOR NUMBER',13,10
            DB      '   N   - INCREMENT PHYSICAL SECTOR NUMBER',13,10
            DB      '   R   - READ CURRENT SECTOR',13,10
            DB      '   W   - WRITE CURRENT SECTOR',13,10
            DB      '   Esc - RETURN TO DOS',13,10
            DB      '$'
ADDRESS     DW      0
SET         DB      0
BLOCK       DB      0
LINE        DB      0
RETRY       DB      0
SCRVAL      DB      0                   ;BUFFER IS ON SCREEN IN <> 0
DSPSTART    DW      0                   ;DISPLAY OFFSET IN BUFFER
HEXTBL      DB      '0123456789ABCDEF'
BUFFER      DB      8*512 DUP(?)
DSEG        ENDS
;ESTABLISH ENTRY LINKAGE FROM DOS
```

```
CSEG    SEGMENT PARA    PUBLIC  'CODE'
START   PROC    FAR
        ASSUME  CS:CSEG,DS:DSEG,SS:STACK,ES:DSEG
        MOV     AX,DSEG
        MOV     DS,AX
        MOV     APREFIX,ES      ;SAVE POINTER TO PSP
        MOV     ES,AX
        CALL    INIT
LOOP:   CALL    CMDLIN
        CALL    CMD
        MOV     TBLEND,AL       ;INSURE MATCH
        MOV     BX,OFFSET CMDTBL        ;START OF TABLE
LOOP1:  CMP     [BX],AL         ;CMD FOUND?
        JNZ     TRYNXT          ;TRY NEXT ENTRY
        INC     BX              ;POINT TO ADDRESS
        JMP     WORD PTR [BX]           ;EXECUTE ROUTINE
TRYNXT: INC     BX
        INC     BX
        INC     BX
        JMP     LOOP1           ;TRY NEXT ENTRY
DONE:   CALL    CLRSCN
        MOV     AX,APREFIX      ;PROGRAM SEGMENT PREFIX
        PUSH    AX              ;PUT RETURN SEGMENT ON STACK
        SUB     AX,AX
        PUSH    AX              ;PUT RETURN OFFSET ON STACK
        RET                     ;RETURN TO DOS
START   ENDP
;SUBROUTINES
INIT    PROC
        MOV     DRIVE,0
        MOV     HEAD,0
        MOV     TRACK,0
        MOV     SECTOR,1
        CALL    CLRBUF
        CALL    MENU
        RET
INIT    ENDP
CMENU   PROC
        CALL    MENU
        JMP     LOOP
CMENU   ENDP
MENU    PROC
        CALL    CLRSCN
        MOV     SCRVAL,0                ;SHOW NO BUFFER ON SCREEN
        MOV     DX,OFFSET MENUMSG
        JMP     WRTLN
MENU    ENDP
CLRBUF  PROC
        MOV     AL,0
        CLD
        MOV     DI,OFFSET BUFFER
        MOV     CX,200H         ;LENGTH OF BUFFER
        PUSH    ES
        PUSH    DS
        POP     ES
        REPNZ   STOSB
        POP     ES
        RET
CLRBUF  ENDP
CLRSCN  PROC
        MOV     AX,2            ;CLEAR SCREEN FUNCTION
```

```
                INT    10H                    ;VIDEO HANDLER
                RET
CLRSCN   ENDP
SETCSR   PROC
                PUSH   AX
                PUSH   BX
                MOV    AH,2                   ;SET CURSOR
                MOV    BH,0                   ;PAGE
                INT    10H                    ;VIDEO HANDLER
                POP    BX
                POP    AX
                RET
SETCSR   ENDP
WRTLN    PROC
                DOSCALL 9                     ;WRITE LINE FUNCTION
                RET
WRTLN    ENDP
CRLF     PROC
                MOV    DL,13                  ;CARRAGE RETURN
                DOSCALL 2                     ;WRITE SCREEN FUNCTION
                MOV    DL,10                  ;LINE FEED
                DOSCALL
                RET
CRLF     ENDP
READ     PROC
                CALL   CLRBUF
                CALL   RSECT
                CALL   DISP
                JMP    LOOP
READ     ENDP
WRITE    PROC                                 ;WRITE CURRENT BUFFER TO DISK
                CALL   WSECT
                JMP    LOOP
WSECT:          MOV    RETRY,5
                MOV    FUNC,3                 ;WRITE SECTORS
                JMP    RSECT1
WRITE    ENDP
RSECT    PROC                                 ;READ CURRENT SECTOR
                MOV    RETRY,5                ;SET RETRY COUNT
                MOV    FUNC,2                 ;READ SECTOR CMD
RSECT1:         MOV    NOSECTS,1
                MOV    BUFOFF,OFFSET BUFFER
                MOV    BUFSEG,SEG BUFFER
                CMP    TRACK,42               ;MAXIMUM PHYSICAL TRACK
                JC     RSECT2                 ;VALID PHYSICAL TRACK
                MOV    TRACK,39               ;LIMIT TRACK TO VALID RANGE
RSECT2:  CALL   DISKIO
                JNB    RSECTX                 ;IF GOOD RETURN
                DEC    RETRY
                JNZ    RSECT1                 ;TRY AGAIN
RSECTX:  RET
RSECT    ENDP
DISP     PROC
                MOV    DX,0
                CALL   SETCSR
                MOV    AX,DSPSTART
                MOV    ADDRESS,AX
                MOV    LINE,16
DISP1:          MOV    AX,ADDRESS
                CALL   PRWORD
                MOV    SET,2
```

```
DISP2:    MOV      BLOCK,4
          MOV      CL,2
          CALL     PRBLANK
DISP3:    MOV      CL,1
          CALL     PRBLANK
          MOV      BX,ADDRESS
          CALL     PRMEM
          ADD      ADDRESS,+4
          DEC      BLOCK
          JNZ      DISP3
          DEC      SET
          JNZ      DISP2
          DEC      LINE
          JNZ      DISP1
          CALL     DISPASC            ;DISPLAY ASCII EQUIVALENTS
          MOV      SCRVAL,255         ;SHOW BUFFER ON SCREEN
          RET
DISP      ENDP
DISPASC   PROC
          MOV      DX,1000H           ;CURSOR LOCATION
          CALL     SETCSR
          MOV      AX,DSPSTART
          MOV      ADDRESS,AX
          MOV      LINE,8
DISPASC1:
          MOV      AX,ADDRESS
          CALL     PRWORD
          MOV      CL,8
          CALL     PRBLANK
          MOV      BLOCK,64
          MOV      BX,ADDRESS
DISPASC2: MOV      AL,BUFFER[BX]
          CMP      AL,' '
          JL       DISPASC3
          CMP      AL,7EH
          JBE      DISPASC4
DISPASC3: MOV      AL,'.'
DISPASC4: MOV      DL,AL              ;CHARACTER TO WRITE
          DOSCALL  2                  ;DISPLAY OUTPUT
          INC      BX
          DEC      BLOCK
          JNZ      DISPASC2
          MOV      ADDRESS,BX
          CALL     CRLF
          DEC      LINE
          JNZ      DISPASC1
          RET
DISPASC   ENDP
PRBLANK   PROC
          MOV      DL,32
          DOSCALL  2                  ;DISPLAY OUTPUT
          DEC      CL
          JNZ      PRBLANK
          RET
PRBLANK   ENDP
CMD       PROC
          DOSCALL  8                  ;CONSOLE INPUT
          CMP      AL,40H
          JL       CMDX
          AND      AL,0DFH            ;CONVERT TO UPPER CASE
          MOV      DL,AL
```

```
          PUSH    AX
          DOSCALL 2         ;DISPLAY OUTPUT
          POP     AX
CMDX:     RET
CMD       ENDP
CMDIN     PROC              ;UPDATE COMMAND VARIABLES FROM KEYBOARD
          MOV     CLNPOS,0
          JMP     CMDIN2
CMDIN1:   INC     CLNPOS
CMDIN2:   CALL    CMDPOS    ;POSITION CURSOR TO DESIRED FIELD
CMDIN3:   DOSCALL 7         ;DIRECT KEYBOARD INPUT
          CMP     AL,9      ;TAB
          JZ      CMDIN1    ;ADVANCE TO NEXT FIELD
          CMP     AL,0            ;SPECIAL CHAR?
          JNZ     CMDIN5          ;NO - CONTINUE TESTS
          DOSCALL 7               ;DIRECT KEYBOARD INPUT
          CMP     AL,71           ;HOME KEY
          JZ      CMDINX          ;YES - RETURN TO COMMAND MODE
          CMP     AL,77
          JNZ     CMDIN4          ;NOT ->
          CMP     CCRPOS,0        ;AT 1ST FIELD POS?
          JNZ     CMDIN1          ;NO - TREAT AS TAB
          CALL    INCCSR
          INC     CCRPOS          ;SHOW POS IN FIELD
          JMP     CMDIN3
CMDIN4:   CMP     AL,75           ; <-
          JNZ     CMDIN3
          CMP     CCRPOS,0        ;AT 1ST POS?
          JZ      CMDIN3          ;YES - CAN NOT MOVE LEFT
          CALL    DECCSR
          DEC     CCRPOS
          JMP     CMDIN3
CMDIN5:   CMP     AL,'0'
          JC      CMDIN3          ;< 0
          CMP     AL,':'
          JC      CMDIN6          ;GOOD DIGIT - GO PUT ON SCREEN
          CMP     AL,'A'
          JC      CMDIN3
          CMP     AL,'G'
          JC      CMDIN6          ;GOOD HEX CHAR
          SUB     AL,32           ;CONVERT TO UPPER CASE
          CMP     AL,'A'
          JC      CMDIN3
          CMP     AL,'G'
          JNC     CMDIN3
CMDIN6:   CALL    WRTSCR
          CALL    INCCSR
          INC     CCRPOS
          CMP     CCRPOS,2
          JZ      CMDIN1    ;TAB TO NEXT FIELD
          JMP     CMDIN3    ;GET NEXT KEYPRESS
CMDINX:   CALL    GETTBL          ;USE PROPER TABLE
CMDIX1:   MOV     DX,[BX+SI+5]    ;CURSOR POS
          CALL    SETCSR
          MOV     AL,[BX+SI+4]    ;CONTROL FLAGS
          AND     AL,2
          JNZ     CMDIX2          ;SKIP INPUT
          PUSH    BX
          MOV     BX,[BX+SI+7]    ;OFFSET
          CALL    GFMSCR          ;GET VALUE FROM SCREEN
          MOV     DISK_BASE[BX],AL          ;STORE INTO TARGET
```

```
          POP     BX
CMDIX2:   ADD     BX,9
          LOOP    CMDIX1
          JMP     LOOP
CMDPOS:   CALL    GETTBL          ;USE PROPER TABLE
CMDPOØ:   MOV     BX,CLNPOS
          CMP     CX,CLNPOS
          JNZ     CMDPO1          ;VALID FIELD
          POP     AX              ;KILL RETURN VECTOR
          JMP     CMDINX
CMDPO1:   MOV     AX,9            ;TABLE WIDTH
          MUL     BX
          MOV     BX,AX
          INC     BX
          MOV     AL,[BX+SI+4]    ;FLAGS
          AND     AL,2
          JZ      CMDPO2          ;VALID FIELD
          INC     CLNPOS
          JMP     CMDPOØ
CMDPO2:   MOV     DX,[BX+SI+5]
          CALL    SETCSR
          MOV     CCRPOS,Ø        ;SHOW AT BEGINNING OF FIELD
          RET
GFMSCR:   CALL    CHFSCR          ;GET CHARACTER AT CURRENT CURSOR POS
          MOV     DL,AL           ;SAVE MS DIGIT
          CALL    INCCSR          ;INCREMENT CURSOR
          CALL    CHFSCR          ;GET NXT CHAR
          MOV     AH,DL           ;RESTORE MS DIGIT
          CALL    HEXFCH
          RET
INCCSR:   PUSH    AX
          PUSH    BX
          PUSH    CX
          PUSH    DX
          MOV     BX,Ø            ;PAGE Ø
          MOV     AH,3            ;READ CURSOR POS
          INT     1ØH
          MOV     AH,2            ;SET CURSOR POS
          INC     DL              ;BUMP COL
          CMP     DL,80
          JNZ     INCCS1          ;SAME LINE
          MOV     DL,Ø
          INC     DH
INCCS1:   INT     1ØH
          POP     DX
          POP     CX
          POP     BX
          POP     AX
          RET
DECCSR:   PUSH    AX
          PUSH    BX
          PUSH    CX
          PUSH    DX
          MOV     BX,Ø
          MOV     AH,3
          INT     1ØH
          MOV     AH,2
          DEC     DL
          CMP     DL,255
          JNZ     DECCS1          ;SAME LINE
          MOV     DL,Ø
```

```
          DEC     DH
DECCS1:   INT     10H
          POP     DX
          POP     CX
          POP     BX
          POP     AX
          RET
CHFSCR:   MOV     AH,8
          INT     10H
          RET
WRTSCR:   PUSH    AX
          PUSH    BX
          PUSH    CX
          MOV     BX,0
          MOV     AH,10
          MOV     CX,1
          INT     10H
          POP     CX
          POP     BX
          POP     AX
          RET
HEXFCH:   PUSH    BX
          PUSH    CX
          MOV     BX,AX           ;SAVE ENTRY PARMS
          MOV     AL,AH
          CALL    HEXFC1          ;CONVERT TO HEX DIGIT
          MOV     CX,4
          SHL     AX,CL           ;CONVERT TO MS DIGIT
          MOV     BH,AL
          MOV     AL,BL
          CALL    HEXFC1
          ADD     AL,BH           ;COMBINE INTO ONE BINARY VALUE
          POP     CX
          POP     BX
          RET
HEXFC1:   SUB     AL,'0'
          CMP     AL,10
          JC      HEXFC2
          SUB     AL,7
HEXFC2:   RET
CMDIN     ENDP
PRWORD    PROC
          PUSH    AX
          XCHG    AL,AH
          CALL    PRBYTE
          POP     AX
PRBYTE:   PUSH    AX
          PUSH    CX
          MOV     CL,4
          ROR     AL,CL
          CALL    PRHEX
          POP     CX
          POP     AX
PRHEX:    AND     AL,0FH
          PUSH    BX
          MOV     BX,OFFSET HEXTBL
          XLAT
          POP     BX
          MOV     DL,AL
          DOSCALL 2               ;DISPLAY OUTPUT
          RET
```

```
PRWORD   ENDP
CMDLIN   PROC
         CALL    CLRCMD               ;CLEAR COMMAND LINE
         CALL    GETTBL               ;USE PROPER TABLE
CMDLI1:  MOV     DX,[BX+SI]           ;CURSOR POS
         CALL    SETCSR
         MOV     DX,[BX+SI+2]         ;LABEL
         CALL    WRTLN
         MOV     DX,[BX+SI+5]         ;CURSOR POS
         CALL    SETCSR
         MOV     AL,[BX+SI+4]         ;GET CONTROL FLAGS
         AND     AL,1
         JNZ     CMDLI2               ;DON'T DISPLAY THIS FIELD
         PUSH    BX
         MOV     BX,[BX+SI+7]
         MOV     AL,DISK_BASE[BX]           ;GET VALUE
         CALL    PRBYTE
         POP     BX
CMDLI2:  ADD     BX,9
         LOOP    CMDLI1
         RET
GETTBL:  MOV     SI,OFFSET CLNTBL0    ;POINT TO FORMAT TABLE
         MOV     BX,0                 ;START OF TABLE
         MOV     CX,[BX+SI]           ;TABLE LENGTH
         INC     BX                   ;POINT PAST LENGTH
         RET
CLRCMD:  PUSH    AX
         PUSH    BX
         PUSH    CX
         PUSH    DX
         MOV     DX,1800H
         CALL    SETCSR
         MOV     AX,0A20H             ;WRITE BLANKS
         MOV     BX,0                 ;PAGE
         MOV     CX,80                ;CHAR COUNT
         INT     10H
         POP     DX
         POP     CX
         POP     BX
         POP     AX
         RET
CMDLIN   ENDP
PRMEM    PROC
         CALL    PRMEMW
         INC     BX
         INC     BX
PRMEMW:  MOV     AX,WORD PTR BUFFER[BX]
         XCHG    AL,AH
         JMP     PRWORD
PRMEM    ENDP
RDNXT    PROC
         INC     SECTOR
         CMP     SECTOR,10            ;PAST LAST SECTOR?
         JNZ     RDNXTX
         MOV     SECTOR,1
         XOR     HEAD,1               ;SWITCH HEADS
         JMP     RNTRK                ;INCREMENT TO NEXT TRACK
RDNXTX:  JMP     READ
RDNXT    ENDP
RDPRV    PROC
         DEC     SECTOR
```

```
          CMP      SECTOR,0
          JNZ      RNTRKX
          MOV      SECTOR,9
          XOR      HEAD,1             ;SWITCH HEADS
          JMP      RLTRK              ;DECREMENT TRACK AND READ
RDPRV     ENDP
RNTRK     PROC
          INC      TRACK
          CMP      TRACK,40           ;PAST LAST TRACK
          JNZ      RNTRKX             ;NO - GO READ
          MOV      TRACK,0
RNTRKX:   JMP      READ
RNTRK     ENDP
RLTRK     PROC
          DEC      TRACK
          CMP      TRACK,255
          JNZ      RLTRKX
          MOV      TRACK,39
RLTRKX:   JMP      READ
RLTRK     ENDP
CNTRL     PROC
          DOSCALL  7                  ;DIRECT INPUT REQUEST
          SUB      AL,59              ;INDEX TO F1
          JC       CNTRLX
          CMP      AL,3               ;HIGHER THAN DEFINED?
          JNC      CNTRLX             ;YES - IGNORE
          CBW
          SHL      AX,1
          MOV      BX,AX
          JMP      CNTTBL[BX]
CNTRLX:   JMP      LOOP               ;FLUSH CONTROL CHARACTER
CNTRL     ENDP
EDITHEX   PROC
          CMP      SCRVAL,0           ;BUFFER ON SCREEN
          JNZ      EDITH0             ;YES - DON'T REDRIVE
          CALL     DISP               ;DISPLAY CURRENT BUFFER
EDITH0:   MOV      DX,7               ;UL OF HEX DISPLAY
          CALL     SETCSR
          MOV      CCRPOS,0
          MOV      SET,0
          MOV      BLOCK,0
          MOV      LINE,0
          MOV      BX,0
EDITH1:   DOSCALL  8                  ;CONSOLE INPUT
          CMP      AL,'0'
          JC       EDITH8             ;CHECK FOR CONTROL CHARS
          CMP      AL,':'
          JC       EDITH2             ;GOOD NUMERIC DIGIT
          CMP      AL,'A'
          JC       EDITH1             ;INVALID
          CMP      AL,'G'
          JC       EDITH2             ;GOOD HEX DIGIT
          SUB      AL,32              ;CONVERT TO UPPER CASE
          CMP      AL,'A'
          JC       EDITH1             ;INVALID
          CMP      AL,'G'
          JNC      EDITH1             ;INVALID
EDITH2:   CALL     WRTSCR             ;PUT ON SCREEN
          CALL     UPDBUF             ;AND IN MEMORY
EDITH3:   INC      CCRPOS             ;-> ENTRY
          CMP      CCRPOS,8
```

```
          JNZ      EDITH7          ;UPDATE CURSOR ON SCREEN
EDITH4:   MOV      CCRPOS,0        ;TAB ENTRY
          INC      BLOCK
          CMP      BLOCK,4
          JNZ      EDITH7
          MOV      BLOCK,0
          INC      SET
          CMP      SET,2
          JNZ      EDITH7
EDITH5:   MOV      SET,0           ;NEW LINE ENTRY
          INC      LINE
          CMP      LINE,16
          JNZ      EDITH7
EDITH6:   CALL     DISPASC         ;RETURN TO COMMAND MODE ENTRY
          JMP      LOOP
EDITH7:   CALL     EDHCSR          ;UPDATE CURSOR AND MEMORY POINTERS
          JMP      EDITH1
EDITH8:   CMP      AL,9            ;TAB
          JNZ      EDITH9
          JMP      EDITH4
EDITH9:   CMP      AL,13           ;<CR>
          JNZ      EDITH10
          MOV      CCRPOS,0
          MOV      BLOCK,0
          JMP      EDITH5          ;NEW LINE
EDITH10:  CMP      AL,0            ;CONTROL CODES
          JZ       EDITH11
          JMP      EDITH1          ;GET NEXT CHARACTER
EDITH11:  DOSCALL  8               ;CONSOLE INPUT
          CMP      AL,71           ;HOME KEY
          JZ       EDITH6          ;GO TO COMMAND MODE
          CMP      AL,77           ;->
          JNZ      EDITH12
          JMP      EDITH3          ;INCREMENT CURSOR
EDITH12:  CMP      AL,75           ; <-
          JNZ      EDITH15
          CMP      LINE,0
          JNZ      EDITH13
          CMP      SET,0
          JNZ      EDITH13
          CMP      BLOCK,0
          JNZ      EDITH13
          CMP      CCRPOS,0
          JNZ      EDITH13
          JMP      EDITH1          ;ALREADY AT UL CORNER
EDITH13:  DEC      CCRPOS
          JNS      EDITH14
          MOV      CCRPOS,7
          DEC      BLOCK
          JNS      EDITH14
          MOV      BLOCK,3
          DEC      SET
          JNS      EDITH14
          MOV      SET,1
          DEC      LINE
EDITH14:  JMP      EDITH7          ;UPDATE CURSOR
EDITH15:  CMP      AL,72           ;UP ARROW
          JNZ      EDITH17
          CMP      LINE,0          ;ALREADY AT TOP?
          JNZ      EDITH16         ;NO - GO DECREMENT
          JMP      EDITH1          ;IGNORE REQUEST
```

```
EDITH16: DEC     LINE
         JMP     EDITH7          ;UPDATE CURSOR
EDITH17: CMP     AL,80           ;DOWN ARROW?
         JZ      EDITH18         ;YES
         JMP     EDITH1          ;IGNORE ALL OTHERS
EDITH18: CMP     LINE,15         ;ALREADY AT BOTTOM?
         JNZ     EDITH19         ;NO - GO INCREMENT
         JMP     EDITH6          ;RETURN TO COMMAND MODE
EDITH19: INC     LINE
         JMP     EDITH7          ;UPDATE CURSOR
;UPDATE CURSOR AND MEMORY POINTERS
EDHCSR:  PUSH    AX
         PUSH    CX
         PUSH    DX
         MOV     CL,9
         MOV     AL,BLOCK
         MUL     CL
         CMP     SET,0
         JZ      EDHCS1
         ADD     AL,38
EDHCS1:  ADD AL,CCRPOS
         ADD AL,7
         MOV     DL,AL
         MOV     DH,LINE
         CALL    SETCSR
         MOV     CX,3
         MOV     AL,BLOCK
         CBW
         SHL     AX,CL
         MOV     BX,AX           ;BLOCK*8
         MOV     CL,64
         MOV     AL,LINE
         MUL     CL
         ADD     BX,AX           ; + LINE*64
         CMP     SET,0
         JZ      EDHCS2
         ADD     BX,32           ; + SET*32
EDHCS2:  MOV     AL,CCRPOS
         CBW
         ADD     BX,AX           ; + CCRPOS
         POP     DX
         POP     CX
         POP     AX
         RET
;UPDATE BUFFER WITH HEX INPUT
UPDBUF:  PUSH    AX
         CALL    HEXFC1          ;CONVERT TO BINARY
         PUSH    DX
         PUSH    CX
         PUSH    BX
         MOV     DL,AL
         SHR     BX,1            ;TRUE BUFFER OFFSET
         MOV     AL,BUFFER[BX]
         JNC     UPDBU1          ;GO UPDATE MS NIBBLE
         AND     AL,0F0H         ;ISOLATE MS NIBBLE
         ADD     AL,DL           ;COMBINE WITH NEW DATA
         JMP     UPDBU2
UPDBU1:  AND     AL,0FH          ;ISOLATE LS NIBBLE
         MOV     CL,4
         SHL     DL,CL           ;MOVE INPUT TO MS NIBBLE
         ADD     AL,DL           ;COMBINE WITH OLD DATA
```

```
UPDBU2: MOV     BUFFER[BX],AL   ;UPDATE BUFFER
        POP     BX
        POP     CX
        POP     DX
        POP     AX
        RET
EDITHEX ENDP
EDITASC PROC                    ;EDIT ASCII DISPLAY
        CMP     SCRVAL,0        ;BUFFER ON SCREEN?
        JNZ     EDITA0          ;YES - DON'T REDRIVE
        CALL    DISP            ;ENSURE CURRENT DISPLAY
EDITA0: MOV     DX,100CH        ;U L CORNER OF ASCII AREA
        CALL    SETCSR
        MOV     LINE,0
        MOV     BLOCK,0
        MOV     BX,0
EDITA1: DOSCALL 8               ;CONSOLE INPUT
        CMP     AL,7FH
        JNC     EDITA1
        CMP     AL,' '
        JL      EDITA6
        MOV     BUFFER[BX],AL   ;PUT IN BUFFER
        CALL    WRTSCR          ;AND ON SCREEN
EDITA2: INC     BLOCK
        INC     BX
        CMP     BLOCK,64
        JNZ     EDITA5          ;SAME LINE
EDITA3: MOV     AL,BLOCK        ;CARRIAGE RETURN FUNCTION
        CBW
        SUB     BX,AX
        MOV     BLOCK,0
        INC     LINE
        ADD     BX,64           ;NEXT LINE IN BUFFER
        CMP     LINE,8          ;END OF AREA?
        JNZ     EDITA5          ;NO - CONTINUE
        JMP     EDITAX
EDITA5: MOV     DH,LINE
        ADD     DH,16
        MOV     DL,BLOCK
        ADD     DL,12
        CALL    SETCSR          ;SET NEW CURSOR POSITION
        JMP     EDITA1          ;GET NEXT KEYPRESS
EDITA6: CMP     AL,13           ;CARRIAGE RETURN
        JZ      EDITA3
        CMP     AL,0            ;CONTROL CHAR?
        JNZ     EDITA1          ;IGNORE ANY OTHER INPUT
        DOSCALL 8               ;CONSOLE INPUT
        CMP     AL,77
        JZ      EDITA2          ;->
        CMP     AL,75           ;<-
        JNZ     EDITA9
        CMP     BLOCK,0         ;BEGINNING OF LINE?
        JNZ     EDITA8          ;NO - JUST DECREMENT
        CMP     LINE,0          ;TOP OF SCREEN?
        JZ      EDITA1          ;YES - IGNORE
        DEC     LINE
        MOV     BLOCK,1
EDITA8: DEC     BX
        DEC     BLOCK
        JMP     EDITA5          ;SET NEW CURSOR
EDITA9: CMP     AL,71           ;HOME KEY?
```

```
              JNZ      EDITA10         ;NO
              JMP      EDITAX
EDITA10: CMP      AL,72           ;UP?
              JNZ      EDITA12
              CMP      LINE,0          ;TOP OF SCREEN?
              JNZ      EDITA11         ;NO
              JMP      EDITA1          ;IGNORE
EDITA11: SUB      BX,64
              DEC      LINE
              JMP      EDITA5
EDITA12: CMP      AL,80           ;DOWN?
              JZ       EDITA13         ;YES
              JMP      EDITA1
EDITA13: CMP      LINE,7   ;LAST LINE?
              JNZ      EDITA14
              JMP      EDITAX
EDITA14: ADD      BX,64
              INC      LINE
              JMP      EDITA5
EDITAX:  CALL     DISP
              JMP      LOOP
EDITASC ENDP
DISPCB   PROC                     ;DISPLAY CURRENT BUFFER
              CALL     CLRSCN
              CALL     DISP
              JMP      LOOP
DISPCB   ENDP
DISKIO   PROC
              PUSH     ES
              PUSH     BX
              PUSH     CX
              PUSH     DX
              MOV      AH,FUNC         ;DISK COMMAND
              MOV      AL,NOSECTS      ;NUMBER OF SECTORS
              MOV      CL,SECTOR
              MOV      CH,TRACK
              MOV      DL,DRIVE
              MOV      DH,HEAD
              MOV      BX,BUFOFF       ;BUFFER OFFSET
              MOV      ES,BUFSEG       ;BUFFER SEGMENT
              INT      13H             ;DISK BIOS CALL
              MOV      STATUS,AH       ;SAVE RETURNED STATUS
              POP      DX
              POP      CX
              POP      BX
              POP      ES
              RET
DISKIO   ENDP
CSEG     ENDS
              END      START
```

Part IV

Programming the Silicon

Chapter 15
DIRECT SCREEN HANDLING

In prior chapters, we have treated the display screen in the same way as any other input/output device. However, both the IBM Monochrome Display Adapter and the IBM Color/Graphics adapter differ from all of the other PC I/O devices in that they each use a technique called "memory-mapped video." This means that the video generation circuitry scans a display buffer which is also addressable by the microprocessor. It is not necessary to use either DOS function calls or BIOS interrupt calls to update the video screen. Instead, the programmer can simply move the character to be displayed to the proper position in the display buffer.

The IBM Monochrome Display Adapter contains a display buffer of 4096 bytes located physically on the adapter board and addressed at the fixed address range of B8000H to B0FFFH. The Color/Graphics adapter, because of the additional information necessary to do all-points-addressable graphics, contains 16K bytes in the range B8000H to BBFFFH. This range can be used as 8 pages of 40×25 characters, 4 pages of 80×25 characters, or as a single graphics page.

In all cases, half of the memory locations are used to contain the characters to be displayed, and the other half are used for the associated attribute bytes. (The format of an attribute byte is discussed in Chapter 11.) Each attribute byte immediately follows its associated character in the display buffer. This organization strongly influences the preferred programming style. For example, if we want to move a character string directly to the screen using a REP MOVSB instruction, then we would have to build the string with the attribute characters already interleaved with the characters. On the other hand, a coding sequence like that shown in Figure 15.1 will automatically insert a constant attribute byte into the character string as it is moved, because the LODSB instruction will get the next character into the AL register without disturbing the contents of AH, while the STOSW instruction stores both AL and AH and increments DI accordingly.

Figure 15.1—Direct String to Screen Example

```
;Register on entry:
;DS:SI -> Character String Terminated by 00H.
;ES:DI -> Starting Position in Screen Buffer.
;AH = Attribute Character.

LOOP:     LODSB              ;GET NEXT CHARACTER IN AL
          CMP   AL,0         ;END OF STRING?
          JZ    EXIT         ;YES - RETURN TO CALLER
          STOSW              ;STORE CHARACTER & ATTRIBUTE
          JMP   LOOP         ;GO DO NEXT
EXIT:     RET                ;RETURN TO CALLER
```

The other interesting aspect of memory-mapped video is that the buffer memory can be read as well as written. This not only allows the programmer to determine the current contents of a screen location, but also to save that information while a help screen, menu, or other information is temporarily displayed. The screen can then be restored to its prior state without having to recreate the information. We make use of this capability in this chapter's sample program, SUBLIM (Figure 15.2). SUBLIM is a program which will periodically place a short message on the screen, leave it displayed for a specified time, and then restore the original screen contents. Depending upon the parameters specified, the result can be anything between a barely noticeable flicker to the equivalent of a flashing neon sign.

SUBLIM has been designed to accept all of its input parameters on the command line so that it can be placed in a batch file, like AUTOEXEC.BAT. In addition, multiple invocations of the program— with the same or different parameters—are automatically chained together. This allows some very interesting combinations of effects.

SUBLIM is invoked by specifying the row and column where the message is to be displayed, the length of time the message is to remain on the screen, and the length of time until the message will be redisplayed. For convenience in specifying short time intervals, all time parameters are in internal clock pulses. These pulses occur about 18.2 times per second, so a specification of 91 would provide about a 5-second interval. Default values are provided for all numeric parameters. The specification:

SUBLIM 13,37,3,91, Hi There

would result in the message "Hi There" being displayed approximately in the middle of the screen every five seconds, and remaining there for about one-sixth of a second.

The program begins by skipping over the code which will remain resident to the initialization code at label INIT. After initializing the screen to 80×25 mode, it then issues a BIOS call to determine if the current screen is the Monochrome adapter or the Color/Graphics adapter. Based on the result, it stores the correct segment address for that adapter at the label SCRSEG.

The next task is to interpret the input parameters. The numeric parameters are parsed and converted from decimal to binary by the subroutine GPARM. Each invocation of GPARM returns the next parameter from the input string, assuming that the DS:SI register pair is unchanged between calls. Any character lower than a numeric is accepted as a delimiter, so the user can invoke the program with the parameters separated by spaces, commas, periods, etc. Any field beginning with an alphabetic character is assumed to be the start of the desired message, the defaults are taken for all remaining numeric variables.

The program then gets and saves the current value of the 1CH interrupt vector. This vector is invoked by the system timer interrupt routine after it updates the system clock and checks for system timeout conditions. This current value is then replaced by the address of NEWTIM, which will thereafter get control on every timer interrupt. Finally, the initialization code writes a message to the screen indicating successful execution, and returns to DOS with a terminate and stay resident request. The DS:DX register pair for this request is set so that only the interrupt handling code will remain resident. The initialization code will be released by DOS.

From this point on, the user can run any other DOS-based program at will. However, about every 55 milliseconds, NEWTIM will obtain control of the system. Each time that occurs, it will decrement a counter—NXTON if it is waiting for the right time to display a message, or NXTOFF if a message is currently on the screen.

In either case, if the counter does not become zero, then the routine exits by jumping to the address of the previous interrupt handler. This not only is a good-neighbor policy to any other program which may be monitoring timer interrupts, but allows this program to be multipally invoked.

If NXTON goes to zero, we load DS with the proper

segment address from SCRSEG and SI from the calculated screen offset in SADDR. The ES:DI pair are set to the address of MSGAREA. The length of the message is loaded from MSGLEN to CX. A REP MOVSB instruction then moves the current contents of the screen to the save area. (Note that since we are working with both characters and attribute bytes, all lengths and line widths throughout the program are twice what one normally thinks of.) Following the save, the register sets are reversed, and the message (with its attribute bytes) is moved to the screen. The program then initializes NXTOFF by setting it equal to ONTIM, and exits as before.

When NXTOFF goes to zero, the program restores the original screen contents, sets NXTON to OFFTIM and exits. This process cycles forever. The only way to shut off SUBLIM is to re-IPL the system.

Figure 15.2—Subliminal Message Display Program

```
PAGE      60,132
TITLE     SUBLIM - Subliminal Message Display Program
PAGE
;-----------------------------------------------------------------
;ESTABLISH COMMON SEGMENT FOR INITIALIZATION CODE
;-----------------------------------------------------------------
COMSEG    SEGMENT PARA PUBLIC 'CODE'
          ASSUME  CS:COMSEG
          ORG     80H                    ;UNFORMATTED PARAMETER AREA
PARMLEN   DB      0                      ;LENGTH OF PARAMETER STRING
PARMS     DB      127 DUP (?)            ;PARAMETER STRING
          ORG     100H
START     PROC    FAR
          JMP     INIT                   ;INITIALIZATION CODE
;-----------------------------------------------------------------
;RESIDENT DATA AREAS
;-----------------------------------------------------------------
OLDTIM    DD      0                      ;OLD TIMER INTERRUPT VECTOR
OFFTIM    DW      90                     ;TIME BETWEEN MESSAGES
ONTIM     DW      1                      ;TIME MESSAGE DISPLAYED
NXTOFF    DW      0                      ;TIME TO NEXT RESTORE
NXTON     DW      90                     ;TIME TO NEXT SAVE
MSGLEN    DW      80                     ;LENGTH TO DISPLAY
SADDR     DW      1860                   ;SCREEN STARTING POSITION
CON10     DB      10                     ;CONSTANT FOR DECIMAL ROUTINE
SCRSEG    DW      0                      ;SCREEN SEGMENT
MSGAREA   DW      80 DUP (0720H)         ;MESSAGE TO DISPLAY
MSGSAVE   DW      80 DUP (?)             ;SAVED SCREEN IMAGE
```

```
;-------------------------------------------------------------
;NEW TIMER INTERRUPT ROUTINE
;-------------------------------------------------------------
NEWTIM: STI                             ;ALLOW INTERRUPTS
        PUSH    DS
        PUSH    ES
        PUSH    SI
        PUSH    DI
        PUSH    CX
        PUSH    CS
        POP     DS              ;ESTABLISH ADDRESSABILITY TO DS
        ASSUME  DS:COMSEG       ;KEEP ASSEMBLER INFORMED
        CMP     NXTOFF,0        ;TIME TO NEXT RESTORE
        JZ      TSTON           ;NO ACTION IF ALREADY ZERO
        DEC     NXTOFF          ;COUNT DOWN FIELD
        JNZ     EXIT            ;EXIT IF TIME STILL REMAINS
        MOV     ES,SCRSEG       ;ES NOW POINTS TO SCREEN BUFFER
        MOV     SI,OFFSET MSGSAVE
        MOV     DI,SADDR        ;STARTING POSITION ON SCREEN
        MOV     CX,MSGLEN       ;MESSAGE LENGTH
        REP MOVSB               ;RESTORE SCREEN CONTENTS
        MOV     CX,OFFTIM       ;TIME BETWEEN MESSAGES
        MOV     NXTON,CX        ;TIME TO NEXT MESSAGE
        JMP     EXIT            ;EXIT ROUTINE
TSTON:  CMP     NXTON,0         ;MESSAGE PENDING?
        JZ      EXIT            ;NO - EXIT ROUTINE
        DEC     NXTON           ;COUNT DOWN FIELD
        JNZ     EXIT            ;EXIT IF TIME STILL REMAINS
        MOV     SI,SADDR        ;STARTING POSITION ON SCREEN
        MOV     DI,OFFSET MSGSAVE
        MOV     CX,MSGLEN       ;MESSAGE LENGTH
        PUSH    DS
        PUSH    DS
        POP     ES              ;ES NOW POINTS TO COMSEG
        MOV     DS,SCRSEG       ;DS NOW POINTS TO SCREEN
        REP MOVSB               ;SAVE SCREEN CONTENTS
        POP     DS              ;RESTORE DATA SEGMENT
        MOV     ES,SCRSEG       ;DESTINATION SEGMENT
        MOV     SI,OFFSET MSGAREA
        MOV     DI,SADDR        ;SCREEN STARTING POSITION
        MOV     CX,MSGLEN       ;MESSAGE LENGTH
        REP MOVSB               ;MOVE MESSAGE TO SCREEN
        MOV     CX,ONTIM        ;TIME MESSAGE DISPLAYED
        MOV     NXTOFF,CX       ;TIME TO NEXT RESTORE
EXIT:   POP     CX
        POP     DI
        POP     SI
        POP     ES
        POP     DS
        ASSUME  DS:NOTHING,ES:NOTHING,SS:NOTHING
        JMP     OLDTIM          ;GO TO NEXT INTERRUPT HANDLER
;-------------------------------------------------------------
;NON-RESIDENT DATA
;-------------------------------------------------------------
MSG1    DB      'Subliminal Message Routine Now Resident'
        DB      13,10,'$'
;-------------------------------------------------------------
;INITIALIZATION CODE
;-------------------------------------------------------------
        ASSUME  DS:COMSEG,ES:COMSEG
INIT:   CALL    CLRSCN          ;CLEAR THE SCREEN
```

```
;DETERMINE BUFFER LOCATION
          MOV      AH,15            ;CURRENT VIDEO STATE
          INT      10H              ;VIDEO BIOS CALL
          MOV      BX,0B000H        ;ASSUME MONOCHROME
          CMP      AL,7             ;IS IT?
          JZ       SETBUF           ;YOU BET!
          MOV      BX,0B800H        ;NOPE - MUST BE COLOR
SETBUF:   MOV      SCRSEG,BX        ;SAVE SCREEN SEGMENT
;GET SETUP PARAMETERS - ROW,COL,ON,OFF,MESSAGE
          CMP      PARMLEN,0        ;CHECK FOR PARMS
          JZ       PARMX            ;NO PARMS PASSED
          MOV      SI,OFFSET PARMS  ;POINT TO PARAMETER STRING
          MOV      DI,OFFSET MSGAREA    ;AND MESSAGE SAVE AREA
          CALL     GPARM            ;GET STARTING ROW
          CMP      AX,0             ;SPECIFIED?
          JZ       PARM1            ;NO - USE DEFAULT
          DEC      AX               ;CORRECT FOR ORIGIN
          MOV      BL,160           ;COLUMNS PER ROW
          MUL      BL               ;OFFSET OF CHOSEN ROW
          MOV      BX,AX            ;SAVE ROW
          CALL     GPARM            ;GET STARTING COLUMN
          CMP      AX,0             ;SPECIFIED?
          JZ       PARM0            ;NO - TREAT AS 1
          DEC      AX               ;CORRECT FOR ORIGIN
          SHL      AX,1             ;ALLOW FOR ATTRIBUTES
          ADD      BX,AX            ;ADD COLUMN POSITION
PARM0:    MOV      SADDR,BX         ;STARTING SCREEN POSITION
PARM1:    CALL     GPARM            ;GET ON TIME
          CMP      AX,0             ;SUPPLIED?
          JZ       PARM2            ;NO - USE DEFAULT
          MOV      ONTIM,AX         ;TIME MESSAGE DISPLAYED
PARM2:    CALL     GPARM            ;GET OFF TIME
          CMP      AX,0             ;SUPPLIED?
          JZ       PARM3            ;NO - USE DEFAULT
          MOV      OFFTIM,AX        ;TIME BETWEEN MESSAGES
          MOV      NXTON,AX         ;TIME TO FIRST MESSAGE
PARM3:    LODSB                     ;GET MESSAGE CHARACTER
          CMP      AL,13            ;CARRIAGE RETURN?
          JZ       PARMX            ;DONE
          STOSB                     ;PUT CHAR IN MESSAGE AREA
          INC      DI               ;SKIP ATTRIBUTE CHARACTER
          ADD      MSGLEN,2         ;COUNT CHAR AND ATTRIBUTE
          JMP      PARM3            ;GO DO IT AGAIN
;GET OLD TIMER INTERRUPT VECTOR
PARMX:    MOV      AH,35H           ;GET INTERRUPT VECTOR
          MOV      AL,1CH           ;INTERRUPT NUMBER
          INT      21H              ;DOS SERVICE CALL
          MOV      OLDTIM,BX        ;OFFSET
          MOV      OLDTIM+2,ES      ;SEGMENT
;-------------------------------------------------------------
;SET NEW TIMER INTERRUPT VECTOR
;-------------------------------------------------------------
          MOV      AH,25H           ;SET INTERRUPT VECTOR
          MOV      AL,1CH           ;INTERRUPT NUMBER
          MOV      DX,OFFSET NEWTIM ;NEW INTERRUPT ADDRESS
          INT      21H              ;DOS SERVICE REQUEST
;-------------------------------------------------------------
;ISSUE INITIALIZATION MESSAGE
;-------------------------------------------------------------
          MOV      DX,OFFSET MSG1   ;INITIALIZATION MESSAGE
          CALL     PRINT            ;DISPLAY MESSAGE
```

```
;----------------------------------------------------------------
;TERMINATE BUT STAY RESIDENT
;----------------------------------------------------------------
DONE:     MOV     DX,OFFSET MSG1    ;PAST RESIDENT CODE
          INT     27H               ;TERMINATE AND STAY RESIDENT
START     ENDP
;----------------------------------------------------------------
; SUBROUTINES
;----------------------------------------------------------------
CLRSCN    PROC                      ;CLEAR SCREEN
          PUSH    AX
          MOV     AX,2
          INT     10H
          POP     AX
          RET
CLRSCN    ENDP
PRINT PROC
          PUSH    AX
          PUSH    DX
          MOV     AH,9
          INT     21H
          POP     DX
          POP     AX
          RET
PRINT     ENDP
GPARM     PROC                      ;GET NUMERIC PARAMETER
          LODSB                     ;GET CHARACTER
          CMP     AL,' '            ;LEADING BLANK?
          JZ      GPARM             ;YES - IGNORE
          CMP     AL,'0'            ;BELOW DECIMAL RANGE?
          JNC     GPARM1            ;NO - CONTINUE
          CMP     AL,13             ;END OF INPUT?
          JNZ     GPARM0            ;NO PROBLEM
          DEC     SI                ;IN CASE CALLED AGAIN
GPARM0:   XOR     AX,AX             ;RETURN ZERO
          RET
GPARM1:   CMP     AL,'A'            ;ALPHABETIC?
          JC      GPARM2            ;NO PROBLEM
          DEC     SI                ;FOR STRING MOVE
          JMP     GPARM0            ;RETURN ZERO
GPARM2:   PUSH    BX
          PUSH    CX
          PUSH    DX
          XOR     BX,BX             ;INITIAL VALUE
GPARM3:   SUB     AL,'0'            ;CONVERT TO BINARY
          JC      GPARMX            ;NOT DECIMAL
          CMP     AL,10
          JNC     GPARMX            ;NOT DECIMAL
          CBW                       ;CONVERT TO WORD
GPARM4:   MOV     CX,AX             ;SAVE DIGIT
          MOV     AX,BX             ;FORMER VALUE
          MUL     CON10             ;TIMES 10
          MOV     BX,AX             ;SAVE RESULT
          ADD     BX,CX             ;ADD PREVIOUS VALUE
          LODSB                     ;GET NEXT DIGIT
          CMP     AL,13             ;END OF LINE?
          JNZ     GPARM3            ;NO - GO HANDLE DIGIT
          DEC     SI                ;FOR NEXT CALL
GPARMX:   MOV     AX,BX             ;RETURN RESULT
          POP     DX
          POP     CX
          POP     BX
          RET
GPARM     ENDP
COMSEG    ENDS
          END     START
```

Chapter 16
GRAPHIC PRIMITIVES

The graphic routines provided in Chapter 12 ultimately relied on the use of a BIOS call to place a point on the screen. This approach has two major limitations. First of all, it is slow. The calculations required to turn a row and column designation into a single bit position within the screen buffer are lengthy. When only a few points are being plotted the time lag is not noticeable; but painting a solid area, on the other hand, is painfully slow. The other problem is that the BIOS point routine works only if the Color/Graphics adapter is the currently active screen driver. Many users have both display adapters, and there are many applications where it would be useful to place graphics on the color display while concurrently displaying text on the monochrome display. Both of these limitations can be overcome by directly programming the CRT controller chip on the display adapter and plotting points by turning on bits in the display buffer.

The first step is to initialize the 6845 CRT controller chip. This chip is a very versatile unit which can be

189

programmed in a variety of ways by loading different values into its 18 data registers. A summary of these registers is shown in Figure 16.1. Registers 0–3 control the horizontal timing, registers 4–9 control the vertical timing, registers 10–11 control the shape and location of the cursor, registers 12–13 control the displayed page, and registers 14–15 control the shape and location of the cursor as well as record the location on the screen detected by the light pen.

Figure 16.1—6845 Data Registers

Register	Description	Value
R0	Horizontal Total Register	56
R1	Horizontal Displayed Register	40
R2	Horizontal Sync Position Register	45
R3	Horizontal Sync Width Register	10
R4	Vertical Total Register	127
R5	Vertical Adjustment Register	6
R6	Vertical Displayed Register	100
R7	Vertical Sync Register	112
R8	Interlace Mode Register	2
R9	Maximum Scan Line Register	1
R10	Cursor Start Register	6
R11	Cursor End Register	7
R12	Start Address Register – High Byte	0
R13	Start Address Register – Low Byte	0
R14	Cursor Location Register – High	0
R15	Cursor Location Register – Low	0
R16	Light Pen Register – High	–
R17	Light Pen Register – Low	–

To fully understand the tricks that can be played with this device requires a technical knowledge of video display circuitry, but to duplicate the functions provided by BIOS requires only that the registers be loaded with the values given in the table. The only trick to this is that the data registers are not directly accessible. There are only two port addresses allocated to the chip, as shown in Figure 16.2. One of these is the chip address register, the other the current data register. To load a data register, it is first necessary to put its address in the address register and then to place the data into the data register. This is done in the sample program at label INTG1, which loops until all of the registers have been loaded.

The 6845 knows nothing about color, intensity, or various other control functions of the adapter card. This information is provided through a set of I/O port addresses as shown in Figure 16.2

Figure 16.2—Color/Graphics I/O Ports

```
Port Address                Register Function
------------                ------------------

3D0H            6845 Address Register (Also 3D2, 3D4, 3D6)
3D1H            6845 Data Register    (Also 3D3, 3D5, 3D7)
3D8H            Mode Control Register
3D9H            Color Select Register
3DAH            Status Register
3DBH            Clear Light Pen Latch
3DCH            Pre-set Light Pen Latch
```

The mode control port controls the choices of character mode versus graphics, and color versus black and white. The color select register determines the choice of color palettes, and the selection of the background color and intensity. The status register contains bits that determine the status of the light pen and also when horizontal and vertical retrace operations are taking place. This latter information can be used to update the screen without causing the "green lightning" which is often seen during direct memory update operations.

Once initialization is complete, the remaining task is to place dots on the screen by turning on the appropriate bits in the display buffer. This is a little trickier in graphics mode than it was for character displays, which explains why plotting points via the BIOS point routine is a bit slow. The display buffer is divided into two halves. The first half controls the even scan lines, and the second half controls the odd scan lines. This is caused by the nature of the interleafing circuitry in the video monitor. This also explains why, when you do a BLOAD of a screen image from a BASIC program, the picture first appears streaked and then fills in with a second pass through the screen.

The memory use is contiguous within each scan line, however, since it takes two bits to describe one of four colors for a dot, each byte of storage controls four consecutive dots. To turn on or off a specific dot requires locating the byte containing the significant bits, shifting the bits for the particular dot to the proper location in a register, and ORing, ANDing, or XORing the register into the screen memory.

When there are just a few dots to be plotted, speed is not so important, and the technique used by the BIOS routine is sufficient. When there are a set of related points to plot, it is much faster to work directly in memory locations and update all of the bits within one byte (where possible) than it is to go through the complete row and column to buffer offset calculations for each dot.

The sample program for this chapter (Figure 16.3) illustrates the techniques necessary for running both the Monochrome adapter and the Color/Graphics adapter concurrently, with different displays on each. The program begins by checking the current video mode. If the Monochrome adapter is currently in control, then the program assumes that a Color/Graphics adapter also exists and proceeds to initalize it. Otherwise, it assumes that only one monitor (the color display) exists. In that case it saves the current mode before re-initializing it in graphics mode. In either case, initialization consists of looping through the table of register values and outputing them to the 6845 controller.

Next, the initialization routine (COLORON) calls SETBGD to set the palette colors (Green, Red, Yellow) and the background color (Black). These defaults can be changed by moving the new values to the variables PALCLR for the desired palette, the BGDCLR for the new background color, and then calling SETBGD again. Finally, COLORON sets the ES register to point to the beginning of the display refresh buffer on the Color/Graphics adapter cards.

The subroutine DEMO issues a couple of functions to illustrate use of the graphic primitives, CIRCLE and LINE. CIRCLE uses the same algorithm used in Chapter 12. The only difference is that the POINT routine no longer calls the BIOS set point function. Instead, it performs its own row and column-to-buffer offset calculations. The one concession it makes to speed is that it uses a table look-up function to determine the starting location for the specified row instead of going through the check for odd or even line and adding 8192 to index into the second half of the buffer if the line address is odd.

LINE is also similar to the corresponding function in Chapter 12. However, it makes use of the fact that it intends to step across the screen one dot at a time to avoid recalculating the screen offset for every point. This is an example of making tradeoffs; in this case increased program space for faster execution time.

As DEMO steps through its graphic displays, it also writes messages to the Monochrome adapter to report on its progress. This is done using the BIOS windowing functions. The idea is that the Monochrome screen would have several windows in effect and that the rest of the screen should not be affected by these messages. The message routine checks the console flag and suppresses the message if the Monochrome display is not available.

When the final graphics figure is complete, or at the end of any figure if CTRL-break has been pressed, DEMO returns control to the main routine, which calls COLOR-OFF to return the color monitor to its original state if it was the only available display. If the Monochrome display was the primary monitor, then the Color/Graphics adapter is left initialized with the display intact.

Figure 16.3—Sample Program for Twin Monitors

```
            PAGE     60,132
            TITLE    TWOMON - Direct Control of Graphics Adapter
            PAGE
;-------------------------------------------------------
;STACK SEGMENT
;-------------------------------------------------------
STACK    SEGMENT PARA STACK 'STACK'
         DB      64      DUP ('STACK   ')
STACK    ENDS
;-------------------------------------------------------
;PROGRAM PREFIX SEGMENT
;-------------------------------------------------------
PREFIX   SEGMENT AT 0
         ORG     80H
CMDCNT   DB      ?
CMDLIN   DB      80 DUP(?)           ;COMMAND LINE BUFFER
PREFIX   ENDS
;-------------------------------------------------------
;DATA SEGMENT
;-------------------------------------------------------
DSEG     SEGMENT PARA PUBLIC 'DATA'
APREFIX  DW      0                   ;PREFIX SEGMENT ADDRESS
SYSSEG   DW      40H                 ;SYSTEM SEGMENT ADDRESS
SCRSEG   DW      0B800H              ;SCREEN SEGMENT ADDRESS
DUALC    DB      0                   ;DUAL CONSOLES IF NON-ZERO
MODSAV   DW      0                   ;ORIGINAL EQUIPMENT FLAGS
BGDCLR   DB      0                   ;BACKGROUND COLOR (BLACK)
PALCLR   DB      0                   ;PALETTE COLORS (G,R,Y)
CURCOL   DB      0                   ;CURRENT COMBINED COLOR VALUES
COLOR    DW      0                   ;COLOR FOR LINES
X1       DW      0                   ;POINT VALUES
X2       DW      0                   ;POINT VALUES
Y1       DW      0                   ;POINT VALUES
Y2       DW      0                   ;POINT VALUES
ABORT    DB      0                   ;CTL-BREAK FLAG
;-------------------------------------------------------
; GRAPHICS INITIALIZATION VALUES
;-------------------------------------------------------
GRAFVAL  DB      38H                 ;HORIZONTAL TOTAL
         DB      28H                 ;HORIZONTAL DISPLAYED
         DB      2DH                 ;H. SYNC POS
         DB      0AH                 ;H. SYNC WIDTH
         DB      7FH                 ;VERTICAL TOTAL
         DB      06H                 ;VERTICAL ADJ
         DB      64H                 ;VERTICAL DISPLAYED
         DB      70H                 ;V. SYNC POS
         DB      02H                 ;INTERLACE MODE
```

```
          DB        Ø1H               ;MAX SCAN LINE
          DB        Ø6H               ;CURSOR START
          DB        Ø7H               ;CURSOR END
          DB        ØØH               ;START ADDRESS H.
          DB        ØØH               ;START ADDRESS L.
COLORV    DB        Ø
CMODE     DB        Ø                 ;[1=XOR, Ø=OR]
RADIUS    DW        Ø
DENOM     DW        Ø
NUMER     DW        Ø
XX        DW        Ø
YY        DW        Ø
XP        DW        Ø
YP        DW        Ø
NOTTER    DW        Ø
CLRMSK    DB        ØØ111111b,11ØØ1111b,1111ØØ11b,11111100b
COLMSK    DB        ØØØØØØØØb,ØØØØØØØØb,ØØØØØØØØb,ØØØØØØØØb ; Color Masks
          DB        Ø1ØØØØØØb,ØØØ1ØØØØb,ØØØØØ1ØØb,ØØØØØØØ1b
          DB        1ØØØØØØØb,ØØ1ØØØØØb,ØØØØ1ØØØb,ØØØØØØ1Øb
          DB        11ØØØØØØb,ØØ11ØØØØb,ØØØØ11ØØb,ØØØØØØ11b
DIR       DW        Ø
ADRTBL    EQU       $          ; Vertical Address Table
          .XLIST
ADR       =         Ø
          REPT      1ØØ
          DW        ADR
          DW        ADR+8192
ADR       =         ADR+8Ø
          ENDM
          .LIST
MSG1      DB        "Now let's draw a circle in the middle$"
MSG2      DB        "And finally, a green border.$"
MSG3      DB        "First we draw a red block . . .$"
DSEG      ENDS
;------------------------------------------------
;EXTRA SEGMENT FOR ACCESS TO SYSTEM VARIABLES
;------------------------------------------------
SYSTEM    SEGMENT AT 4ØH
          ORG       1ØH
EQUIP_FLAG DW       ?                 ;INSTALLED HARDWARE
SYSTEM    ENDS
;------------------------------------------------
;CODE SEGMENT
;------------------------------------------------
CSEG      SEGMENT PARA PUBLIC 'CODE'
START     PROC FAR
          ASSUME    CS:CSEG,DS:DSEG,SS:STACK,ES:PREFIX
;ESTABLISH LINKAGE FROM DOS
          MOV       AX,DSEG
          MOV       DS,AX
          MOV       APREFIX,ES        ;SAVE PREFIX SEGMENT
          CLD                         ;AUTO INCREMENT STRINGS
;SET UP CTL-BRK VECTOR
          MOV       AX,2523H          ;SET VECTOR 23
          MOV       DX,OFFSET BRKADR
          PUSH      DS
          PUSH      CS
          POP       DS
          INT       21H
          POP       DS
;TURN ON ENHANCED CTL-BRK CHECKING
          MOV       AX,33Ø1H
          MOV       DL,1
          INT       21H
          CALL      COLORON           ;INITIALIZE COLOR BOARD
          CALL      DEMO              ;MAIN GRAPHICS ROUTINE
          CALL      COLOROFF          ;RE-INITIALIZE ORIGINAL MODE
;RETURN TO DOS
          MOV       AX,APREFIX        ;PROGRAM SEGMENT PREFIX
          PUSH      AX
```

```
          SUB       AX,AX
          PUSH      AX
          RET
START     ENDP
;-------------------------------------------------
;INITIALIZE COLOR GRAPHICS MODE
;-------------------------------------------------
COLORON PROC
;GET CURRENT VIDEO MODE
          MOV       AH,15
          INT       10H
          CMP       AL,7            ;MONO?
          JNZ       CON1            ;NO
          MOV       DUALC,255       ;SHOW DUAL CONSOLE MODE
;GET AND SAVE EQUIPMENT SAVINGS
CON1:     MOV       ES,SYSSEG
          ASSUME    ES:SYSTEM
          MOV       DI,EQUIP_FLAG    ;GET EQUIPMENT SETTINGS
          MOV       MODSAV,DI        ;SAVE FOR EXIT
          CMP       DUALC,255        ;DUAL CONSOLES?
          JZ        CON2             ;YES - DO NOT SWITCH TO COLOR
          MOV       AX,4             ;SET HIRES COLOR MODE
          INT       10H              ;AND TELL BIOS
;INITIALIZE GRAPHICS ADAPTER TO OUR SPECS
CON2:     MOV       DI,0
          MOV       CX,2000H
          MOV       AX,0B800H        ;GRAPHICS BUFFER SEGMENT
          PUSH      ES
          MOV       ES,AX
          MOV       AX,0
          REP       STOSW            ;CLEAR GRAPHICS SCREEN
          POP       ES
          MOV       CX,14            ;# OF REGS TO INIT
          MOV       DX,3D4H          ;GRAPHICS OUTPUT PORT
          MOV       BX,OFFSET GRAFVAL
          XOR       AH,AH            ;REGISTER COUNTER
INTG1:    MOV       AL,AH            ;REGISTER NUMBER
          OUT       DX,AL
          INC       DX
          MOV       AL,[BX]
          OUT       DX,AL
          DEC       DX
          INC       BX
          INC       AH
          LOOP      INTG1
;NOW SET CONTROL PORTS
          CALL      SETBGD
          MOV       ES,SCRSEG        ;POINT TO DISPLAY BUFFER
          RET
          ASSUME    ES:NOTHING
COLORON ENDP
;-------------------------------------------------
;RESTORE ORIGINAL MODE
;-------------------------------------------------
COLOROFF PROC
          CMP       DUALC,0          ;DUAL CONSULE MODE?
          JNZ       COFFX            ;YES - DON'T SWITCH MODES
          MOV       ES,SYSSEG
          ASSUME    ES:SYSTEM
          MOV       DI,MODSAV        ;ORIGINAL MODE SETTING
          MOV       EQUIP_FLAG,DI
          MOV       AX,2             ;80 COLUMN MODE
          INT       10H
COFFX:    RET
          ASSUME    ES:NOTHING
COLOROFF ENDP
;-------------------------------------------------
;MAIN COLOR GRAPHICS ROUTINE
;-------------------------------------------------
DEMO      PROC
```

```
          CMP      DUALC,0            ;DUAL CONSOLES?
          JZ       DEMO1              ;NO
          CALL     CLEAR
DEMO1:    CMP      ABORT,0            ;CHECK ABORT FLAG
          JNZ      DEMOX              ;ABORT PROCESSING
;DRAW A SOLID BLOCK
          MOV      DX,OFFSET MSG3     ;BOX MESSAGE
          CALL     CTLMSG             ;DISPLAY ON MONO
          MOV      X1,20
          MOV      Y1,180
          MOV      X2,300
          MOV      Y2,20
          MOV      COLOR,2
          CALL     DRAWB              ;DRAW A BOX
          CMP      ABORT,0            ;ABORT REQUESTED?
          JNZ      DEMOX              ;YES - QUIT
;DRAW A CIRCLE
          MOV      DX,OFFSET MSG1     ;CIRCLE MESSAGE
          CALL     CTLMSG             ;PUT IT ON MONO
          MOV      XX,160             ;X ORIGIN
          MOV      YY,100             ;Y ORIGIN
          MOV      RADIUS,40          ;RADIUS
          MOV      NUMER,5            ;ASPECT NUMERATOR
          MOV      DENOM,6            ;ASPECT DENOMINATOR
          MOV      CX,3               ;COLOR
          CALL     CIRCLE
          CMP      ABORT,0            ;ABORT REQUESTED?
          JNZ      DEMOX              ;YES - QUIT
;NOW A RECTANGLE
          MOV      DX,OFFSET MSG2     ;RECTANGLE MESSAGE
          CALL     CTLMSG             ;DISPLAY ON MONO
          MOV      COLOR,1
          CALL     DRAWR              ;DRAW A RECTANGLE
DEMOX:    RET
DEMO      ENDP
;----------------------------------------------------
;CONTROL BREAK INTERRUPT ROUTINE
;----------------------------------------------------
BRKADR    PROC
          PUSH     DS
          PUSH     AX
          MOV      AX,DSEG
          MOV      DS,AX
          MOV      ABORT,255
          POP      AX
          POP      DS
          IRET
BRKADR    ENDP
;----------------------------------------------------
;MONOCHROME SCREEN SUBROUTINES
;----------------------------------------------------
MONO      PROC
CLEAR:    PUSH     AX
          PUSH     BX
          PUSH     CX
          PUSH     DX
          MOV      AX,600H            ;BLANK WINDOW
          MOV      BH,7               ;NORMAL ATTRIBUTE
          MOV      CX,0
          MOV      DX,184FH
          INT      10H
          POP      DX
          POP      CX
          POP      BX
          POP      AX
          RET
SETCSR:   PUSH     AX
          PUSH     BX
          XOR      BX,BX              ;PAGE 0
          MOV      AH,2
```

```
          INT     10H
          POP     BX
          POP     AX
          RET
SCRLUP:   PUSH    AX
          PUSH    BX
          PUSH    CX
          PUSH    DX
          MOV     AX,601H               ;SCROLL UP ONE LINE
          MOV     BH,7
          MOV     CX,1500H
          MOV     DX,174FH
          INT     10H
          POP     DX
          POP     CX
          POP     BX
          POP     AX
          RET
CTLMSG:   CMP     DUALC,255             ;DUAL CONSOLES?
          JNZ     CTLMSX                ;NO - SKIP DISPLAY
          PUSH    DX
          CALL    SCRLUP
          MOV     DX,1700H
          CALL    SETCSR
          POP     DX
          MOV     AH,9                  ;PRINT STRING
          INT     21H
CTLMSX:   RET
MONO      ENDP
;------------------------------------------------
;GRAPHICS SUBROUTINES
;------------------------------------------------
GRAFPAC   PROC
SETBGD:   PUSH    AX
          PUSH    DX
          MOV     DX,3D9H
          MOV     AL,BGDCLR             ;GET COLOR SELECTION
          AND     AL,3FH                ;CLEAR PALLETTE
          TEST    PALCLR,16
          JZ      SETBG0
          MOV     AH,10H                ;SAVE AL FOR NOW...
          JMP     SETBGA
SETBG0:   MOV     AH,0
SETBGA:   TEST    PALCLR,1              ;WANT PALETTE 1?
          JZ      SETBG1                ;NO
          OR      AL,20H                ;TURN IT ON
SETBG1:   OR      AL,AH
          OUT     DX,AL                 ;TELL HARDWARE
          MOV     CURCOL,AL             ;SAVE COMBINED STATUS
          DEC     DX
          MOV     AL,0AH                ;40X25 COLOR GRAPHICS
          TEST    PALCLR,2              ;WANT B&W?
          JZ      SETBG2                ;NO
          OR      AL,4                  ;TURN ON B&W
SETBG2:   TEST    PALCLR,4             ;WANT 640X200?
          JZ      SETBG3                ;NO
          OR      AL,16                 ;TURN ON HIRES B&W
SETBG3:   OUT     DX,AL                 ;TELL HARDWARE
          POP     DX
          POP     AX
          RET
DRAWR:    MOV     SI,X1
          MOV     DI,Y1
          MOV     AX,SI
          MOV     BX,Y2
          MOV     CX,COLOR
          CALL    LINE
          MOV     SI,X1
          MOV     DI,Y2
          MOV     AX,X2
```

```
          MOV     BX,DI
          MOV     CX,COLOR
          CALL    LINE
          MOV     SI,X2
          MOV     DI,Y2
          MOV     AX,SI
          MOV     BX,Y1
          MOV     CX,COLOR
          CALL    LINE
          MOV     SI,X2
          MOV     DI,Y1
          MOV     AX,X1
          MOV     BX,DI
          MOV     CX,COLOR
          CALL    LINE
          RET
DRAWB:    MOV     SI,X1
          MOV     DI,Y1
          MOV     AX,X2
          MOV     BX,DI          ;USE Y2 = Y1 FOR LINES
          MOV     CX,Y2          ;BOTTOM OF BOX
          SUB     CX,BX          ;NUMBER OF LINES TO DRAW
          JNC     DRAWB0         ;COUNT IS POSITIVE
          MOV     DI,Y2          ;THIS IS ACTUAL TOP
          MOV     BX,DI          ;DRAW HORIZONTAL LINES
          NEG     CX             ;MAKE COUNT POSITIVE
DRAWB0:   INC     CX             ;COUNT IS END - START + 1
DRAWB1:   PUSH    SI
          PUSH    DI
          PUSH    AX
          PUSH    BX
          PUSH    CX
          MOV     CX,COLOR
          CALL    LINE
          POP     CX
          POP     BX
          POP     AX
          POP     DI
          POP     SI
          INC     DI             ;NEXT Y1
          INC     BX             ;NEXT Y2
          LOOP    DRAWB1         ;DRAW NEXT LINE
          RET
GRAFPAC   ENDP
POINT     PROC    NEAR           ;[SI=X,DI=Y]
          PUSH    AX
          PUSH    BX
          PUSH    CX
          PUSH    SI
          PUSH    DI
          SHL     DI,1           ;mult y*2 (addr table is 2 bytes wide)
          MOV     DI,ADRTBL[DI]  ;get vert address from table
          MOV     AX,SI          ;save x in si
          AND     SI,3
          SHR     AX,1           ;divide by 4 (4 dots per byte)
          SHR     AX,1
          ADD     DI,AX          ;get addr of byte on screen
          XOR     BX,BX
          MOV     BL,COLORV
          SAL     BL,1           ; color table is 4 by 4 so mult color * 4
          SAL     BL,1
          MOV     AL,CLRMSK[SI]
          MOV     BL,COLMSK[SI+BX]
          CMP     CMODE,1
          JNE     ORIT
          CMP     NOTTER,0
          JNE     XORIT
          XOR     ES:[DI],BL
          JMP     SHORT XORIT
ORIT:     AND     ES:[DI],AL
```

```
            OR        ES:[DI],BL
XORIT:      POP       DI
            POP       SI
            POP       CX
            POP       BX
            POP       AX
            RET
POINT   ENDP


;Draws a circle at center  (XX,YY) with aspect ratio
;numer/denom; radius in column units; color in CX

CIRCLE  PROC      NEAR
            MOV       NOTTER,0
            MOV       COLORV,CL
            MOV       CMODE,CH
            MOV       AX,NUMER        ;GET ASPECT NUMER
            MOV       BX,1000         ;SCALE BY 1000
            IMUL      BX
            MOV       CX,DENOM        ;GET ASPECT DENOM
            IDIV      CX              ;AX=ASPECT*1000
            PUSH      AX              ;SAVE ASPECT
            XCHG      AX,CX           ;GET DENOM IN AX
            MOV       CX,NUMER        ;GET NUMER IN CX
            IMUL      BX              ;SCALE
            IDIV      CX              ;AX=INV ASPECT*1000
            MOV       DENOM,AX        ;SAVE
            POP       AX              ;ASPECT*1000
            MOV       NUMER,AX        ;SAVE

;Y=Y+1 X=X-TAN(INV ASPECT)


            MOV       AX,RADIUS       ;GET RADIUS
            MOV       XP,AX           ;1st PREVIOUS X
            MOV       BX,1000         ;SCALE
            IMUL      BX
            XOR       DI,DI           ;ZERO INIT Y VALUE
CR5:        PUSH      AX
            PUSH      DX
            XOR       BX,BX
            ADD       AX,500          ;ROUND
            ADC       DX,BX
            MOV       BX,1000         ;RESCALE X
            IDIV      BX
            MOV       BX,AX           ;1st quad
            PUSH      BX              ;NEW CALCULATED X
CR5A:       ADD       AX,XX           ;ADD X ORIGIN
            MOV       DX,YY           ;Y ORIGIN
            SUB       DX,DI
            MOV       CX,AX           ;GET X TO PLOT

            NOT       NOTTER

            CALL      CPOINT          ;CALL POINT ROUTINE
            SUB       CX,BX           ;GET 2nd QUAD
            SUB       CX,BX           ;X+ORIGIN
            CALL      CPOINT
            ADD       DX,DI           ;GET 3rd QUAD
            ADD       DX,DI           ;Y+ORIG
            CALL      CPOINT
            ADD       CX,BX           ;GET 4th QUAD
            ADD       CX,BX           ;X+ORIGIN
            CALL      CPOINT
            INC       BX
            CMP       BX,XP           ;X GAP?
            JAE       CR6             ;NO
            MOV       AX,BX           ;SET INTERMEDIATE POINT
            JMP       CR5A            ;GO PLOT IT
```

```
;CX NOW AT ORIGINAL POINT

CR6:    POP     BX              ;CALCULATED X
        MOV     XP,BX           ;PREVIOUS X
        XCHG    CX,BX           ;1st QUAD X
        INC     DI              ;NEW Y
        MOV     AX,DI           ;Y
        MOV     BX,DENOM        ;BX=INV ASPECT*1000
        IMUL    BX
        IDIV    CX              ;TAN*INV ASPECT
        XOR     DX,DX           ;REMAINDER
        MOV     SI,AX           ;SI=TAN*INV ASPECT
        IDIV    BX              ;AX=TAN
        CMP     AX,1            ;TAN=1?
        POP     DX
        POP     AX
        JAE     CR7             ;GO TO NEXT SECTOR
        NEG     SI              ;TO DEC X
        MOV     BX,-1           ;NEGATIVE CARRY
        ADD     AX,SI           ;NEW X VALUE
        ADC     DX,BX           ;HIGH WORD CARRY
        JMP SHORT CR5           ;PLOT NEW POINT

;PLOT 45 TO 90 DEGREES

CR7:    MOV     AX,DI           ;NEXT Y
        MOV     YP,AX           ;INIT PREVIOUS Y
        MOV     BX,1000         ;SCALE
        IMUL    BX              ;DX:AX=Y*1000
        MOV     DI,CX           ;LAST X VALUE
        DEC     DI              ;NEXT X
CR8:    PUSH    AX
        PUSH    DX
        XOR     BX,BX
        ADD     AX,500          ;ROUND
        ADC     DX,BX
        MOV     BX,1000         ;RESCALE Y
        IDIV    BX
        MOV     BX,AX           ;1st QUAD Y
        PUSH    BX
CR8A:   ADD     AX,YY           ;ADD Y ORIGIN
        MOV     CX,XX           ;X ORIGIN
        ADD     CX,DI
        MOV     DX,AX           ;Y

        NOT     NOTTER
        CALL    CPOINT
        SUB     CX,DI           ;2nd QUAD
        SUB     CX,DI           ;X
        CALL    CPOINT
        SUB     DX,BX           ;3rd QUAD
        SUB     DX,BX           ;Y
        CALL    CPOINT
        ADD     CX,DI           ;4th QUAD
        ADD     CX,DI           ;X
        CALL    CPOINT
        DEC     BX
        CMP     BX,YP           ;GAP?
        JBE     CR9             ;NO
        MOV     AX,BX
        JMP     CR8A            ;PLOT INTERMEDIATE POINT
CR9:    POP     BX
        MOV     YP,BX           ;SAVE PREVIOUS Y
        SUB     DX,YY           ;Y-Y ORIGIN
        NEG     DX              ;Y ORIGIN ADJUST
        XCHG    CX,DX           ;CX=Y
        OR      DI,DI           ;90 DEG
        JS      CR11            ;YES, EXIT
        DEC     DI              ;NEW X
```

```
          MOV     AX,DI
          MOV     BX,NUMER        ;ASPECT*1000
          IMUL    BX
          IDIV    CX
          MOV     SI,AX           ;DELTA Y
          POP     DX
          POP     AX
          XOR     BX,BX
          OR      SI,SI           ;SIGN CHECK
          JNS     CR10            ;POSITIVE
          MOV     BX,-1           ;NEGATIVE CARRY
CR10:     ADD     AX,SI           ;NEW X VALUE
          ADC     DX,BX           ;HI WORD CARRY
          JMP     CR8             ;PLOT NEXT POINT
CR11:     POP     AX
          POP     AX
          RET

CIRCLE    ENDP

CPOINT    PROC    NEAR
          CMP     CX,0
          JL      CPOINT1
          CMP     CX,319
          JG      CPOINT1
          CMP     DX,0
          JL      CPOINT1
          CMP     DX,199
          JG      CPOINT1
          PUSH    SI
          PUSH    DI
          PUSH    CX
          MOV     DI,DX
          MOV     SI,CX
          CALL    POINT
          POP     CX
          POP     DI
          POP     SI
CPOINT1:  RET
CPOINT    ENDP

;----------------------------------------

; LINE - Draws lines in normal or XOR mode - real fast!
;        Point routine is internal for highest speeds.

LINE      PROC    NEAR            ;[SI=X1,DI=Y1,AX=X2,BX=Y2]
          MOV     COLORV,CL       ;[CX=COLOR]
          MOV     CMODE,CH
          MOV     NOTTER,0
          MOV     DX,0
          CMP     SI,AX
          JBE     NOXCHG
          XCHG    SI,AX
          XCHG    DI,BX
NOXCHG:   SUB     AX,SI
          MOV     BP,AX           ;BP HOLDS X DIFFERENCE CONSTANT
          SUB     BX,DI
          MOV     CX,1
          JNS     NOTNEG
          NEG     CX
          NEG     BX
NOTNEG:   MOV     [DIR],CX
          MOV     AX,BX           ;SAVE Y DIFFERENCE CONSTANT IN AX
          PUSH    BX
          PUSH    SI
          PUSH    DI
          SHL     DI,1            ;MULT Y*2 (ADDR TABLE IS 2 BYTES WIDE)
          MOV     DI,ADRTBL[DI]   ;GET VERT ADDR FROM TABLE
          MOV     BX,SI           ;SAVE X IN SI
```

```
          AND       SI,3
          SHR       BX,1              ;DIVIDE BY 4 (4 DOTS PER BYTE)
          SHR       BX,1
          ADD       DI,BX             ;GET ADDR OF BYTE ON SCREEN
          MOV       BH,0
          MOV       BL,COLORV
          SAL       BL,1              ;MULT BY 4 (4X4 TABLE)
          SAL       BL,1
          MOV       BL,COLMSK[SI+BX]
          MOV       BH,CLRMSK[SI]     ;MASK FOR COLOR
          CMP       CMODE,1
          JNE       ORIT1
          XOR       ES:[DI],BL
          JMP       SHORT XORIT1
ORIT1:    AND       ES:[DI],BH        ;BH HOLDS CLRMSK
          OR        ES:[DI],BL        ;BL HOLDS COLMSK (4X4)
XORIT1:   POP       DI
          POP       SI
          POP       CX                ;CHANGE TO CX TEMPORARILY
          CMP       BP,CX             ;SO BX IS PRESERVED
          JLE       CASE1
          JMP       CASE2
CASE1:    CMP       [DIR],1
          JNE       CASE3             ;NEGATIVE Y
          MOV       CX,AX
LP1:      DEC       CX
          JS        DONEL1
          INC       DI
          ADD       DX,BP
          CMP       AX,DX
          JA        SKP1
          SUB       DX,AX
          INC       SI
          ROR       BL,1              ;INCREMENT MASKS FOR
          ROR       BL,1              ;CURRENT PIXEL
          ROR       BH,1
          ROR       BH,1
SKP1:     PUSH      AX                ;SAXE AX (Y CONSTANT)
          PUSH      DI                ;SAVE DI (Y)
          SHL       DI,1              ;MULT BY TWO FOR...
          MOV       DI,ADRTBL[DI]     ;TABLE LOOK UP
          MOV       AX,SI             ;SAVE X IN SI
          SHR       AX,1              ;DIVIDE BY 4 (4 PIXELS/BYTE)
          SHR       AX,1
          ADD       DI,AX             ;ADD TO Y-BYTE FOR DEST. BYTE
          CMP       CMODE,1
          JNE       ORIT2
          NOT       NOTTER
          CMP       NOTTER,0
          JNE       XORIT2
          XOR       ES:[DI],BL
          JMP       SHORT XORIT2
ORIT2:    AND       ES:[DI],BH        ;AND SCREEN BYTE WITH OTHER MASK
          OR        ES:[DI],BL        ;BL HOLDS COLMSK (4X4)
XORIT2:   POP       DI                ;RECOVER DI (Y)
          POP       AX
          JMP       SHORT LP1
DONEL1:   RET
CASE3:    MOV       CX,AX
LP3:      DEC       CX
          JS        DONEL3
          DEC       DI
          ADD       DX,BP
          CMP       AX,DX
          JA        SKP3
          SUB       DX,AX
          INC       SI
          ROR       BL,1              ;INCREMENT MASKS FOR
          ROR       BL,1              ;CURRENT PIXEL
          ROR       BH,1
```

```
         ROR     BH,1
SKP3:    PUSH    AX                  ;SAVE AX (Y CONSTANT)
         PUSH    DI                  ;SAVE DI (Y)
         SHL     DI,1                ;MULT BY TWO FOR...
         MOV     DI,ADRTBL[DI]       ;TABLE LOOK UP
         MOV     AX,SI               ;SAVE X IN SI
         SHR     AX,1                ;DIVIDE BY 4 (4 PIXELS/BYTE)
         SHR     AX,1
         ADD     DI,AX               ;ADD TO Y-BYTE FOR DEST. BYTE
         CMP     CMODE,1
         JNE     ORIT3
         NOT     NOTTER
         CMP     NOTTER,0
         JNE     XORIT3
         XOR     ES:[DI],BL
         JMP     SHORT XORIT3
ORIT3:   AND     ES:[DI],BH          ;BH HOLDS CLRMSK
         OR      ES:[DI],BL          ;BL HOLDS COLMSK (4X4)
XORIT3:  POP     DI                  ;RECOVER DI (Y)
         POP     AX
         JMP     SHORT LP3
DONEL3:  RET
CASE2:   CMP     [DIR],1
         JNE     CASE4               ;NEGATIVE Y
         MOV     CX,BP
LP2:     DEC     CX
         JS      DONEL2
         INC     SI
         ADD     DX,AX
         CMP     BP,DX
         JA      SKP2
         SUB     DX,BP
         INC     DI
SKP2:    ROR     BL,1                ;INCREMENT MASKS FOR
         ROR     BL,1                ;CURRENT PIXEL
         ROR     BH,1
         ROR     BH,1
         PUSH    AX                  ;SAVE AX (Y CONSTANT)
         PUSH    DI                  ;SAVE DI (Y)
         SHL     DI,1                ;MULT BY TWO FOR...
         MOV     DI,ADRTBL[DI]       ;TABLE LOOK UP
         MOV     AX,SI               ;SAVE X IN SI
         SHR     AX,1                ;DIVIDE BY 4 (4 PIXELS/BYTE)
         SHR     AX,1
         ADD     DI,AX               ;ADD TO Y-BYTE FOR DEST. BYTE
         CMP     CMODE,1
         JNE     ORIT4
         NOT     NOTTER
         CMP     NOTTER,0
         JNE     XORIT4
         XOR     ES:[DI],BL
         JMP     SHORT XORIT4
ORIT4:   AND     ES:[DI],BH          ;BH HOLDS CLRMSK
         OR      ES:[DI],BL          ;BL HOLDS COLMSK (4X4)
XORIT4:  POP     DI                  ;RECOVER DI (Y)
         POP     AX
         JMP     SHORT LP2
DONEL2:  RET
CASE4:   MOV     CX,BP
LP4:     DEC     CX
         JS      DONEL4
         INC     SI
         ADD     DX,AX
         CMP     BP,DX
         JA      SKP4
         SUB     DX,BP
         DEC     DI
SKP4:    ROR     BL,1                ;INCREMENT MASKS FOR
         ROR     BL,1                ;CURRENT PIXEL
```

```
            ROR     BH,1
            ROR     BH,1
            PUSH    AX              ;SAVE AX (Y CONSTANT)
            PUSH    DI              ;SAVE DI (Y)
            SHL     DI,1            ;MULT BY TWO FOR...
            MOV     DI,ADRTBL[DI]   ;TABLE LOOK UP
            MOV     AX,SI           ;SAVE X IN SI
            SHR     AX,1            ;DIVIDE BY 4 (4 PIXELS/BYTE)
            SHR     AX,1
            ADD     DI,AX           ;ADD TO Y-BYTE FOR DEST. BYTE
            CMP     CMODE,1
            JNE     ORIT5
            NOT     NOTTER
            CMP     NOTTER,0
            JNE     XORIT5
            XOR     ES:[DI],BL
            JMP     SHORT XORIT5
ORIT5:      AND     ES:[DI],BH      ;BH HOLDS CLRMSK
            OR      ES:[DI],BL      ;BL HOLDS COLMSK (4X4)
XORIT5:     POP     DI              ;RECOVER DI (Y)
            POP     AX
            JMP     SHORT LP4
DONEL4:     RET
LINE        ENDP
CSEG        ENDS
            END
```

Part V

Interfaces and Ideas

Chapter 17
BASIC SUBROUTINES

The development of high-level languages in general—
and BASIC in particular—was one of the major steps in
making home computers acceptable to the programmer-
hobbyist. BASIC is easy to understand, simple to use,
and relatively portable between machines ... but as
everyone knows, "There ain't no such thing as a free
lunch." There had to be a trade-off somewhere, and the
trade-off was in speed. Interpretive BASIC is notori-
ously slow.

Another problem with BASIC is its inability to use
the available machine memory. As implemented on the
PC, BASIC uses the first 64KB above DOS. It is limited
to that amount of memory and incapable of handling
any BASIC program larger than 64KB. Even if you've
got a machine with 512KB you're still stuck with
BASIC's 64K work area.

This book is dedicated to the concept that there is
still a need for assembly language where more speed or
function is required than is available in other languages.
But there is a price in programmer productivity. The
compromise is to use both. By writing common subrou-

tines in assembly language you can get both the speed and memory utilization of the low-level code, while preserving the ease and familiarity of BASIC.

If you have worked with assembly language you've probably considered this approach yourself, but you may have gotten discouraged when you tried to develop the BASIC/assembly language interface. IBM's BASIC manual devotes an entire 18-page appendix to the subject, but the suggested procedures are cumbersome and require a lot of manual intervention by the programmer.

Although the systems shown in the manual will certainly work, one of them calls for converting each line of the subroutine into machine code, translating it into hex, and then using POKE to insert the instructions one by one into memory. This is a lengthy and time-consuming procedure. Another suggested way of loading a routine is to use DEBUG to load it into high memory, where it overlays the transient portion of COMMAND.COM. This requires you to reset the system registers and use the DEBUG N command to initialize the parameter passing area.

Besides the actual program load, another problem that has to be dealt with is deciding exactly where in memory to locate the new code. You have your choice of inserting it within the the 64K BASIC work space or, if the BASIC program is too large to allow that, putting it somewhere else in memory. In either case you have to determine the end of BASIC itself, which can vary depending on the device drivers installed in DOS.

Fortunately there is a relatively easy procedure that will let you load assembly subroutines via interpretive BASIC without resorting to POKE, and without having to use DEBUG to find the end of the interpreter work area. This procedure loads the code from within the BASIC program and allows you to invoke it from anywhere in the program with a simple CALL statement.

Let's take as an example a subroutine that converts an input text string to upper case. This is a procedure that is done in countless programs, to let the user enter either upper or lower case letters. To do this in BASIC is both slow and awkward, and involves looping through nested function calls, as shown in Figure 17.1.

Figure 17.1—BASIC Uppercase Translate Routine

```
10    REM  Convert Lower Case to Upper Case
20    FOR Z=1 TO LEN(Z$)
30    MID$(Z$,Z,1) = CHR$(ASC(MID$(Z$,Z,1))
      + 32*(ASC(MID$(Z$,Z,1))>96))
40    NEXT Z
50    RETURN
```

Nobody can seriously maintain that statement 30 is a natural use of the BASIC language. Without the comment, it would take a reasonably experienced programmer just to figure out what the statement does, and an even more advanced one to explain why it works. Compare that to the equivalent function in assembler as shown in Figure 17.2.

Figure 17.2—Assembly Language Upper Case Translate Routine

```
      ;Upper Case Translate Routine
      ;Called with String Address in SI
      ;         and  String Length in CX

XLAT:     CMP  BYTE PTR [SI],'a'      ;LOWER CASE LETTER?
          JC   XLAT1                  ;NO
          AND  BYTE PTR [SI],0DFH     ;CONVERT TO UC
      XLAT1:    INC  SI               ;POINT TO NEXT CHAR
          LOOP XLAT                   ;LOOP UNTIL DONE
          RET
```

Of course, to use this subroutine with BASIC we have to fancy it up a little bit, because there is no way to directly set SI and CX to their assumed values in the BASIC program. The program will actually issue:

CALL XLAT(A$)

This statement will cause BASIC to place the address of the string descriptor for the passed string on the stack and make an intersegment call to XLAT. We will discuss later how BASIC knows where to find XLAT. The string descriptor contains a one-byte length field, followed by a two-byte offset of the string's address within BASIC's data segment. The subroutine, in theory, must not change anything within the descriptor or change the physical length of the string, although it can do anything it wants to the *content* of the string. Due to the actual implementation of BASIC's string handling routines, it is safe to shorten the actual string, but never to lengthen it. Figure 17.3 shows the subroutine expanded to properly handle the passed parameters.

Figure 17.3—Assembly Subroutine Called from BASIC

```
;Translate String to Upper Case

XLAT      PROC FAR
XLAT0:    PUSH BP                     ;Save Caller's Frame
          MOV  BP,SP                  ;Set Frame Pointer
          MOV  SI,[BP+6]              ;String header
          MOV  CL,[SI]                ;String length
          CMP  CL,0                   ;Null string?
          JZ   XLAT3                  ;Yes - exit
          XOR  CH,CH                  ;Clear MSB of length
          MOV  SI,[SI+1]              ;String address
XLAT1:    CMP  BYTE PTR [SI],'a'      ;Lower case char?
          JC   XLAT2                  ;No
          AND  BYTE PTR [SI],0DFH     ;Convert to upper case
XLAT2:    INC  SI                     ;Point to next character
          LOOP XLAT3                  ;Loop until done
XLAT3:    POP  BP                     ;Restore Caller's Frame
          RET  2                      ;Return Flushing Stack
XLAT      ENDP
```

The subroutine is now ready to be loaded, which we will do with a BLOAD instruction from BASIC. However, BLOAD has its own conventions about the format of the object file. It wants to see a seven-byte prefix containing the following information about the file: type, segment, offset, and length. Type is a one-byte field; segment and offset are two-byte (word) addresses; and length is a two-byte field. BASIC will delete this header as it loads the file into memory. One "quick and dirty" way to pass this information to BASIC is to set up a seven-byte prologue at the beginning of the CALLED program which contains the necessary information. Program length is determined by setting up an EQU statement to trap the starting address (BOF) and subtracting that address from EOF, which is defined at the program end. File type is defined as 0FDH which is BASIC's convention for a data file. This technique is illustrated in Figure 17.4.

Figure 17.4—Prologue for a Called BASIC subroutine

```
;Build file prologue for BASIC loader
            DB      ØFDH        ;File type
            DW      ØF77H       ;Default segment
            DW      Ø           ;Default offset
            DW      EOF-BOF     ;Program length
BOF         EQU     $           ;Start of code
            JMP     XLATØ       ;Upper case translate
            JMP     Routine2    ;Some other subroutine
            . . .
XLATØ:      . . .
Routine2:   . . .
EOF         DB      1AH             ;End of File
```

These lines of prologue information establish the segment, offset, and program length variables which will be stripped off by the BLOAD command. The second JMP command opens an entry point to the translate routine. (You would typically include several assembly language routines in one program, in which case there would be an additional JMP command for each routine.) An end of file marker (EOF DB 1AH) is written at the end of the programs, just prior to the

COMSEG ENDS statement, so that the program length can be calculated.

· Because the assembler does not know that BASIC will strip off the seven-byte prologue when the program is loaded, you cannot use absolute jumps or addresses in the remainder of the program. All addressing must be relative or the instruction pointer will be off by seven bytes and wind up in some nebulous never-never land, causing unpredictable results.

The subroutine code can now be assembled and converted into a binary file, after which is it ready be loaded into memory. (Binary files are created from .EXE files by running EXE2BIN against the compiled code and specifying a .BIN extension for the output.) The actual load is done in the CALLing BASIC program, using BLOAD, and depends on using PEEK to retrieve the correct loading address as shown in Figure 17.5

Figure 17.5—BASIC Program Loading Sequence

```
100   'Load machine language subroutines
110   DEF SEG=0
120   MLSEG=PEEK(&H510)+256*PEEK(&H511)+&H1001
130   DEF SEG=MLSEG
140   XLAT=0
150   BLOAD "SUBRTN.BIN",0
```

The success of this routine depends on the fact that DOS maintains the beginning segment address of BASIC's work area at hex 510–511. Adding hex 1000 (64K) to this address provides the ending address of BASIC in segment notation. An extra 16 bytes is then added in to account for the memory management block that follows BASIC. The result of these calculations is an address in free memory above BASIC.

Notice that the entire program, SUBRTN.BIN, is loaded into memory. The translate routine, XLAT, is shown as entry point 0. If there were additional routines in the program they would be numbered with an offset of 3, for the byte length of the JMP command, so that the second one would be equal to 3, the third to 6, and so on.

As we mentioned above, this system requires you to use relative addressing. A tidier solution is to write the machine language program as you normally would, omitting the load information, and then append those seven bytes to the beginning of the compiled and linked code. This scheme allows you to use absolute addressing since the seven load bytes are not present when the program is assembled.

The routine shown in Figure 17.6, BASFMT.ASM, has been written to create the necessary load information for BASIC and insert it at the beginning of a binary (.BIN) assembly language program. This program must be compiled into an .EXE file and linked before it can be run.

Either of these schemes—adding a prologue and using relative addressing, or inserting the load information ahead of the finished code—will let you load and call machine language subroutines via BASIC with a minimum of trouble. If you've been looking for a way to get faster response out of interpretive BASIC, try converting some of your common subroutines to assembly language and interfacing them with one of these methods. You'll be amazed at the difference in response time.

Figure 17.6—BASFMT.ASM

```
PAGE     62,132
TITLE    BASFMT - Convert File to BASIC Load Format
PAGE
;------------------------------------------------------------
;DEFINE STACK SEGMENT
;------------------------------------------------------------
STACK    SEGMENT PARA STACK 'STACK'
```

```
            DB       64 DUP('STACK   ')
STACK    ENDS
;-------------------------------------------------------------
;DEFINE PROGRAM SEGMENT PREFIX
;-------------------------------------------------------------
PREFIX   SEGMENT AT Ø
         ORG      80H
PARMCT   DB       Ø                 ;LENGTH OF PASSED PARAMETERS
PARM     DB       80 DUP (?)        ;UNFORMATTED PARAMETER AREA
PREFIX   ENDS
;-------------------------------------------------------------
;DEFINE DATA SEGMENT
;-------------------------------------------------------------
DSEG     SEGMENT PARA PUBLIC 'DATA'
PARM1    DB       40 DUP (?)        ;INPUT FILE STRING
PARM2    DB       40 DUP (?)        ;OUTPUT FILE STRING
HEADER   DB       ØFDH              ;FILE TYPE
         DW       ØF77H             ;DEFAULT SEGMENT
         DW       Ø                 ;DEFAULT OFFSET
FLENGTH  DW       Ø                 ;FILE LENGTH
HANDLE1  DW       Ø                 ;INPUT FILE HANDLE
HANDLE2  DW       Ø                 ;OUTPUT FILE HANDLE
RCODE    DB       Ø                 ;DOS RETURN CODE
DSUFF    DB       '.BLM',Ø          ;DEFAULT OUTPUT SUFFIX
MSGTBL   DW       MSGØ,MSG1,MSG2
MSGØ     DB       'File Created without Error',13,10,'$'
MSG1     DB       'FILE NOT FOUND',13,10,'$'
MSG2     DB       'Error in Creating Output File',13,10,'
BUFFER   DB       128 DUP (?)       ;FILE BUFFER
DSEG     ENDS
;-------------------------------------------------------------
;DEFINE CODE SEGMENT
;-------------------------------------------------------------
CSEG     SEGMENT PARA PUBLIC 'CODE'
START    PROC     FAR
         ASSUME   CS:CSEG,SS:STACK,DS:PREFIX
;ESTABLISH ADDRESSABILITY TO DATA SEGMENT
         MOV      AX,DSEG           ;ADDRESS OF DATA SEGMENT
         MOV      ES,AX             ;NOW POINTS TO DATA SEGMENT
         ASSUME   ES:DSEG           ;TELL ASSEMBLER
;-------------------------------------------------------------
;START OF MAIN PROGRAM
;-------------------------------------------------------------
         CALL     CLRSCN
         XOR      CX,CX             ;CLEAR LENGTH REGISTER
         MOV      CL,PARMCT         ;GET PARAMETER LENGTH
         MOV      SI,OFFSET PARM    ;POINT TO PARAMETERS
         MOV      DI,OFFSET PARM1   ;INPUT FILE NAME
         CALL     MVPARM
         MOV      DI,OFFSET PARM2   ;OUTPUT FILE NAME
         CALL     MVPARM
         MOV      AX,DSEG
         MOV      DS,AX             ;DON'T NEED PREFIX ANY MORE
         ASSUME   DS:DSEG
         CMP      PARM1,Ø           ;NULL STRING?
         JZ       FILBAD            ;YES
         CMP      PARM2,Ø           ;NULL STRING?
         JNZ      FILEOK            ;NO PROBLEM
         CALL     DNAME             ;USE DEFAULT NAME FOR OUTPUT
         JMP      FILEOK
FILBAD:  MOV      RCODE,1           ;FILE NOT FOUND
         JMP      DONE              ;QUIT
```

```
FILEOK: MOV     DX,OFFSET PARM1  ;INPUT FILE NAME
        MOV     AX,3D00H         ;OPEN FILE FOR INPUT
        INT     21H
        JC      FILBAD           ;ERROR OPENING FILE
        MOV     HANDLE1,AX       ;INPUT FILE HANDLE
        MOV     DX,OFFSET PARM2  ;OUTPUT FILE NAME
        XOR     CX,CX            ;NORMAL ATTRIBUTE
        MOV     AH,3CH           ;CREATE OUTPUT FILE
        INT     21H
        JNC     OPENOK           ;FILES OPENED OK
OUTERR: MOV     RCODE,2          ;CAN NOT OPEN OUTPUT
        JMP     DONE
OPENOK: MOV     HANDLE2,AX
;GET FILE SIZE
        XOR     CX,CX
        XOR     DX,DX
        MOV     BX,HANDLE1
        MOV     AX,4202H         ;POINT TO END OF FILE
        INT     21H
        MOV     FLENGTH,AX       ;SAVE FILE LENGTH
;RESET FILE TO BEGINNING
        XOR     CX,CX
        XOR     DX,DX
        MOV     BX,HANDLE1
        MOV     AX,4200H         ;POINT TO BEGINNING OF FILE
        INT     21H
;WRITE HEADER
        MOV     BX,HANDLE2       ;OUTPUT FILE
        MOV     CX,7             ;LENGTH OF HEADER
        MOV     DX,OFFSET HEADER
        MOV     AH,40H           ;WRITE FILE
        INT     21H
        CMP     AX,CX            ;WRITE OK?
        JNZ     OUTERR           ;OUTPUT ERROR
;COPY INPUT FILE
COPY:   MOV     DX,OFFSET BUFFER
        MOV     CX,128
        MOV     BX,HANDLE1       ;INPUT FILE
        MOV     AH,3FH           ;READ FILE
        INT     21H
        CMP     AX,0             ;END OF FILE?
        JZ      CLOSE            ;YES
        MOV     CX,AX            ;WRITE NO OF BYTES READ
        MOV     BX,HANDLE2       ;OUTPUT FILE
        MOV     AH,40H
        INT     21H
        CMP     AX,CX            ;ALL BYTES WRITTEN?
        JNZ     OUTERR           ;NO
        CMP     AX,128           ;FULL BUFFER READ?
        JZ      COPY             ;YES, READ NEXT
CLOSE:  MOV     AH,3EH           ;CLOSE FILE
        INT     21H
;-------------------------------------------------------------
;RETURN TO DOS
;-------------------------------------------------------------
DONE:   MOV     AX,DSEG
        MOV     DS,AX            ;ENSURE ADDRESSABILITY
        XOR     BX,BX
        MOV     BL,RCODE
        SHL     BX,1
        MOV     DX,MSGTBL[BX]    ;ADDRESS OF ERROR MESSAGE
        CALL    PRINT
```

```
          MOV     AH,4CH          ;EXIT
          MOV     AL,RCODE        ;SET RETURN CODE
          INT     21H             ;TERMINATE PROGRAM
START     ENDP
;------------------------------------------------------------
;SUBROUTINES
;------------------------------------------------------------
CLRSCN    PROC                    ;CLEAR SCREEN
          PUSH    AX
          MOV     AX,2
          INT     10H
          POP     AX
          RET
CLRSCN    ENDP
PRINT     PROC
          PUSH    AX
          MOV     AH,9
          INT     21H
          POP     AX
          RET
PRINT     ENDP
MVPARM    PROC                    ;MOVE ONE PARAMETER FROM PREFIX
          CMP     CX,0            ;ANY STRING LEFT?
          JZ      MVPARY          ;NO - EXIT
MVPAR0:   LODSB                   ;GET 1ST CHAR
          CMP     AL,' '          ;LEADING BLANK?
          JNZ     MVPAR1          ;NO
          LOOP    MVPAR0          ;DELETE LEADING BLANK
MVPARX:   DEC     CX              ;ADJUST COUNT FOR DELIMITER
MVPARY:   MOV     AL,0            ;END OF STRING
          STOSB
          RET
MVPAR1:   STOSB
          LODSB
          CMP     AL,' '          ;TERMINATING BLANK?
          JZ      MVPARX          ;YES - DONE
          CMP     AL,','          ;COMMA IS VALID TERMINATER
          JZ      MVPARX
          CMP     AL,0DH          ;CR?
          JZ      MVPARX
          LOOP    MVPAR1          ;GET NEXT CHARACTER
          JMP     MVPAR1
MVPARM    ENDP
DNAME     PROC                    ;COPY NAME AND ADD DEFAULT PREFIX
          MOV     SI,OFFSET PARM1
          MOV     DI,OFFSET PARM2
DNAME1:   LODSB
          CMP     AL,'.'          ;DELIMITER?
          JZ      DNAME2          ;YES
          CMP     AL,0            ;END OF STRING?
          JZ      DNAME2          ;YES
          STOSB
          JMP     DNAME1          ;LOOP TIL DONE
DNAME2:   MOV     SI,OFFSET DSUFF ;DEFAULT SUFFIX
          MOV     CX,5
          REP     MOVSB
          RET
DNAME     ENDP
CSEG      ENDS
          END     START
```

Chapter 18
COPY-PROTECTION SCHEMES

If you have been reading this book because you want to write programs for commercial sale, sooner or later you and your distributor will have to make a decision about employing a copy-protection scheme. There are basically three choices: buy protected diskettes on which to put your programs, develop your own protection scheme, or leave your software unprotected. This is not an easy choice.

There is no doubt that for every legitimate copy of a program sold there are some number of bootleg copies floating about. For some popular and expensive programs such as one of the top spreadsheet packages, there are undoubtedly many more pirated copies than there are legitimate ones. This has led many people to conclude that tougher and tougher copy-protection schemes are needed. Despite these facts, there is a line of argument that says that copy protection costs the software author more than it can possibly save. Before discussing specific copy-protection techniques, let me present some of these arguments.

First of all, the use of copy protection limits the

number of sales, especially in the business market-place. Most companies have enough data processing backgrounds to understand the value of backup copies. No matter how swiftly a company will replace a damaged diskette or how little they charge for the service, for at least a day or two the user will be unable to run the program. If that program is essential to his business, then his business suffers. Imagine a small business owner explaining to five or six employees that their paychecks cannot be written until the replacement copy of the accounts payable program is received from the distributor. Many companies will flat-out refuse to buy any copy-protected software.

Additionally, people are learning to expect that programs will be easy to use. Most copy-protection methods will not allow the program to be run from the hard disks that are now becoming common, without having the original diskette in the floppy drive. Having to rummage around through a pile of diskettes to find the protection key for a program that is on the hard disk is a sure way to develop a strong dislike for that program. More and more users are refusing to buy software that will not run freely from the hard disk.

The second problem is that copy-protection schemes don't work. Mostly what they do is develop a market for specialized copy programs that can copy the diskettes anyway. The escalating war between the developers of copy-protect schemes and the developers of "nibble" copiers does nothing but increase development and distribution costs for the software companies and increase the price paid by the legitimate user.

The third problem is the calculation of the "losses" due to piracy. These are usually based on the "street value" theory. If a program has a list price of $500 and if an estimated 10,000 illegal copies have been made, then the software developers are out of pocket to the tune of $5 million. With that much money at stake, drastic measures are called for.

This logic ignores several key facts. First of all, list price has little to do with anything. The list price includes a very healthy markup for the retailer, one which today's competition generally does not allow him to collect. Most software is available in stores or by mail at discount prices. Businesses that buy in quantity get still bigger discounts.

Secondly, the "street value" theory assumes that there are no costs in the manufacturing and distribution of software. A pirated copy may not make any money for the developer, but it doesn't cost anything either. It even increases the sale of blank diskettes, which benefits the industry if not the software houses.

But the biggest flaw is the assumption that if the software were adequately protected, each of those pirated copies would have been purchased instead of copied. The pirate has many more choices than just those two. He can pirate some competitor's product which is not as well protected, buy a less functional—and therefore cheaper—product, write his own, or do without. Many people would use a $500 integrated product that they get for free, but would make do with a $29.95 simple single-function program if they actually had to pay for it.

Finally, pirated copies are good advertising. Most companies will pay for their copies. The risk of being sued for large sums of money as well as the resultant bad publicity will keep them honest. The illegal copies are mostly in the hands of individuals who probably wouldn't have paid for them anyway. The large software houses spend millions of dollars to develop brand recognition in the marketplace. The actual lost profits due to stray copies probably are a more cost-effective method of advertising than television commercials.

On the other side of the coin, if copying is too easy, if there is no advantage to having a legitimate copy, then you will soon have no customers.

How should you protect your software, then? First of all, provide good, extensive (but not exhaustive) documentation. Despite the availability of excellent copying machines, books, magazines, and newspapers are still doing fine. Copying a manual, especially one professionally printed and bound, is a lot more work than just coping a diskette, and results in a document that is not only difficult to use, but shouts to all the world that it is an unauthorized copy.

Serialize your distribution copies, and provide a prepaid post card for registering users. Provide good customer support by mail or by phone, but always check the serial number against your registration list. Provide periodic update releases with fixes and new features. Give a significant discount on these new releases to your registered users.

When unauthorized copies start showing up, and they will, check the serial numbers to determine the original buyer and threaten legal action. Most casual copiers are not sophisticated enough to find and alter the serial number before making a copy for their friends.

These techniques will not put a stop to illegal copying, but they will pretty much ensure that most of those copies will end up with people who don't really need them enough to justify buying them. But what about programs such as arcade games, where there is no documentation, no support, no new releases, and the sales are mostly to individuals rather than companies? Well, perhaps you will decide to copy protect these after all.

The first copy-protection schemes for the IBM PC were pretty simplistic. IBM itself, used to operating in an environment where regular backups were standard, decided against protecting any of the system software developed under its name, such as DOS and the various language compilers. Those companies which did decide on protection did just enough to fool the standard utilities, which was not difficult. One of the early word processing programs just left track 5 unformatted. The DISKCOPY program supplied by IBM as part of DOS quit on any unrecoverable error. This technique was easily overcome by simply writing a copy program that issued a message and continued whenever it encountered an error.

More inventive was the scheme used by Infocom for its text adventure games. The standard PC diskette is formatted with 512 byte sectors. Infocom wrote tracks which had one 1024-byte sector on each track, along with the several of the normal 512-byte sectors. In addition, the 1024-byte sectors had non-standard sector numbers. This caused the standard copy programs to miss the large sectors entirely. It was the existence of this scheme that was responsible for the development of the first of the true "nibble" copiers for the IBM PC—System Backup. (The term "nibble copier" is a misnomer for the IBM. The term comes from the sophisticated copy programs written for the Apple computers, where data was actually recorded on the diskette a nibble—4 bits—at a time.)

To handle such schemes as Infocom's, the copy programs had to figure out what sectors were really on each track. The best way to accomplish this with the IBM diskette adapter board is to issue a READ ID command. This command asks the controller chip to return the sector header of the next sector to pass under the read/write head. The header contains the cylinder number, head number, sector number, and size code for the sector. By sitting in a loop until the sector first encountered comes around again, the program can build a list of all the sectors on a given track. With this information, it is a simple matter to issue the correct read and write commands to copy the track. The only real trick is that IBM did not support either READ ID or READ TRACK commands as part of its diskette BIOS routines. System Backup had to start using its own diskette driver routines.

Personal Software's VisiCalc carried the war a step further. They figured out that the READ ID command reported the first ID field it was able to read without error. The sector header, in addition to the data fields described above, also has some error checking information—a CRC field. Personal Software placed a record on track 39—the last track—which had an error in the header's CRC field. A READ ID command would not detect this sector, but a VERIFY command with the correct sector number supplied would return a unique error code. The diskette would appear to copy properly, but the VisiCalc loader routine would fail to get the proper error code and know that the copy was a forgery. System Backup and the very few other good copy programs soon solved this problem, discovering that such an error can be created by de-selecting the write head just as the CRC characters are being written. Of course this requires a carefully controlled and precise timing loop.

Another step in the escalating war was to lie about the way the sectors were formatted. When formatting a track, it is possible to put any information one wishes into the sector header. The sector ID is always correct, because that is the only place the ID appears, but one can play games to one's heart's content with the cylinder and head numbers as well as the size code. These measures were also soon countered. Adding timing information to the READ ID loop determined the physical size of the sectors, and the customized diskette drivers had little difficulty separating physical and logical track IDs.

As it became apparent that anything that could be created on an IBM PC could be copied on an IBM PC, the protectors had to make a major move in the battle. There are other disk controller chips than the one used in the IBM PC. Some of these can produce formats which can be read by the PC but not duplicated. One program has a copyright notice written in the gap following a sector which claims to be bigger than it really is. By issuing a READ TRACK command, the gap information will be read as the second half of the gimmicked sector.

The ultimate in this genre is the scheme that uses a laser to burn a hole in the diskette. The protected diskette attempts to write over the spot where the hole is and then reads back what it has written. If the exact error remains in the exact place, then the diskette is good. In all the other cases, it is deemed a forgery. At first glance this technique would seem to be foolproof. No standard PC can burn a laser hole in a diskette. But at least one of the copy programs has solved that problem too. It loads a resident routine which notes the error condition on the protected diskette. When the copy is run, the routine intercepts the attempt to verify the diskette and returns the information necessary to fool the program.

The moral of all this is that it is fairly easy to protect software against the typical user who will make a copy for a friend with the standard utility programs. But it is not economically feasible to create a protection scheme which will stand up to the attempts of a dedicated professional. Furthermore, an attempt to claim that one has developed such a scheme is viewed as a challenge in many quarters. The war is not yet conceded by either side, but like most wars, it is probably safer to stay out of the battle.

Appendix A
IBM PC MACROASSEMBLER INSTRUCTION SET

Instruction Set—By Function

Data Movement Instructions

MOV   Move
XCHG   Exchange
XLAT   Translate
LDS   Load data segment register
LEA   Load effective address
LES   Load extra segment register
PUSH   Push word onto stack
PUSHF   Push flags onto stack
POP   Pop word off of stack to destination
POPF   Pop flags off of stack
LAHF   Load AH from flags
SAHF   Store AH in flags

Arithmetic Instructions

ADC   Add with carry
ADD   Addition

AAA   ASCII adjust for addition
AAD   ASCII adjust for division
AAM   ASCII adjust for multiplication
AAS   ASCII adjust for subtraction
CBW   Convert byte to word
CWD   Convert word to doubleword
DAA   Decimal adjust for addition
DAS   Decimal adjust for subtraction
DIV   Divide
IDIV   Integer division, signed
IMUL   Integer multiply
MUL   Multiply
NEG   Negate (form is 2's complement)
SBB   Subtract with borrow
SUB   Subtract

Compare Instructions

CMP   Compare two operands
CMPS,CMPSB,CMPSW   Compare byte or word string

Logical Instructions

AND   Logical AND
NOT   Logical NOT
OR   Logical inclusive OR
TEST   Test (logical compare)
XOR   Exclusive OR

String Primitive Instructions

CMPS,CMPSB,CMPSW   Compare byte or word string
LODS,LODSB,LODSW   Load byte or word string

MOVS,MOVSB,MOVSW   Move byte or word string
SCAS,SCASB,SCASW   Scan byte or word string
STOS,STOSB,STOSW   Store byte or word string

Program Counter Control Instructions

CALL   Call a procedure
JA,JNBE   Jump if above, if not below or equal
JAE,JNB   Jump if above or equal, if not below
JB,JNAE,JC   Jump if below, if not above or equal, if carry
JBE,JNA   Jump if below or equal, if not above
JCXZ   Jump if CX is zero
JE,JZ   Jump if equal, if zero
JG,JNLE   Jump if greater, if not less nor equal
JGE,JNL   Jump if greater or equal, if not less
JL,JNGE   Jump if less, if not greater nor equal
JLE,JNG   Jump if less or equal, if not greater
JMP   Jump
JNC   Jump if no carry
JNE,JNZ   Jump if not equal, if not zero
JNO   Jump if no overflow
JNP,JPO   Jump if no parity, if parity odd
JNS   Jump if no sign, if sign positive
JO   Jump on overflow
JP,JPE   Jump on parity, if parity even
JS   Jump on sign
LOOP   Loop until count complete
LOOPE,LOOPZE   Loop if equal, if zero
LOOPNE,LOOPNZ   Loop if not equal, if not zero
RET   Return from a procedure

Processor Control Instructions

CLC   Clear carry flag
CMC   Complement carry flag

CLD   Clear direction flag
CLI   Clear interrupt flag (disable)
ESC   Escape
HLJ   Halt
IN   Input byte or word
INT   Interrupt
INTO   Interrupt if overflow
IRET   Interrupt return

Rotate and Shift Instructions

LOCK   Lock bus
NOP   No operation
OUT   Output byte or word
RCL   Rotate left through carry
RCR   Rotate right through carry
ROL   Rotate left
ROR   Rotate right
SAL,SHL   Shift arithmetic left, shift logical left
SAR   Shift arithmetic right
SHR   Shift logical right
WAIT   Wait

Instruction List—Alphabetic

AAA   ASCII adjust for addition
AAD   ASCII adjust for division
AAM   ASCII adjust for multiply
AAS   ASCII adjust for subtraction
ADC   Add with carry
ADD   Addition
AND   Logical AND
CALL   Call a procedure
CBW   Convert byte to word

CLC   Clear carry flag
CLD   Clear direction flag
CLI   Clear interrupt flag (disable)
CMC   Complement carry flag
CMP   Compare two operands
CMPS,CMPSB,CMPSW   Compare byte or word string
CWD   Convert word to doubleword
DAA   Decimal adjust for addition
DAS   Decimal adjust for subtraction
DEC   Decrement destination by one
DIV   Division, unsigned
ESC   Escape
HLT   Halt
IDIV   Integer division, signed
IMUL   Integer multiply
IN   Input byte or word
INC   Increment destination by 1
INT   Interrupt
INTO   Interrupt if overflow
IRET   Interrupt return
JA,JNBE   Jump if above, if not below or equal
JAE,JNB   Jump if above or equal, if not below
JB,JNAE,JC   Jump if below, if not above or equal, if carry
JBE,JNA   Jump if below or equal, if not above
JCXZ   Jump if CX is zero
JE,JZ   Jump if equal, if zero
JG,JNLE   Jump if greater, if not less nor equal
JGE,JNL   Jump if greater or equal, if not less
JL,JNGE   Jump if less, if not greater nor equal
JLE,JNG   Jump if less or equal, if not greater
JMP   Jump
JNC   Jump if no carry
JNE,JNZ   Jump if not equal, if not zero
JNO   Jump if no overflow
JNP,JPO   Jump if no parity, if parity odd

JNS   Jump if no sign, if positive
JO   Jump on overflow
JP,JPE   Jump on parity, if parity even
JS   Jump on sign
LAHF   Load AH from flags
LDS   Load data segment register
LEA   Load effective address
LES   Load extra segment register
LOCK   Lock bus
LODS,LODSB,LODSW   Load byte or word string
LOOP   Loop until count complete
LOOPE,LOOPZE   Loop if equal, if zero
LOOPNE,LOOPNZ   Loop if not equal, if not zero
MOV   Move
MOVS,MOVSB,MOVSW   Move byte or word string
MUL   Multiply, unsigned
NEG   Negate, form is 2's complement
NOP   No operation
NOT   Logical NOT
OR   Logical inclusive OR
OUT   Output byte or word
POP   Pop word off stack of destination
POPF   Pop flags off stack
PUSH   Push word onto stack
PUSHF   Push flags onto stack
RCL   Rotate left through carry
RCR   Rotate right through carry
REP,REPZ,REPE,REPNE,REPNZ   Repeat string
   operation
RET   Return from procedure
ROL   Rotate left
ROR   Rotate right
SAHF   Store AH in flags
SAL,SHL   Shift arithmetic left, shift logical left
SAR   Shift arithmetic right
SBB   Subtract with borrow

SCAS,SCASB,SCASW   Scan byte or word string
SHR   Shift logical right
STC   Set carry flag
STD   Set direction flag
STI   Set interrupt flag (enable)
STOS,STOSB,STOSW   Store byte or word string
SUB   Subtract
TEST   Test (logical compare)
WAIT   Wait
XCHG   Exchange
XLAT   Translate
XOR   Exclusive OR

GLOSSARY

ANALOG—A way of representing one type of physical property in terms of another. A lot of early computers were analog machines, and researchers sometimes still use them, but the majority of computers in commercial use are digital devices. Analog is also used to describe a peripheral device, like a mouse, that produces directional information which a computer can translate into screen display data.

APA—All Points Addressable, a type of graphics that allows direct mapping between screen coordinates and computer memory.

APPLICATION—A set of computer programs which work together to perform some generalized function, like inventory management or financial tracking. Application code is generally written for some end-user and is more likely to be in a high-level language than in assembler.

ARRAY—A matrix of numbers or letters that can be searched by the computer in order to retrieve the same number or word multiple times. Each item in an array is called an "element."

ASCII—American Standard Code for Information Interchange, the standard 7-bit coded character set that is used in most microcomputer systems. ASCII is actually an 8-bit code, but the high-order bit is used for parity checking.

ASSEMBLER—A computer program that is used to convert the source code typed in by a programmer into object code that is understandable by the computer. This term is also used in casual reference to assembly language, i.e. "It was written in assembler."

BACKUP—Any copy of a program, file, or entire diskette that is kept in case of damage to the original. The process of making the copy is often called "backing up" or "making a backup."

BASIC—A popular high-level language used extensively on microcomputers.

BAUD—The rate at which information is exchanged between computers, or between a computer and its input-output devices.

BINARY—A numbering system that only allows two characters, 0 and 1. In a binary system, there are only two choices, such as YES and NO, or ON and OFF. All computers store information in binary form, but programmers generally work in a more convenient mode, like decimal or hexadecimal.

BIOS—Basic Input/Output System, the logical section of a computer that maintains the addresses of connected devices and lets the computer communicate with its printer, display, and other external equipment.

BIT—Binary digIT, the smallest piece of information that a computer can process. Bits are usually moved, read, and updated in sets of eight, called a byte.

BOOT—To start up a computer system. A "warm boot" is done on the IBM PC by pressing the CTRL, ALT, and DEL keys while the computer is running. A "cold start" or "boot" is starting up the machine from scratch by turning on the power switch.

BOOTSTRAP—A technique that lets a computer or other device start itself up with minimal outside help, from the phrase "lifting yourself up by your bootstraps." The bootstrap program on the IBM PC automatically starts up and tries to read the main load sequence from a diskette in the A: drive. If there is no diskette available, the bootstrap program loads a version of BASIC from ROM.

BUFFER—A section of memory that is used for temporary storage of information. Typically, buffers are used to hold data that comes in from a keyboard or communications line, or to hold formatted data before it is transmitted or moved to a more permanent storage location.

BUG—An error in a program, a glitch or mistake. The process of locating and correcting bugs is called "debugging."

BUS, BUS STRUCTURE—The signal or set of wires that carries binary coded addresses from a microcomputer's CPU chip (the Intel 8088 in the case of the

IBM PC) through the rest of the computer; also referred to as the "address bus."

BYTE—A set of eight consecutive bits of information.

CHANNEL—A logical or physical unit in the computer that controls data flow, such as an I/O Channel.

CHARACTER—A single letter, number, or other symbol.

CLONE—A computer designed to imitate a competitor's machine as closely as possible, usually produced for economic reasons.

COPROCESSOR—An extra device that does some of the work for a computer's CPU. A coprocessor usually has some features that are missing in the main processor. For example, the Intel 8087 coprocessor chip, which is required in the IBM PC for APL programming, supplies the special keyboard handling for APL's symbol set.

CPS—Characters Per Second, used as a measurement of transmission speed for printers and some other devices.

CPU—Central Processing Unit, the section of a computer that does the actual calculations. When the CPU is a single chip, like the Intel 8088 in the IBM PC, it is often referred to as an MPU (microprocessing unit).

CRC—Cyclic Redundancy Check, a special character used to ensure data integrity during transmission or memory testing.

CRT—Cathode Ray Tube, the common computer display monitor, which uses such a tube.

CURSOR—The symbol that is displayed on the computer screen to show where the next typed character will display, or to prompt the user for input. The cursor is generally shown as a short blinking line or a small block, but it can be any character, depending on the machine and the software.

DEFAULT—A setting that the computer uses unless it is told otherwise. Defaults are pre-set values which can be changed or overridden under software control.

DIRECTORY—The list of programs and files on a diskette.

DIRECTORY PATH—The series of directories that will be checked in turn to locate a specific program or file. Directory paths are used in operating systems that support sub-directories, like DOS 2.0, XENIX, UNIX, etc.

DISK DRIVE—The phonograph-like mechanism that reads and writes on diskettes for microcomputers and on disk packs for larger machines.

DISKETTE—A flat square envelope of heavy plasticized paper that contains a thin flexible disk. Diskettes, also called "floppy disks" and "floppies," are used to store information, and are usually 5¼" or 8" in diameter, depending on the disk drives that handle them.

DISPLAY—The television-like screen on which a computer shows information. A display can be a CRT, liquid crystal, or any other sort of technology. Also called a "monitor" or "screen."

DMA—Direct Memory Access.

DOS—Disk Operating System, the set of programs that communicate between a computer and its disk drives.

DOUBLE DENSITY—This term refers to the amount of information that can be stored on a diskette. The IBM PC has double-density disk drives and formats diskettes as double density.

DOUBLE-SIDED DRIVE—A disk drive with two read/write heads, one for each side of the diskette.

DUAL DRIVE—A computer system that has two disk drives.

ENTER, RETURN—The key on the computer keyboard that is used to tell the system that input is complete. The ENTER key is usually in the same position as the RETURN key on an electric typewriter.

EPROM—Erasable Programmable memory, a read-only I/C chip that can be erased with ultraviolet light and re-programmed.

FIELD—A section of a file record or input string that contains one specific piece of information, like a zip code, program name, or memory address.

FILE—A section of space on a diskette or tape that can be referred to by name and is used to store information. A file can be broken down into sub-groupings, like blocks, records and fields.

FIRMWARE—Memory chips (I/C's) that have a program permanent written into them, also referred to as ROM, PROM, and EPROM, depending on whether the programs within the chips can be erased and changed.

FORMAT—The process of writing blank tracks onto a diskette so that it can be used by a computer, or the way the completed tracks are written on the diskette. Format is a general term that is used to refer to the way data is organized, such as "What is the format of the inventory record?"

GRAPHICS—Symbols produced by writing, drawing, or printing, as opposed to characters from the keyboard.

HARDCOPY—Information printed on paper instead of being displayed on the computer's monitor.

HARD DISK—A storage device similar to a disk drive, except that the actual recording surface cannot be removed from the machine. Hard disks have a lot more capacity than diskettes and may contain 10, 20, or even 40 million bytes of information.

HARDWARE—Physical computer equipment, such as the machine itself, the monitor, printer, etc. (Compare SOFTWARE.)

HEAD—The device that moves across the surface of a diskette, reading or writing information. A double-sided drive has two heads, one for each side of the diskette.

HEX, HEXADECIMAL—A numbering system that has 16 possible values. These values are traditionally numbered from 0 through F. In hexadecimal, the next number after F is 10.

HERTZ—A unit of frequency, one cycle per second.

HIGH-LEVEL—Any computer language where the programmer does not have to move information around byte by byte. BASIC, COBOL, and FORTRAN are high-level languages. Assembly language is regarded as low-level.

HIGH-ORDER—The far left position in a character string, byte, or other series. In the binary group 10000000 the 1 is the high-order bit.

HOST—The main computer in a network, or any computer with terminals connected to it.

I/C—Integrated Circuit, an electronic circuit that is produced in miniature and enclosed in a small rigid plastic case. I/C's are also called "chips."

I/O—Input/Output, any logical or physical device that is concerned with information flow in and out of the computer.

INTERPRETER—A computer program that translates source code line by line, as it is executed, into computer instructions. Programs that run under an interpreter are usually slower to execute than those that are compiled and are much slower than assembly language.

INTERRUPT—To stop an action in such a way that it can be resumed later. Interrupt is also used as a noun to refer to some specific computer commands.

K, KB—Abbreviations for Kilobyte, pronounced "Kay." Although it is more precise to use the term KB, popular usage prefers the single letter—as in "64K memory board."

LOG, LOGGED—Identified to the computer, as in "logged on." The log-on procedure for a computer may consist of entering a name and password. Log can also refer to the process of printing or spooling all of the communication between a computer terminal and the host, for security or archival purposes.

LOOP—A series of computer instructions that are repeated over and over some set number of times, or until something specific happens. Loops can contain other loops, and may become quite complex.

LOW LEVEL—A computer language which requires the programmer to handle information one or two bytes at a time. Assembly languge is a low-level language. FORTH, which has both high-level and low-level commands, is sometimes regarded as a low-level language.

LOW-ORDER—The far right position in a character string, byte, or other series. (Compare HIGH-ORDER.)

MACHINE LANGUAGE—Any language that is used directly by a computer, without translation. This is also used rather loosely as a term for the computer's instruction set.

MAINFRAME—A large multiuser computer used in major business operations. Mainframes may have several hundred terminals connected to them and are able to do a wide variety of tasks concurrently.

MEG, MEGABYTE—A million bytes of storage. Microcomputers do not yet have this kind of capacity, although it's a common term for mainframe storage. In the microcomputer environment the term is usually used in reference to hard or fixed disks.

MEMORY—The physical and logical locations within a computer where data and programs are stored.

MEMORY ADDRESS—A two-byte value that indicates a particular location in computer memory.

MEMORY MAP—A list of memory locations that can be accessed and used by a computer. Adding additional memory to a computer is useless unless the new locations are also added to the memory map so that the computer "knows" they are available.

MICROPROCESSOR—The section of a microprocessor that executes instructions. In the IBM PC family of computers this is the Intel 8088 (except for the PC AT, which uses the Intel 80286 chip).

MNEMONIC—A memory aid or abbreviation that usually consists of two or three characters in place of a more complicated series of words, such as CRT, ROM, etc.

MODE—A means of operation, such as graphics mode, text mode, decimal mode, or hex mode.

MODEM—Modulator-Demodulator, a device that converts electronic signals from the computer into tones that can be sent across telephone lines.

MONITOR—A device or person that keeps track of a process or operation. In data processing this term is used almost exclusively for the display terminal that is attached to a computer.

MONO, MONOCHROME—A computer display screen that only shows two colors, usually green on black, amber on black, or white on black. Also, specifically, the IBM Monochrome display unit.

MULTIPLEXER—A device that combines two or more sequences into an interleaved series. Multiplexers are used in data communications and in voice lines.

OBJECT, OBJECT CODE—Program instructions which have been translated into information the computer can understand, through a compiler or assembler. (Compare SOURCE CODE.)

OFF-LINE—Not logically connected to the computer. If a device is attached to the computer but is not available for use, it is referred to as off-line.

ON-LINE—Attached to the computer both physically and logically and ready for use. A device which is in communication with a computer is on-line.

OPERATING SYSTEM—A set of computer programs that control its basic functions, like reading diskettes and displaying information on the screen. DOS, CP/M, UNIX, and XENIX are all operating systems.

PARAMETER—A piece of information entered as part of a command to the computer and used in some process, e.g. "What are the FORMAT command parameters?"

PIXEL—Picture Element, a point on the display screen that can be set to light, dark, or a particular color. Graphics displays allow you to set each pixel individually, whereas text displays allow only character groupings to be changed.

PRINTED CIRCUIT BOARD—A piece of non-conducting material that has an electronic circuit attached to one or both surfaces. Some PC boards are combined together to make sandwiches of four and six layers. PC boards are usually produced from fiberglass that has a layer of metal adhered to it. The circuit is produced by etching away the metal so that only the desired paths are left.

PROGRAM—A series of computer instructions that are stored together and used to produce some particular result when executed in sequence.

PROM—Programmable Memory, an I/C chip that can have a program permanently stored within it. Some PROMs can be erased and reused, while others are limited to a single programming and have to be discarded if the software becomes obsolete.

RANDOM ACCESS—Retrieving a particular piece of information from a file without having to read all of the other records. Diskettes and hard disks are random access devices, since the read/write heads can go directly to any location on them without having to read the rest of the data. Tape handlers are sequential access devices.

REGISTER—A two-byte memory location that is used in assembly and other low-level programming. The IBM PC has four general purpose registers: AX, BX, CX, DX.

ROM—Read Only Memory, a computer chip that can be read but not changed. ROM is used to store programs, and is especially valuable for bootstrap loaders and some basic system code. (Compare FIRMWARE.)

ROM BIOS—An input/output system that is permanently built into read-only memory.

SEGMENT—A logical division of memory in the IBM PC computers. Segments can be up to 64K in size, and are used to separate complex tasks.

SEQUENTIAL ACCESS—Any means of memory access that requires all of the prior records to be read before the one that is wanted can be found. Tape handlers are sequential access devices. (Compare RANDOM ACCESS.)

SOFTWARE—The files and programs used by a computer. Software is stored on diskettes or tape and may be saved as hardcopy listings. (Compare HARDWARE, FIRMWARE.)

SOURCE, SOURCE CODE—The program instructions that are actually typed in by a programmer, before they have been translated into object code for the computer's benefit. (Compare OBJECT CODE.)

SPOOL, SPOOLING—Channeling information into a disk or tape file instead of sending it directly to an I/O device, like a printer. This allows the computer to process information more rapidly, since it doesn't have to wait for the relatively slow peripheral device to catch up.

STACK—A special section of computer memory that is used to keep track of addresses and data. Information can be saved on the stack by the programmer, and it is used by the operating system to hold subroutine addresses and return locations.

STRING—A series of letters or numbers. ABCDEF is an alpha string, and 342156 is a numeric string.

SUBROUTINE—A series of instructions, within a program, that is referred to by a name or address and is used to do something specific, like printing an error message, or clearing the display. A subroutine is generally invoked by other sections of the program and is used to avoid repetition within the code.

SYSTEM FILES—Special files, used by the operating system, and written on the the system tracks of a diskette. In the IBM PC environment these files are IBMBIO.COM and IBMDOS.COM.

SYSTEM TRACKS—The sections on a formatted diskette that are reserved for use by the operating system.

TAPE—A medium for storing information for sequential access. Since random access devices are faster, tapes are now generally used for archival purposes instead of daily operations in large commercial installations. Some low-cost home computer systems do use tapes, and these are generally the same sort of cassettes used for recording and playing music.

VIRTUAL MEMORY—An advanced memory storage technique that allows a computer to address more memory than it actually has. Although virtual memory is used on large mainframe computers it is not yet available for home systems. The IBM PC/XT 370 uses a modified form of virtual memory.

WARM BOOT—Resetting the computer while it is running. On the IBM PC this is done by pressing the CTRL, ALT, and DEL keys at the same time.

Appendix B
SAMPLE PROGRAM LIST

The source code for the following programs is printed in this book. Readers who would like to purchase a diskette with both the source code and executable object code should contact Workman and Associates, 112 Marion Avenue, Pasadena, CA 91106.

CHARSET—Demonstration of alternate character sets.
DATETIME—Display of date and time using DOS function calls.
DISKEDIT—Display and alter diskette sectors.
GRAPHICS—Line and circle routines using BIOS all-points-addressable capability.
HEBRU—Graphics display using non-standard characters (Hebrew alphabet).
MCOPY—Copy program that displays the amount of space occupied by each program and issues a warning if there is insufficient room on the diskette for the copy.
MDIR—Displays system and hidden files by using the file control block.
MDIR2—Display system and hidden files by using stream I/O techniques.

PRZER—A display subroutine that uses DOS character
          calls.
SAMPLE—DOS calling conventions for .COM files.
SCAN—Simple file display program.
SCAN2—File display using stream I/O.
SCAN3—File display using video BIOS calls.
SKELETON—Skeleton assembly program.
SUBLIM—A screen display program which flashes a
          message and then restores the background.
TWOMON—Display routines using concurrent monitors.
XKEY—Keyboard translation routine.

INDEX